continued . . .

REDNECK
CINDERELLA

LuAnn McLane

A SIGNET ECLIPSE BOOK

SIGNET ECLIPSE
Published by New American Library, a division of
Penguin Group (USA) Inc., 375 Hudson Street,
New York, New York 10014, USA
Penguin Group (Canada), 90 Eglinton Avenue East, Suite 700, Toronto,
Ontario M4P 2Y3, Canada (a division of Pearson Penguin Canada Inc.)
Penguin Books Ltd., 80 Strand, London WC2R 0RL, England
Penguin Ireland, 25 St. Stephen's Green, Dublin 2,
Ireland (a division of Penguin Books Ltd.)
Penguin Group (Australia), 250 Camberwell Road, Camberwell, Victoria 3124,
Australia (a division of Pearson Australia Group Pty. Ltd.)
Penguin Books India Pvt. Ltd., 11 Community Centre, Panchsheel Park,
New Delhi - 110 017, India
Penguin Group (NZ), 67 Apollo Drive, Rosedale, North Shore 0632,
New Zealand (a division of Pearson New Zealand Ltd.)
Penguin Books (South Africa) (Pty.) Ltd., 24 Sturdee Avenue,
Rosebank, Johannesburg 2196, South Africa

Penguin Books Ltd., Registered Offices:
80 Strand, London WC2R 0RL, England

First published by Signet Eclipse, an imprint of New American Library,
a division of Penguin Group (USA) Inc.

First Printing, March 2009
10 9 8 7 6 5 4 3 2 1

Redneck Cinderella is dedicated to Kim and Terri.
You gotta kiss a lot of toads . . .

ACKNOWLEDGMENTS

Thanks to country music fans who are spreading the word about my Southern-fried books. Your encouraging e-mails and message-board posts help to keep my fingers on the keyboard.

I'd like to extend a special thanks to my editor, Lindsay Nouis. Your enthusiasm brings out the best in my writing, and you have been a pleasure to work with.

As always, thanks so much to my agent, Jenny Bent. Your continued support, encouragement, and insight are highly valued and appreciated.

Prologue

"I'll get it, Daddy," I shout from where I'm washing the supper dishes.

"Okay, Jolie," he calls back from his workshop just off the kitchen. He's busy whittling Christmas ornaments for a craft show and I don't want to interrupt him. This year's drought hurt our tobacco crop, so what started out as a therapeutic hobby now brings in much-needed income. Another sharp rap at the front door has me grabbing a towel and hurrying through the living room to see who might be coming our way on such a cold night.

"Hold your horses," I grumble. Our farm is miles from town, so it's not as if we often have visitors just dropping in for social calls. After wiping my wet hands, I toss the dish towel over my shoulder and open the door. *Oh wow* rings in my head but doesn't reach my mouth. Now, I'm not usually one to be rendered speechless, but when I see who is on our doorstep, I get tongue-tied and flustered.

"Jolie Russell?" our visitor asks.

"Ughaaaa." Forgetting about my tongue-tied situation, I then try to respond but manage only this weird noise, which I then disguise as a sneeze. "Chu." Sometimes you just have to think on your feet.

"God bless you."

This time I'm smart enough to merely nod while rubbing my finger beneath my nose as if I really did sneeze.

"You are Jolie and your daddy is Wyatt Russell, correct?"

"Last time I checked."

He gives me a half grin. "Good. The name and address on your mailbox were faded and I wanted to be sure I hadn't taken a wrong turn in the dark. Cody Dean." He extends his hand and I give him a firm handshake just like my daddy taught me.

"H-hey there," I manage to sputter. Of course, like everybody else in Cottonwood, Kentucky, I'm already well aware of who he is. Cody, the elder son of Carl Dean, is back from his fancy Ivy League education to take over his daddy's company. The Dean family is like royalty here in Cottonwood, with Cody being the prince. I also know that Dean Development has been buying up farmland for subdivisions all over Cottonwood, and I suddenly get light-headed at the prospect of why Cody is paying us a visit, because I'm pretty sure it isn't to ask me on a date.

Ha! No, I'm certain he isn't here to take little ole me out to dinner. Back in high school, having him ask me out was my secret fantasy. I bet he doesn't even remember that we had a chemistry class together. I got a dog-gone C in the course, much to Daddy's dismay, because I was too busy gawking at Cody when I should have been taking notes. Of course, he never noticed me, except for the day I caused a minor chemical explosion. Had I been paying attention to my experiment instead of looking his way, the incident would never have occurred. To say he's out of my league would be the understatement of the year, which leaves me to wonder if he's going to make us an offer to buy our acreage. My heart starts beating wildly at the prospect.

"Sorry to have stopped by unannounced, but may I come in?"

"Oh . . . why sure—where the hell are my manners?" I blurt out, and then wish my tongue had remained tied. "I mean, um, please, come on in," I amend softly, since I tend to shout when I get jittery, even when it's not necessary. With a smile that goes wobbly on me, I step aside for him to enter. As he passes me I get a whiff of expensive-smelling aftershave that makes me want to pant after him like a lovesick puppy. I firmly remind myself that it's been almost six years since high school and I need to conduct myself in an adult manner. Oh, but he's wearing a slick leather bomber jacket and fancy-looking black jeans and don't ask me why, but I have a sudden, silly urge to take the dish towel from my shoulder, roll it up tightly, and zap him on the butt. "Pop a squat," I offer, and gesture toward the sofa. "Um, I mean, have a seat." God, I suck at this.

"Thank you." Cody's tone is refined, but the hint of amusement in his blue eyes has my chin coming up a notch. Mercy, did he know I was ogling his backside? I make a mental note to keep my eyes on his face. Admittedly, I'm a bit lacking in social graces, having lost my mama at the tender age of ten. I'm more at home fishing and four-wheeling with guys than dressing up for dinner dates, not that shaking Cody's hand didn't give me a hot little tingle that traveled all the way to my toes. I might be a little rough around the edges, but I still have all my girl parts, and Cody Dean is making all of those particular areas stand up and take notice. But I remind myself that I'm no longer a teenager and that unrequited love is a long and lonely road. Cody Dean is here for a reason, but it sure isn't to romance me.

When his gaze sweeps the room, pride stiffens my backbone. Unlike him, we might not have much, but although everything is old and outdated, it's clean and as neat as a pin. I'm starting to get a little out of sorts as I watch him look around our humble home with what seems like open curiosity.

"What brings you here?" My blunt question carries slightly more bite than intended.

Cody's dark eyebrows shoot up at my tone. "A business proposition," he answers smoothly. "Is your father home, Jolie?"

Oh, holy crap. I tamp down the don't-mess-with-me attitude that tends to land me in hot water, putting a smile back on my face. "Why yes, he is. I'll get him. Um, make yourself at home."

"Thanks." He inclines his neatly cropped head and sits down on the sofa. I hope he thinks it's an expensive antique instead of an ancient hand-me-down, but then beat myself up for caring. Cottonwood is a fairly small town, but it has a large social gap between old Southern money and dirt-poor farmers. Carl Dean has been known to be hard-nosed in his business dealings, but it's been rumored that Cody is trying to soften the family reputation for ruthlessness.

My knees are a little shaky as I walk toward the doorway, but I suddenly remember my manners. "Would you like something to drink? Sweet tea?" I'm about to add crumpets just for fun, but I'm not sure what a crumpet is and I'm quite sure we don't have any. About the best I could do is Oreos, and that's if Daddy hasn't eaten them all. Well, okay, I might have had one or two, starting with the icing first. The finer points of Southern hospitality must be in me somewhere, but because we so rarely have visitors, except for those who come for outdoor activities like four-wheeling, fishing, and such, I have few opportunities to practice those finer points. Still, I'm trying. "Anything?"

"No, thank you," he says, but then adds, "On second thought, a bottle of water would be nice."

Well, la-di-da. "Um, all I have is plain old water from the cistern." My daddy thinks that buying bottled water is the dumbest damned thing ever imposed upon the American public, and I'm pretty much with him on that one. When Cody hesitates I add, "We're fresh out of Perrier, but the tank is clean."

His mouth twitches as if he isn't sure if he should smile or not, but then he waves a hand at me. "That's okay. I'm fine. Don't go to any trouble."

"Oh, it's no bother." Of course I'm going to bring him a glass of water just to be ornery. I'm bad that way. "I'll go find Daddy."

I walk slowly out of the room, wishing I were wearing something better than worn jeans and a George Strait T-shirt, but when I get to the kitchen I scurry into the workshop. "Daddy!" I say in what is a whisper for me but what is a normal tone for most folks. "Guess who's sittin' on our very own sofa?" Daddy blows sawdust off an angel, but when he opens his mouth to make a guess I blurt, "Cody Dean!" *Dean* comes out so high-pitched that our old mutt, Rufus, lifts his head and whines.

"Ya don't say." Daddy frowns and looks down at the angel with a critical eye.

"He wants to talk to you!" I tell him.

When Daddy doesn't move, I reach over and tug him by his flannel shirt. "Hurry," I urge, and all but drag him from the room. Although I love the farmhouse, I hate raising tobacco, the very crop that's responsible for the death of my mama. "Just a second." I pause to draw a glass of water from the faucet and make a mental bet with myself as to whether Cody will drink it.

When we enter the living room, Cody politely stands up and shakes my daddy's hand. "Nice to meet you, Mr. Russell. May I have a few minutes of your time?"

Daddy nods, but I see the stubborn set of his jaw and my hope plummets. He eases down into the overstuffed chair while I march over and hand Cody the glass of water.

"Thank you," he says, and while looking at me drains half the contents before setting it on the scarred coffee table. He gives me an I'm-on-to-you smile, and I can't help but grin back at him. His smile deepens, causing a little dimple in his left cheek, and I have to grab the back of Daddy's chair for support. I hang out with guys all the time, and while I've been sweet on one or two of them, none have ever turned me inside out with a mere smile.

"So, what brings you here?" Daddy asks, even though we suspect the reason. Rufus, who must sense the excitement in the air, sits back on his haunches and we all three look expectantly at Cody.

After clearing his throat, Cody leans forward and

rests his elbows on his knees. "There's no reason to beat around the bush, Mr. Russell. I'd like to make you an offer for your land."

"I'm not interested," Daddy tells him.

What? "Daddy, hear him out," I say.

Cody shoots me a grateful glance. "I'm prepared to offer three million."

When my knees give way I grab on to the back of the chair so hard that my fingernails dig into the nubby fabric.

"Sorry, Cody," Daddy says.

Oh no! A little whimper escapes me.

"Three and a half million," Cody counters, and I breathe a sigh of relief. Who knew that Daddy could bargain like this? I arch an eyebrow in an expression that says, *See, we're not as stupid as we look.*

"Money isn't the issue, son. This here land is where I lived with my dear wife, Rosie. I'll never leave it."

Oh . . . emotion suddenly clogs my throat. I can't argue with his reasoning, but I also have to think that Mama somehow has a hand in this sudden windfall. Color me crazy, but I tend to feel her presence now and then.

Cody steeples his fingers and for a long moment remains silent, but then says, "You don't have to leave your land. I'll set aside your plot and you can keep several of the wooded acres as well. Now, you *would* have to rebuild. Mr. Russell, this isn't going to be your average subdivision. I'm proposing a gated community with upscale homes. I might add that this would bring in much-needed tax dollars to Cottonwood."

Daddy shakes his head. "Who could afford homes like that around these parts?"

"Kentucky horse money. I've done my homework. There are plenty of wealthy Kentuckians. These homes will sell quickly. Of course, we would build your house first."

Daddy slowly runs a hand down his face and then looks back at me. "Jolie? What do you think?"

I kneel down beside the chair and put a hand on his arm. "Daddy, I know that Mama would want this for you. It seems like a good thing all around." I squeeze his arm. "It's okay to do this," I assure him, and then hold my breath.

My daddy's eyebrows draw together and he gazes down at me for a moment before looking over at Cody. "Son, do we have a few days to think this through?"

"I'm sorry, Mr. Russell. I have other property in mind as well and time is of the essence."

Daddy sighs. "Well then, would you give us a minute or two?"

"Yes, sir, of course," Cody answers with a little less determination and a bit more understanding.

"All righty then." After standing up, Daddy takes my hand gives my arm a tug. "We'll be back in a bit."

"Take your time," Cody says.

"Thank you," Daddy responds. I'm suddenly very proud of my father. He might not run in the same circles as Carl Dean, but my daddy is a hardworking man of honor and conviction, and they don't come any better. I'm irritated that Cody is forcing us into a decision this quickly and I wonder if this is a business tactic to put the hat on us and seal the deal. But when I toss a questioning glance his way, his dark head is bent toward the floor and he seems to be deep in thought.

Reaching the doorway, I look over my shoulder. As if

Cody feels my gaze upon him, he suddenly looks up. When our eyes meet I feel an unexpected jolt of heat. His own eyes widen a fraction and I wonder if he feels it too. But then I tell myself I'm crazier than a June bug in May and quickly turn my head.

My tummy is doing flip-flops as I follow Daddy and Rufus into the workshop. What had begun as an ordinary winter night suddenly feels surreal. Trying to clear my head, I inhale a sharp breath that smells of sawdust and paint and then turn my attention to my father.

"Jolie-girl, what should we do?" He sits down in his whittling chair and rests his elbows on his knees.

"Oh, Daddy, don't get me wrong. I love this farm. But I hate the constant struggle and worry on your shoulders." I hesitate and then add, "And you know how I feel about the tobacco." Lung cancer from smoking took my mother's life. She was so beautiful and vibrant. Watching her suffer haunts me to this day.

He closes his blue eyes and swallows hard while absently scratching Rufus behind the ears. "Daddy." I put my hand on his shoulder. "You deserve this."

After a long sigh my father looks up as if he's asking my mama for guidance and then, as if getting his answer, nods slowly. "Let's do this, baby girl."

My smile trembles a bit when he stands up and pulls me into his arms.

"You're sure?"

"Yes," he answers gruffly, and then kisses the top of my head. "Now let's go tell Mr. Cody Dean the good news."

Entering the living room, Daddy looks Cody Dean straight in the eye, extends his hand, and says, "Son, you have a deal."

Cody smiles and grasps Daddy's hand. "Congratulations, Mr. Russell." He glances at me and inclines his head. "And you too, Jolie. I'll have the paperwork drawn up tomorrow, but I trust your handshake is binding."

And just like that, we're millionaires.

1

The Icing on the Cake

"Noooo! Rufus, don't you even think about it!" I warn my crazy dog when the toy poodle he adores scampers across our front lawn. Rufus doesn't pay one bit of attention to me and takes off down the driveway in hot pursuit of Misty. "Git back here!" From recent experience I know this will likely end badly. With a groan of pure frustration, I stop washing my truck and toss my soapy sponge to the pavement with a squish before hightailing after him.

"Rufus! Stop!" But he's totally enamored of the yappy little beast and ignores my command. Of course, he has no idea that he is completely out of his league. I'd be willing to bet that uppity little Misty is well aware of the fact and is entertaining herself at his expense. Although, with all the other pedigreed pets in the neighborhood, perhaps Misty is attracted to the underdog, I think to myself, and then snicker at my little pun.

"Rufus!" I yell, in between panting. He's pretty darned quick for a mutt that is mostly basset hound. "Ouch!" Stubbing my toe, I make a mental note to get an invisible fence. How he can run so fast on those stubby legs is beyond me, and the fact that he got a head start is in his favor. With my bare feet slapping against the sidewalk, I notice that the neighbors are stopping to gape at me in my bikini top and cutoff jeans, but what else is a person supposed to wear while washing a muddy truck? Not that anyone else in this neighborhood would even consider washing his or her own vehicle. I let out another yelp when I step on a stone, drawing even more unwanted attention to my bouncing breasts, and it takes everything in me not to flip my audience the bird.

When I notice fancy cars parked in front of Misty's house, I let out a breathless groan, knowing there must be some sort of gathering going on, most likely another la-ti-da rich-people brunch in the backyard. "Oh lord, help me," I mutter when I see Rufus making quick progress in that direction. I refer to most of the big-ass houses here in Copper Creek by where the dogs live, since even though Misty can be a pain in the butt, I pretty much like the pets better than the uppity owners.

The lush lawn slows Rufus's progress enough that I catch up with him around the corner of the huge house, but just as I'm ready to grab him, he spots Misty and lets out a happy howl, drawing attention from the crowd of impeccably dressed people. I swear I've never seen so many big floppy hats in my life, and they are suddenly all turned toward me.

The clinking of glasses and chatter stop. The only sounds are my labored breathing and the lyrical notes of a harp playing in the background. Half-naked, wet, and panting, I'm having one of those I-wish-I-were-anywhere-but-here moments, but I have way too much Russell pride to let them know. "Hey there, how y'all doin'?" With a smile, I give them a little wave of my fingers, but I'm met with wide-eyed stares and silence. Ignoring the rebuff, I glance around, hoping to locate Rufus.

Beads of perspiration form on my forehead, and I do believe the temperature is closing in on ninety degrees even though it's early. The pool glistens invitingly in the background, and you would have thought at least a few of the guests would have worn a swimsuit, but then again, I don't think these people ever break a sweat.

The young harpist, looking confused, seems to wonder if she should keep on plunking away and decides to compromise by playing ever so lightly. I wish I had the nerve to shout for her to crank it up with some Lynyrd Skynyrd, but of course I don't since I've gotten in enough trouble lately, and we haven't even lived here for a year. And truthfully, although I'm standing with my hands on my hips, trying to appear confident, the fact is I'm shaking on the inside . . . not that I'd ever let on.

When Mason Worthington, the owner of the house, heads my way, I try to smile, but I fear my smile is more of a cringe. "May I help you, Ms. Russell?" he asks in a voice as smooth as single-barrel bourbon. He reminds me of the Kentucky Fried Chicken Colonel. I want to ask for a bucket of Extra Crispy, but I compose myself.

"I'm here to git my dog. He came this way chasin' after Misty. Have you seen him?"

"I'm afraid not." He arches one bushy white eyebrow as he nervously glances around. I'm guessing he doesn't want Rufus and Misty to, you know, hook up.

"Oh . . . crap," I mutter when I see Misty's curly little head peeking out from beneath a long white tablecloth. On top of the round table is a tiered cake; I do recall hearing something about Mason Worthington and his wife celebrating their fiftieth anniversary, not that Daddy and I were invited. Rufus, who I now see was side-tracked by the buffet table droppings, spots Misty too and with a happy bark makes a mad dash for the pesky poodle. With his head bent in determination, he takes off and might have caught her, but he trips over one of his floppy ears and does two sideways rolls in the grass before coming up looking disoriented. He barks, as if trying to clear his head.

"Rufus, come here!" I plead, and grab a slice of ham as incentive. He looks longingly at the meat flapping in my hand, but then Misty yaps, drawing his attention. When she runs beneath the table again, Rufus chooses puppy love over food and hurries her way.

Well, hellfire.

Rufus runs straight for the long tablecloth and then tugs on the edge to get to Misty's hiding place. "No!" I yell, but it's too late. I watch, along with the rest of the party, as the anniversary cake creaks back and forth in slow motion as if it's in an earthquake. "Oh no," I whimper, but aside from the bride and groom ornament taking a swan dive to the ground, the cake remains standing. Thank God! A collective sigh of relief ripples through the crowd. But when yapping Misty emerges from beneath the table with Rufus in howling pursuit, the top tier slides to the left, creating the Leaning Tower of Cake. For a dramatic moment it remains that way but then, just when I'm thinking total disaster has been avoided, the rest of the cake follows, sliding tier by tier and creating a white heap on the green grass.

Everyone, including me, gasps, except for a tow-headed toddler dressed in a frilly pink dress. Clapping with glee, she waddles over, trips over the bride and groom, and falls face-first into the cake. "Cassidy! You poor baby!" her mother croons when Cassidy starts to wail. Her mother hurries over, but then slips sideways in the slick icing and lands as if she's sliding into second base. The harpist, caught up in the moment, picks up the tempo and, as if working with the soundtrack in a movie, sets the music to the sudden chaos.

With a glare in my direction, the cake-smeared mother picks up her cake-smeared toddler. "Are you *happy*?" she asks me with a lift of her chin.

Sensing this is a rhetorical question, I choose to remain silent even though it's on the tip of my tongue to answer, *Yes*. Misty, the real culprit in the whole mess, scampers over and starts scarfing down anniversary cake as if there's no tomorrow. Rufus, of course, isn't far behind.

"Misty, no! Baby doll, you're going to get sick!" Mason Worthington whines, and hobbles over to scoop her up in his arms. Once again I'm on the receiving end of a glare. I'm about to remind him that Misty caused this ruckus by running through *my* yard, but seeing my opportunity, I dive for my dog. With a bark of protest he sidesteps me on his stubby legs and I come up with nothing but air and a face full of icing. "Well . . . hell!" I curse, but luckily my expletive is muted by my mouthful of sweet buttercream.

"Here, you might need this," offers a smooth, deep voice I would know anywhere. Cody Dean. Trying not to act like I'm totally humiliated, I come up to my knees and take the napkin from his outstretched hand. After wiping the goop from my face, I finally look up. I'm about to thank him, when Marissa Clayton, the petite blonde he's with, puts her hand over her mouth and *snickers*, making my words die in my throat and steam come out of my ears. She's dressed in a floral sundress and a white, wide-brimmed hat. Soft waves of hair fall to her exposed, lightly tanned shoulders. With dazzling white teeth and perky breasts, she's standing there looking down her perfect little nose at me just like she used to do in high school. Hmmm, but back then her nose was bigger and her breasts smaller . . .

Without saying a word I slowly lick a dab of icing from the corner of my mouth and silently count to ten since I'm very close to giving Marissa a hard shove right smack dab into the heap of cake. Some of my intention must be written on my face, because her eyes widen slightly and she takes a step backward, sinking the pointy heels of her sandals into a glob of cake. "Eeeew," she whines, and once again I'm on the receiving end of a glare. What is it with these people? This is not my fault!

Cody's dark eyebrows draw together before turning a sympathetic smile in my direction. I should be grateful, but for some reason the fact that he feels sorry for me angers me even more than Marissa's snicker.

"Allow me." When Cody extends his hand to assist me to my feet, I think about refusing, but Marissa's little hiss has me accepting his offer.

"Thank you," I mumble while trying to ignore the warm tingle I get from his touch as he tugs me to my feet. I'm feeling a bit smug that Marissa looks peeved; then suddenly the slippery icing causes my fingers to slide from his and I tumble backward, landing on my ass in the cake with an audible splat. Marissa covers her mouth and giggles, and a titter ripples through the crowd. Heat creeps up my neck to my face and I want the ground to open up and swallow me.

"Sorry, Jolie," Cody says with such sincerity that I believe him, but the sympathy in his deep blue eyes causes another wave of humiliation to wash over me, especially when Marissa now sports a smirk. Even in the toughest of times I've never been one for tears, so the sudden emotion that bubbles up in my throat is unexpected and causes me a bit of a panic.

The very last thing I want to do is cry.

The guests hover with expectation. I suppose this is more action than they bargained for at an otherwise stuffy and boring brunch. If I weren't so embarrassed, I might find this situation funny or, better yet, start a food fight. Instead, I bite the inside of my cheek hard and swallow the moisture clogging my throat. When Cody extends his hand again, a hot rush of anger staves off my tears and I manage something close to a glare . . . well, I hope so, anyway. If I thought my voice wouldn't come out a gurgle, I might just tell him, *Bite me*, and when Marissa's shiny red lips twitch I decide to try. Then, out of the corner of my eye, I spot Brett Dean, Cody's younger brother, heading my way, holding none other than Rufus in his arms.

"This little guy belong to you?" Brett asks with a twinkle in his blue eyes, which are a shade lighter than Cody's. Although he's a bit shorter and more muscular, the two definitely look like brothers.

"I guess I'll claim him," I answer with a slight smile. Thank goodness my voice is only a little shaky. "Oh, don't let him get icing on your shirt."

"No big deal." Brett glances down at his green polo and shrugs. He's dressed a bit more casually than most of the guests and doesn't seem to mind an icing smudge or two. I recall that while Cody was the serious scholar back in high school, Brett was the hell-raiser athlete, graduating the same year as me. He went to college on a baseball scholarship and now, instead of falling into the family business, coaches at Cottonwood High School while teaching American history. Good for him.

"How about I carry him back home for you?"

"Thanks," I answer gratefully. I notice that although Marissa is clinging to Cody, her gaze lingers on Brett. Their eyes meet and although I'm no expert in such matters since I've never had a real boyfriend, I swear something passes between them. It was rumored that Brett's wild ways kept him at odds with his daddy, but I guess that's the way of the second son having to measure up to someone like Cody. While we never ran in the same circles, Brett was always nice to me, and right now I'd like to give him a big hug . . . well, except I'm covered with cake.

"Ready?" he asks, and I nod.

"Sorry," I announce to everyone in general, glad that my usually spunky nature is returning. It really was Misty's fault, when you get down to brass tacks, but I do feel sorry about the mess . . . well, a little bit, anyway. With a stiff nod to Cody and Marissa, I follow Brett, who is carrying big ole Rufus with ease. I have a strong urge to glance over my shoulder at Cody, but I refrain and turn my attention to Brett and Rufus. The crazy mutt doesn't protest and I'm betting he's plumb worn out. *Serves him right*, I think with a shake of my head, but when he looks over at me with those big, sad basset hound eyes, I know I won't stay mad at him.

"Thanks for coming to my rescue," I tell Brett when we reach the sidewalk.

"Are you kidding? I was bored stiff. Mason Worthington is some sort of distant relative on my mother's side, but I only went for the free food. Since I was already finished eating, I should be thanking you. Those kinds of events aren't my thing."

"Mine either."

"Of course, I was looking forward to a slice of cake," he adds with a sigh.

For a second I think he's serious, but then he grins. "Oh, stop!" I tell him, but his grin is infectious and I laugh, thinking he's my kind of guy. I wonder if his hand will give me a hot tingle like Cody's did and I think I might want to find out. Boy, I hope so, especially after seeing Cody cozying up with Marissa Clayton, even though I know that any romantic notions I have where Cody is concerned will always be pure fantasy.

"This is where you live, right?" Brett asks when we reach my long driveway.

I look up at the white, pillared, Southern-style mansion and nod slowly. The old red pickup truck parked in the driveway looks out of place, just like I feel most of the time. "Hard to believe sometimes, but yes."

"So, how do you like living here?" Brett asks as we walk up the brick-paved path.

While I'm wondering how to answer, Rufus squirms out of Brett's arms and hurries around back toward his doghouse. "That's where you belong," I shout after him, and Brett laughs. After inhaling a deep breath I say, "The house is pretty and I love the swimmin' pool."

Brett arches one eyebrow. "But?"

"Daddy and I aren't exactly"—I shrug and then

finish—"accepted." My brave I-don't-care smile wobbles a bit at the corners, but I quickly recover and then roll my eyes. "Whatever." After glancing down at my cake-smeared cutoffs, I manage to grin. Brett seems down-to-earth and even though I'm half dressed with clumps of cake, mostly on my butt, I find myself pretty much at ease. Of course, being a tomboy, I always did get along with guys, but lately it seems that I've been longing for more than friendship. Glancing over at my half-washed truck I say, "I can't imagine why we're not welcomed with open arms."

Brett laughs again. "Well, if it's any consolation, I was born into all this and never fit in. I sometimes wonder if I wasn't switched at birth." But then his grin fades and he says, "Listen, Jolie, don't let these people intimidate you."

"I'm not easily intimidated."

"I get that about you. But growing up with money has a way of making people think they're somehow superior." He gives me a deadpan look. "Believe me, they're not."

"Not even Marissa Clayton?"

"Especially her," he answers tightly.

"Really?" I ask, and purse my lips as if in thought. "Am I wrong, or are you protesting just a bit too much?"

Brett jams his hands in his pockets and shoots me a half grin. "Okay, yeah, she's a snob and wants my money-making brother, not a high school teacher." He shrugs. "I'm not even sure I like her."

"But she sets your pants on fire?" I casually ask while I walk over to pick up the garden hose.

Brett tosses his dark head back and laughs. "Yeah, I think you nailed it."

"I call 'em like I see 'em." While grinning over at him I start squirting off my cake-encrusted toes.

"Kinda like you and my brother."

My grin fades. "What?" I scoff with a wave of my hand.

He arches an eyebrow.

"Do I act as if I like him?" Oh lord, will the humiliation never cease?

"It's in the way you look at him," Brett says, and flutters his eyelashes.

"I do *not* bat my eyes." Holy crap. Do I? But then Brett laughs, and I sigh with relief before pointing the nozzle in his direction.

"Hey, don't," he pleads with his hands up, not that I really would squirt him anyway. "It's really more the way Cody looks at you."

I'm reconsidering hosing him down when I realize from his expression that he's serious. "What?"

"Cody didn't like me coming to your rescue one bit."

"What do you mean?" I ask.

"He wanted to be your hero."

My heart pumps harder. "Wait a minute. How do you know this?"

Brett's eyes crinkle with amusement. "Because I've made it my job to get under his skin over the years. He hides it well, but I'm an expert at getting his goat. I can read him like a book. Jolie, he couldn't take his eyes off you when you came running into the backyard. I saw his eyes darting around looking for your dog."

"Well, yeah, just like everyone else at the party." I'm not really buying into this. "Wait, so you carried Rufus home just to tick off your brother?"

"No. That was just the icing on the cake."

Of course I have to groan, but then I say softly, "So do you think Cody . . . likes me?" I put my hands to my cheeks. "Dear lord, did I really just ask you that?"

Brett looks at me carefully and I realize he probably doesn't want to get my hopes up.

"Don't worry," I say. "I know he's way out of my league. He could never go for a little ole redneck like me." I jab my thumb at my chest.

Brett takes a step closer to me. "I think Cody is fascinated by you, Jolie."

"Really?" My heart skitters around in my chest again. "Why do you say that?"

"Whenever I'm around him, your name seems to come up."

"Probably not in a good way, though. I know the neighbors don't always take a liking to our outdoor activities." I swing my hand toward my half-washed truck. "But you know, this is my home. I should be able to wash my truck in my very own driveway or fish in Copper Creek. I know we've gotten a bit rowdy here and there, playing some corn hole and tossing back some beer, but this is our property and Daddy and I are used to doin' as we please. Am I wrong in my way of thinkin'?"

Brett shakes his head. "No. I'm sure this has been quite a transition for you."

"Ya think?" I try to joke.

"You must be overwhelmed . . ."

"Oh, I hear a big *but*." I put my hands on my hips. "Let me have it, Brett."

"Neighborhoods like these have rules, as stupid as some of them seem."

"You mean like the one that says we have to ask permission to have a garden? Or that we can't have a shed in the side yard?" With a small lift of my shoulders I continue. "I realize we are different than the rest of these people, but it's hard to conform to a lifestyle I don't even understand. Everyone stares, and not in a good way. It sucks not to be liked."

"Well, Cody would like you if he allowed himself the chance to get to know you, Jolie." He shrugs. "But people like him and Marissa can't see past their noses."

"Do not clump your brother together with Marissa," I tell him, but I realize there is some truth to his statement. "I guess we're doomed for unrequited love," I tell him in my best Scarlet O'Hara voice. I bat my eyes for good measure, making him laugh.

"There's more than one way to skin a cat," he tells me in a thoughtful voice that has me curious.

"Just what are you gettin' at?" I ask Brett. Rufus, who must have thought he had enough of a time-out, comes lumbering around the house to the driveway. When I shoot him an I'm-still-ticked-at-you look, he hangs his head and drags his ears, but as always those sad eyes get to me. "Oh, come here, you old mutt." After kneeling down to scratch behind Rufus's ear, I look up at Brett. "Well?"

Brett bends down and scratches Rufus's other ear. "I just had an interesting idea pop into my head," he says, but then fails to elaborate.

"Oh, don't even think about not tellin' me."

"I will, Jolie, but first I have to see if it's even possible."

"What?"

He shakes his head as if reconsidering. "It was just a fleeting thought that came from out of nowhere."

"Oh, come on!"

Brett looks at me for a long moment and then says, "You promise you won't be offended?"

"Well, that's a tough request," I tell him. "Obviously, I'm not going to like what you're gonna say, but shoot."

Brett rocks back on his heels. "You forgot to promise."

"What are we—ten?" I roll my eyes. "Okay. I'm not easily intimidated *or* offended."

"Keep in mind it's not my intention to offend you," Brett says.

When he pauses again I have the urge to give him a shove. "Oh, for Pete's sake, just tell me what's on your mind!"

2

No Offense, But . . .

Brett opens his mouth, but then he threads his fingers through his dark hair. "What am I thinking? I don't know you that well, Jolie. I can't even believe we're having this conversation."

"Well, but we are." I shrug. "If it helps, I feel as if I can trust you." But then again, maybe I'm just desperate for a friend. "So just tell me what's on your mind." I lick my lips and taste the remaining sweetness of buttercream icing while waiting none too patiently for his response. "Please."

Brett looks at me thoughtfully and then gives me a slow smile. "All right."

"Thanks." While scratching behind Rufus's ear, my fingers brush against his. I'm not sure whether the touch was on purpose, but there's no tingle, just a warm, comfortable feeling. Well, damn, I think to myself. Why do I have to be attracted to the wrong brother? But then it really does hit me. "I need a friend, Brett. Someone who understands this whole world I've been thrown into. You can help me, can't you?"

Brett looks up from Rufus's fur and into my eyes. He nods slowly. "Yeah, I think I can, Jolie."

"Oh, thank you!" I think about throwing my arms around him, but I'm not really a spontaneously hugging kind of girl.

"Okay, but this is the part where you can't take offense."

"I promise!" I assure him even though I'm not so sure and my optimistic mood deflates a little. I just won't let it show. I've gotten really good at not letting my hurt feelings show.

"You mentioned how you don't feel as if you and your daddy are . . . accepted."

"That's putting it mildly." I nod slowly. "You know, I sorta talked Daddy into selling our land and building this monster." I wave my hand toward the house. "I wanted him to be able to fish and hunt and whittle. Just kick back and enjoy life, you know?" My throat closes up. "He's worked his fingers to the bone and then lost Mama on top of it all," I gruffly explain, and then have to clear my throat in order to continue. "And now I wonder if we made the right decision. Sometimes I don't know when to keep my mouth shut." When my voice cracks Brett puts his hand over mine, and I'm suddenly embarrassed. He's little more than a stranger and I'm opening up to him with things I haven't voiced to anyone . . . well, except in prayers to my mama.

Rufus, who often reads my moods, nudges my leg with his cool nose and whines. When he turns his doleful eyes up to me, I give him a reassuring neck rub. "Daddy and I just don't fit into this hoity-toity world."

"What if you could?"

My gaze snaps up to meet Brett's. "Right . . . ," I scoff.

"The neighbors look at me and Daddy as if we're Ellie Mae and Jed Clampett."

"Who?"

"The Beverly Hillbillies."

"You're not that bad, Jolie."

"Oh, really?" My laugh is a bit brittle. "You should have seen the look on Cordelia Crawford's face when Daddy caught a mess of fish in Copper Creek last week and proceeded to clean them on the back patio. Miss Cordelia watches us from her deck as if we're her own personal reality TV show. Daddy thinks it's funny."

Brett laughs. "I already like your father."

"Yeah, well, just to give you a heads-up as to what you're gettin' yourself into."

"Sounds like he has a good-ole-boy attitude about the whole thing, Jolie."

While absently scratching Rufus beneath his chin I say to Brett, "You know, come to think of it, Daddy tends to look at our situation with a laid-back sense of humor . . . not unlike Jed Clampett."

"And you?"

I wrinkle my nose. "I tend to get ticked."

"Whoof!" Rufus barks, and takes off after a bird.

"Good luck with that!" I holler after him, then turn back to Brett, who is grinning at me. "What?"

"Nothing." His grin widens, and I wonder what it is about me that amuses him.

"You'd think he'd realize after the millionth time that there's no way he's ever gonna catch a darned bird," I explain.

"Yeah, you'd think." Brett grins. "You have to give him credit for his determination and undying persistence. Not giving up goes a long way."

"All right, Brett, enough small talk. Tell me what's on your mind."

"Okay, Jolie, are you ready?"

"You betcha."

"There's this very nice woman, Ms. Abigail Marksberry, who teaches family life management at Cottonwood High School."

"Family life management?"

Brett inclines his head. "A modern version of home economics."

"I already know how to cook and sew."

"Well, she also teaches speech and etiquette classes on the side."

"There are people who really do that?"

"Oh sure." Brett nods. "It's mostly for business-related reasons. She helps her clients become polished in business settings."

"Oh." I nod as if I understand.

"She comes from old Southern money but fell on hard times and turned her knowledge into a career."

While pursing my lips I nod slowly, suddenly knowing where this is going and not sure if I like it.

"Jolie, she's an expert in instilling poise and confidence in people. I can even see it in her high school students."

"Is she mean?" I ask.

He laughs. "No."

"Bossy?"

"Well, yeah, I suppose it's part of her job description."

I nibble on the inside of my cheek. "And you think she can make me and Daddy over?"

"Yeah, I do . . . not that I think you need it. But you

know, if it's your goal to fit in, then you should give it some thought."

"What makes you think Miss Abigail would take on this sort of job?" I ask.

He pauses, then says, "This is between you and me, okay?"

I scoot closer to him on the driveway. "Gotcha. My lips are sealed." He chuckles when I make a show of locking my lips and throwing away the key. "Is everything I do funny?" I ask him.

He smiles. "No, just cute."

I feel a little blush creep into my cheeks since I don't get called things like *cute* too often, especially by a hot guy. I'm usually treated like one of the boys, but I never was much into girlie things. There was always too much work to be done to worry about hair and makeup. Lately I've been wondering if I've been missing out. After getting myself under control I ask, "Are you gonna hold me in suspense forever?"

When his blue eyes take on a serious expression, I pipe down and give him my full attention. "As I said, Miss Abigail's family fell on hard times financially. Most of her friends deserted her and she was no longer invited to the parties and events as she had been in the past."

"Those jackasses!" I sputter, then wish I had used a more feminine phrase, but then again I don't think I know any.

"You got that right." When Brett nods in agreement, I breathe a sigh of relief.

"So in other words, she has an ax to grind," I say.

"I guess you could put it that way." Brett pauses and then continues. "I don't want to influence you, but"—he grins—"wouldn't it be fun to show these people a thing or two?"

"These people are *your* people, Brett," I respond.

He lifts his shoulders. "Mmmm, not so much. I'm perfectly content with my simple lifestyle instead of all the drama. Don't get me wrong. I love my parents and Cody too. I've just chosen a different, um, unpretentious path."

"Your own path." I'm beginning to like him even more.

"Yep. I still get invited to functions and attend family events. But other than that, I do my own thing."

"Good for you."

He grins. "Thanks. Most people think I'm crazy for not following in my father's footsteps like Cody did." But then his grin fades a little. He plucks a blade of grass from the edge of the lawn and fiddles with it.

"It must have been tough following someone as ambitious as Cody," I tell him quietly. "I hope I'm not overstepping my bounds by saying that."

"Not at all," he assures me with a wave of his hand, and then grins. "Ambitious? That's a polite way of saying someone as smart as Cody." He shakes his head. "Yeah, I've always had a bad case of second-son syndrome. Got all my attention by raising hell," he admits with a laugh.

"I can relate to that." When I give him a high five, he laughs, and I continue. "So, I'm guessing you want to help me prove a point?"

He shrugs again but then nods. "I'm a teacher. I love proving points. Plus, it'll be fun. What do ya say? Are you game?"

"I dunno. It would take a miracle to turn me into a soft-spoken Southern belle. This here Abigail Marksberry would have her work cut out for her."

Brett arches one eyebrow. "Jolie Russell, you don't give yourself enough credit. You're smart, pretty, and you think on your feet."

"And on my butt too."

He laughs. "Yeah. And I think we can have you ready for the Cottonwood ball at the end of the summer."

"Wait a minute." My eyes widen. "You're kiddin'. That's like a black-tie affair or whatever you call it. Written up in the paper and everything."

"Yeah, and you can be my date. I always go to that one because the auction raises so much money for charity."

I swallow hard and flick a dab of crusty icing from my elbow.

"It would be a blast to turn heads, Jolie. Knock their socks off." He gives me a you-can-do-this smile.

"Good lord, I would be like a redneck Cinderella."

Brett laughs. "I like that. So, what do ya say?"

I'm still not totally convinced I can pull it off. "I'll think on it, okay?"

"Fair enough. But in the meantime, I'll give Miss Abigail a call and see if she's interested, even though I'm pretty sure she'll jump all over this. Since we're on summer break she should be available." He pushes himself to his feet and then politely lends me a hand.

"Whatever I decide to do, I hope we can be friends."

"You can count on that," he promises, and then gives me a knuckle bump. "I'll give you a few days to make up your mind."

"Thanks, Brett."

"You betcha."

I watch him walk down the long driveway before I pick up the garden hose. I start squirting the remaining crumbs and icing off my feet while thinking that this day

started off normally, but then I shake my head and a
chuckle escapes me. No, normal has been long gone since
we sold our farm and built this house in Copper Creek
Estates.

After glancing around at my butt, I lift the nozzle and
use it as a shower to wash away the remaining mess.
While I'm squirting, I ponder Brett's unexpected offer,
thinking how good it would feel to hold my head high in
this neighborhood instead of feeling like an unwanted
outsider. But then again, I'm not quite certain I really
want to fit in with people I don't know if I could ever actually like! Oh, but boy oh boy, Brett sure is right that it
would be fun to show them all up.

Angling my head to the side, I let the cool water slide
over my shoulders and down my back. No longer a sticky
mess, I decide I might as well finish washing my truck.
Just as I turn to start hosing the front fender, Rufus barks
and starts down the driveway. "No! Don't you dare!"
Thinking he is once again in hot pursuit of Misty, I spin
around and blast water in the face of none other than
Cody Dean. I'm so shocked that for an insane moment I
continue to give him a good soaking like a fireman dous-
ing a fire.

"Whoa!" When Cody sputters and takes a step backward, I drop the nozzle to the concrete with a clank.

"Sorry!" Stuck on full blast, the hose snakes around on
the driveway while Rufus howls. The poor dog must
think it's alive. It sure looks like it is. "Come back here!"
I yell as if that might help, and go zigzagging after it like
a crazy person, joined by my equally crazy dog. "Stop!"
I actually shout as if the hose will obey my command.
Rufus thinks I'm yelling at him and gives me a guilty
look, but then starts barking again. "Ouch!" I let out a

yelp of pain when I stub my already stubbed toe and start hopping on one foot.

"Just turn it off," Cody shouts.

"What?" I blink at him while nursing my throbbing toe. Water is sliding off every part of him and his hair is plastered to his head. The thought goes through my brain that he manages to look damned good dripping wet.

"The hose. Where do you turn it off?"

"Oh . . . right!" Duh! I hobble over to the faucet and crank it clockwise. "Sorry, I wasn't thinkin' straight." He has that effect on me, but I leave that part out. While nibbling on the inside of my cheek, I look at him with big I'm-so-sorry eyes. It usually works with Daddy. The thought crosses my mind that if this situation had happened to Brett, we'd probably both laugh.

"It's no big deal," Cody assures me in his perfectly polite way, but I can't quite read his expression. I decide I'd better tread softly. I'm having a hard time not bursting into a fit of laughter since hosing him down is sort of a big deal in my book. Had he hosed me down, even unintentionally, as I did to him, I wouldn't be standing there so calmly.

"It was an accident," I feel compelled to explain.

Cody smiles. "I had that figured out."

"Good. I wanted to be sure. There are lots of stories about me floatin' around, and I didn't want this to be fodder for the gossip mill."

"Believe me, I don't plan on starting any gossip about you, Jolie."

"Why, thank you." I consider doing a curtsy, but I'm not sure if he would laugh or be offended.

"Not necessary." When he looks at me—rather *intently*, I guess is the word—it dawns on me that I'm standing here sopping wet too, but without much clothing covering me. I wonder what brings him here, but I'm not sure if it's polite to ask, so I refrain.

A bikini top and cutoff shorts are my usual attire for a variety of outdoor summer activities, and I'm not usually self-conscious about my body. Now, I'm aware that I'm built fairly nicely, especially since I'm no stranger to hard physical work, but I'm suddenly wishing for one of those beach cover-ups, even though I'm pretty sure I don't own such a thing. I'm coming to find there are many feminine items lacking in my meager wardrobe. I keep meaning to do something about it, but I'm not sure where to begin. Brett was right. I need help.

Now would be a good time to come up with something witty or cute, but I'm too focused on how his shirt is plastered to his very nice chest. Cody might have been a scholar instead of an athlete, but he's no stranger to working out, that's for sure. A hot tingle slides down my back, and oh, heaven help me, I suddenly feel my traitorous nipples tighten in my bikini top, making my desire for a beach cover-up even more intense.

"Would you happen to have a towel handy?"

My eyes widen. Ohmigod, he must surely notice my nipples looking pointy like on a mannequin at the mall and is no doubt reading my mind. "Um . . . ," I stammer.

"I'm sopping wet," he explains.

At first I don't get what he's saying since I'm busy begging my brain to send nipple shrinkage messages south. Oh, he meant a towel for *him*. "Oh, sure! A towel. Yes. A towel." I know I'm babbling a bit loudly, but I can't seem to stop myself. "Follow me into the pool. I mean . . . oh, you know what I mean." When he looks at me as if I'm a little loopy, I turn and head toward the pool house, hoping there aren't any more crumbs smashed to my butt. Then I wonder if he's looking at my butt and if I should give him a little hip action, but since I'm likely to burst into a fit of laughter if I even attempt such a thing, I simply walk in a normal fashion. But then I hear a squishing sound and glance down at my feet.

"The squishing is coming from my soggy shoes," he explains. I wince, knowing he's wearing some fancy leather tasseled loafers that likely cost a mint. While how much things cost probably doesn't even enter his mind and should no longer matter to me, being frugal is in my blood. No matter how rich we are, I know I'll always pinch pennies. It's just who I am.

"Sorry 'bout your shoes," I mumble as we approach the pool house that's nicer than my old home.

"It's no big deal," Cody assures me in a voice laced with humor.

My backbone gets a little stiffer as I wonder if he's laughing at me like everyone else in the neighborhood. But then, thinking I might be overreacting, I let it slide. Daddy had a few of his buddies over to play some poker the other night and I hope there aren't any Budweiser bottles strewn about. I hold my breath as I open the door, but when I see everything is as neat as a pin, I remind myself we have a maid. "Whew!"

"Pardon?" Cody says.

"Oh, nothin'. Sometimes this new lifestyle is difficult to comprehend and I feel as if any moment I'll wake up in my old bedroom, snuggled beneath my worn quilt," I admit. "I know we've been here for close to a year, but it's my first summer not working the farm and it really feels . . . weird." I'm not quite sure why I just divulged my personal thoughts to him and I feel heat creep into my cheeks.

"Oh." He gives me an odd, almost guilty look that makes me wonder what this visit is all about.

The air conditioner kicks on with a soft hum, and I shiver as I pull a couple of fluffy towels from the linen closet. "Here you go." I walk over to Cody, who is politely dripping onto a colorful throw rug by the door. None of the decor was my or Daddy's doing. Some fancy interior designer lady did up the entire house since Daddy and I were clueless. While I like it all well enough, it doesn't really feel like home to me.

"Thanks," he replies, and when my fingers barely brush his, I get another hot tingle. I shiver, but this time it's not because of the cool air.

"Cold?"

"No . . . oh, I mean, *yes*," I lie, and then wrap a towel around me as if I'm freezing. I do a fake little shiver for good measure. Then, since he covers his face with the towel and starts vigorously drying his hair, I have the opportunity to stare at the play of muscle in his biceps and chest without him knowing. "If you need a dry shirt and shorts, I could probably round something up," I offer, hoping he doesn't realize it's a blatant effort on my part to see some skin. "I have plenty of large T-shirts and maybe some gym shorts that might do the trick."

After lowering the towel, he hesitates long enough for me to realize he doesn't exactly like the idea, but his clothing is so saturated that he finally nods. "Okay, sure."

"I'll see what I can find," I tell him. But then I can't stand it any longer and have to ask, "What brings you here, Cody?" My heart beats a little faster, with a part of me hoping he's come to his senses with the realization that Marissa is a snotty, pretentious bitch and the decision to give a real woman a try—namely, you know, *me*. But when he suddenly clears his throat and appears uncomfortable, my hopes are dashed.

"We need to have a little talk if you have a few minutes," he says.

I give him a smile while nodding, but I'm thinking this can't be good.

3

Indecent Exposure

I'm wondering just what our little talk is going to entail while I make my way to the guest bedroom closet. Some of my guy friends from my life before money come over once in a while to party and swim, so there's an abundance of leftover clothing. Their visits, however, have become few and far between and they treat me, I don't know . . . *different*, making me want to scream that the money and big house haven't changed who I am and never will. At least I hope not. If I ever start flitting around, acting uppity and snooty like Marissa, I'd want to be shot and tagged like a doggone deer. Snagging a pair of blue Nike shorts and a UK Wildcats T-shirt, I return to the main room.

"This should do," I tell him. When he looks at the clothing a bit skeptically, I get somewhat miffed. "It's washed. We have a laundry room out here." I know my tone is a little defensive, but I can't help it.

"I was just wondering if it belongs to your boyfriend."

"Oh . . . no," I reply without the bite this time. "It's from what I call the lost and found. I don't have a boyfriend," I admit, then quickly add, "At the moment," so he doesn't think I'm a big loser. "I'm, you know, in between relationships. How 'bout you?" If he declares his undying love for Marissa, I just might have to hose him down on purpose.

Cody accepts the clothing and then shrugs. "I've been too busy developing Copper Creek Estates to do much dating."

"Oh." He didn't exactly answer my question, but I decide that pressing the issue would be too forward. I do have to wonder if his question about my availability was simple curiosity or an interest in me. But then I give my brain a mental shake. There's no way Cody Dean is considering asking me out. *Is there?* I peer at him more closely. Is this what our little talk is going to be about? My heart beats faster at the prospect and I'm suddenly anxious to find out. "You can change in the bathroom," I tell him, and point to the door at the opposite end of the room.

"Thanks." When he sloshes across the beige tile I watch his progress, and after the door closes behind him a little sigh escapes me. Then, deciding I need a quick change too, I hurry to the bedroom in search of dry clothes.

After slipping on a clean pair of cutoffs, I tug a white tank top over my bikini bra. Better, I think to myself, until I make the mistake of glancing at my reflection in the oval, floor-length mirror. Instead of delicate and petite like Marissa, I'm sturdy and tall. Her sleek blond hair had been swept back from her face with a fancy clip whereas my unruly mane of chestnut brown has a mind of its own. I touch my face while remembering Marissa's flawless skin and frown at the smattering of freckles across my nose. I know they could be hidden with foundation, but my attempts at applying makeup had always left me looking as if I needed to be on a street corner. Mascara and lip-gloss are about all I can manage. After an *oh, well* sigh, I head back to the main room.

"Wow," I say rather loudly when I see Cody dressed in the shorts and T-shirt. In my mind he looks even better in casual clothes.

" 'Wow,' what?" He angles his almost-dry head at me in question.

"W-wow, it feels better to be in dry clothes." I quickly cover up the real meaning of my outburst while thinking I need to learn not to say what I'm thinking out loud. Daddy tells me I wear my emotions on my sleeve, so I guess I'll have to work on that as well. Maybe Miss Abigail can assist me in learning to be more discreet.

"Yes, it sure does," Cody agrees with a slight smile. "I tossed my wet stuff in the dryer. I hope that's okay?"

"Oh, sure. I should have offered." I notice that his shoes are dangling from his fingertips. "Those should dry out nicely in the sun." When Cody frowns as if having second thoughts, I point my thumb over my shoulder toward the door. "You wanna take them outside and then have our little . . . talk?" For some silly reason I feel as if I should bat my eyes, but I refrain.

"Mmm . . . maybe we should do this another time."

"Oh." My mood deflates a little, but then I give him a perky smile. "My daddy always says there's no time like the present." Since I have lingering hope he's going to ask me out, I try to think of another reason for him to stay. "You have to wait for your clothes to dry anyway." But then, thinking I sound too desperate, I continue. "Or you could come back later." I want to add that we could grill some supper by the pool, but I don't have enough nerve. Yet when he appears indecisive, I decide to go for it. "I'm thinking about ribs on the barbecue for dinner. You're welcome to join me," I offer in a quieter-than-usual tone. I hold my breath and wait, and my heart plummets when he gives me a you're-getting-the-wrong-idea expression. Feeling heat creep into my cheeks, I quickly amend my invitation. "I was thinking about asking a few people over and thought you might drop by for a bite, you know . . . *too*." But then I snap my fingers. "Oh, sorry, what am I thinking? I already have dinner plans."

"With a friend?" Cody asks casually. I'm not sure if he's calling my bluff or if he actually believes me and is simply curious.

"Um, yes, with Brett," I reply when his name pops into my head. *Oh, why did I do that?*

Cody's eyebrows rise, and he gives me a look I can't quite read. "My brother, Brett?"

"Yes." I draw out the word, giving it several extra syllables as if he had nerve to doubt that Brett would ask me out. Of course, since it's a flat-out fabrication, it requires a bit of acting on my part. I put the heel of my hand to my forehead. "It had totally slipped my mind." I give *mind* a few extra syllables too.

When something akin to annoyance passes over Cody's features, I fear he's catching on to my nonsense. Horrified, I'm thinking about coming clean, when Cody murmurs, "So that's why Brett brought your dog home."

"Your brother was being a nice guy, Cody," I tell him as I head back outside.

"I don't doubt that." Cody follows me and places his shoes on a nearby umbrella table before sitting down in a lounge chair next to the glistening pool. "But he obviously had other intentions as well."

"What does that mean?" My tone is a bit defensive, which is silly since I'm making all of this up. I'm also feeling guilty since lying isn't in my nature, but still, I can't keep my mouth shut as I sit down next to him. "Why shouldn't your brother have dinner with me?"

Cody looks at me in surprise. "I didn't mean it that way."

"Then how did you mean it?" I can't believe I have the nerve to ask, but he's getting me riled up. I sit up straighter in the lounge chair and wait for his answer.

Cody looks over at me as if he's a little confused at his own reaction. If I didn't know better I'd think he was jealous. But I do know better, so I drop my line of questioning to ask, "What really brings you here, Cody?"

Appearing uncomfortable once again, he sits up from his leaned-back position and rubs his hands together as if trying to decide how to tell me what's on his mind.

"Oh, for Pete's sake, I'm a big girl. Just spit it out," I encourage, but then lace my hands together to keep him from seeing them tremble. I'm getting a bad feeling in the pit of my stomach.

Cody clears his throat and then says, "At a recent HOA meeting there was some . . . um, concern over some of the activities you and your father conduct on your property."

"HOA?"

"Home Owners Association," he clarifies.

"Oh . . . right, the people who said we couldn't have a shed in the side yard or a garden bigger than a postage stamp."

"This is a gated community and we have rules that

have to be followed, Jolie." His tone is gentle and indulgent, but instead of soothing me, it ticks me off.

"I'm aware of that fact." Deep down I know he's trying to be nice, but he's making me feel as if he's talking to a two-year-old. I raise my chin and in a deep, serious adult voice ask, "Could you elaborate?"

"Sure." He politely inclines his head. "For example, hunting isn't permitted."

"Of course not. Nothin' is in season right now," I scoff.

"No, I mean ever."

"Ever?" I frown at Cody and forget to keep my voice down. "But I thought that's why we kept the back ten acres?"

Cody slowly shakes his head. "The rules apply to all the property within Copper Creek Estates. Technically, you should have to tear down the barn."

My eyes widen.

"But since it was already standing and is pretty much hidden from the street, I lobbied to allow you to keep it."

I suppose I should thank him, but the words stick in my throat.

"Fishing in Copper Creek is permitted on your own property as long as you catch and release."

"What would be the point of that?" I sputter.

"Don't shoot the messenger," he says with a small smile. When I don't smile back he clears his throat again. "An open flame is allowed only in grills and fire pits."

"No bonfires?"

"Just fire pits. Decorative ones." He shakes his head again. "You know, this is all spelled out in your handbook. Have you read it?"

"Of course," I tell him in a tight little voice. Of course, I'm lying through my teeth.

He looks at me skeptically, but instead of disputing my declaration he says, "You should review it, Jolie. We take the rules seriously. It's for your own good as well. These regulations keep the value of your property strong. You wouldn't want your next-door neighbor to put up a chain-link fence or park an RV in her backyard."

I personally don't see the problem with either of those things, so I remain mute on the matter.

"And technically there isn't a rule about riding your four-wheeler or dirt bikes, because quite frankly we didn't think it would be an issue, but there have been complaints about the noise."

I'm getting a very strong urge to shove him into the pool.

"And you need to keep Rufus on a leash and contained in your yard. I suggest an electric fence."

I lean forward and force myself not to shout. "Rufus is usually obedient."

"I'm sure he is, but this isn't the first time, Jolie."

"Today's incident was Misty's fault!" This time I can't keep from getting loud. "That poodle is a little hussy!"

Cody starts to smile but then realizes I'm serious. "Granted, you aren't the only one who has dog issues in this neighborhood. Jolie, it's not my intention to offend you or to single you and your father out."

"Like I haven't heard that one before," I mumble under my breath.

"Excuse me?"

"Nothin'." I wave a dismissive hand in the air. "Anything else?" I ask in a tired voice. When he hesitates I say, "Oh, why hold back now?" I roll my eyes, half joking, but when his blue eyes remain serious, I brace myself for what he's going to lay on me next.

"I'm not trying to pick on you, but there have been complaints about some recent, uh, gatherings in your backyard."

"Daddy and his friends get a little rowdy once in a while, but it's all in good fun. They're all hardworkin' people and like to cut loose once in a while."

"Didn't the last party get a visit from the sheriff?"

I glance in the direction of Cordelia Crawford's house and wrinkle my nose. "Yes. But it wasn't Daddy's fault. Tucker Jones spiked the lemonade with white lightnin'."

"And there was some indecent exposure?"

"If you mean that Miss Cordelia got herself mooned, then, yes. She deserved it for callin' the cops. They were just laughin' and carryin' on a little too much. That's all." I know I'm getting loud, so I make an effort to calm down. "All I'm sayin' is she should just get a life and stop snoopin' over here all the time."

Cody leans forward in the lounge chair and rests his elbows on his knees. "People pay a premium for the privilege of living in this neighborhood. We have to hold to certain standards. Word is getting around and it's starting to have an effect on sales of the remaining lots."

My eyes widen even though his tone is gentle. "Wait, you're tellin' me that people are shying away from Copper Creek Estates because of Daddy and *me*?" The word *me* is a mere squeak. "We aren't the only ones who have had a loud party or two or have a dog run around the neighborhood." Completely agitated, I jump to my feet.

"Jolie, please calm down." Cody stands up and gives my shoulder a reassuring squeeze. I glance at his hand, then back at his face, and then give him a big shove into the pool. Okay, I made that last part up, but I sure want to shove him into the pool.

Or kiss him.

I know that both reactions are irrational, but I'm not thinking clearly at the moment. I also realize he's not purposefully trying to be mean, but he's basically calling Daddy and me white trash with money. "So, I suppose I was the topic of conversation at the Worthington party."

Cody fails to respond, but when he averts his gaze I know I'm right.

"And I just bet Marissa Clayton was the ringleader." I mumble this more to myself than to him, but his silence confirms my suspicion. At least I think it does, but I have to ask, "Or was it you, Cody?"

His eyebrows rise. "I was the one who suggested that you and your father remain here, remember?"

"Sure, to get what you wanted." I lean close and poke him in the chest rather hard, you know, to make my point. Surprised, Cody opens his eyes wide and stumbles backward toward the pool. Oh crap! Knowing he's going to take a tumble, I reach out and grab his shirt in an effort to save him from going in. "Ohmigod!"

4

Making a Splash

"Ahhh!" I yell as I go tumbling into the water right along with Cody. Water splashes as I land on top of him and we sink into the deep end of the pool. I'm still in shock, but he at least has the sense to kick his legs. We bob to the surface, sputtering and coughing, and for some reason I'm still clinging to his shirt. I guess this leads Cody to think I can't swim, so he wraps one arm around me and tries to make his way to the edge of the pool. I'm about to explain that I'm a strong swimmer and don't need rescuing, when I spot Rufus running at full speed on his stubby little legs. "No! Don't!" I yell at my crazy dog, who must suddenly think he's Lassie and needs to save me.

Fat chance. Unlike me, Rufus is not a strong swimmer. Because of their weight in the front and their short legs, basset hounds struggle in the water. Rufus is no exception. He makes it about three feet into the pool before his eyes bug out with a what-was-I-thinking expression, and although he's frantically doing the dog paddle, he starts to sink. "Lemme go!" I tell Cody, and try to push away so I can save my dog.

"Calm down," Cody croons, and tightens his arm around me, evidently thinking I'm in a panic because I'm drowning. When I struggle against his hold, he continues to croon. "Jolie, it's okay. I've got you."

"I need to get Rufus!" I tell him.

"Dogs can swim. He's fine."

I answer with a kick to his shin.

"Ouch! Stop! I can get you to safety if you quit struggling," Cody says.

"I don't need savin'!" I try to squirm away, causing us both to go under, but I somehow manage to break free. By this time Rufus is swiftly sinking, so I dive deep and grab a handful of fur. Now, he's a heavy dog, so getting him to the surface is no easy task. I somehow do it, but unlike me, Rufus really *is* in a state of panic and starts to wiggle and squiggle. We both begin another swift descent until a strong arm encircles us and brings us up to the surface.

Although it's a struggle, Cody hauls Rufus and me over to the side of the pool. With a grunt, Cody puts a hand on Rufus's soggy butt and heaves him over the side of the pool. He lands with a plop and then turns around to peer over the edge as if to make sure I'm okay.

"Woof!" Rufus seems proud of his rescue attempt.

"Silly-ass dog," I mumble, but then have to smile. I suppose it was kind of brave since he was well aware that he sucks at swimming.

"You okay?"

I turn my head to look at Cody, who is breathing hard and appears somewhat confused. "Well, yeah," I answer in a sort of snippy tone, but then decide I should show some appreciation for his rescue attempt. "Thank you for saving my dog, but for the record, I've been swimmin' since I was little. My mama taught me." I have more to say, but a drop of water that slides down his cheek and lands on his lips fascinates me and I totally lose my train of thought.

"Oh." He seems a little disappointed that his efforts were for naught. I know I'm supposed to be mad at him for something, but for the moment the reason escapes me. When he licks away the drop of water, I have to swallow a whimper. His mouth, I decide, is gorgeous and I have a sudden urge to run the tip of my finger over his full bottom lip, which is crazy since such an action is totally out of character for me. My heart thumps faster when I wonder how he would react if I did such a thing. Of course, I don't nearly have the nerve . . . do I? It suddenly occurs to me that I'm twenty-four years old and still unsure of myself as a woman. But one thing I know for certain is that I long to be held and kissed by Cody Dean. Perhaps I should just lean closer and do it.

Cody remains silent as if he's collecting his thoughts as well. We're both clinging one-handed to the side of the pool and mere inches separate our bodies. The sun feels warm beating down on my head. The cool water gently laps against my skin and I'm wondering if it might be better just to kiss him instead of doing the fingertip thing.

"I'm not trying to run you out of the neighborhood, Jolie."

Okay, *that's* a mood killer, bringing me back to the unfortunate reality that if I think for a moment that Cody Dean is interested in me, I'm barking up the wrong tree.

"Really? Well, I don't suppose you'd be too terribly sad to see a For Sale sign perched on my front lawn."

Cody shakes his head. "Jolie, I came here with the best of intentions. I hope you realize that."

"Yeah, well, you said your piece. Now take your good intentions and just . . . *go*." I try for a firm I-don't-care tone and almost accomplish it, except that my voice cracks a bit on the word *go*. I cough as if I have pool water in my throat.

"Jolie," Cody softly begins, but his sympathetic expression somehow gets my goat, so I push off from the wall and swim away. As soon as my toes touch the bottom, I whip around with the intention of telling him to take a flying leap, or something along those lines, not realizing that he's followed me and is oh-so-very close. Suddenly I'm nose to nose—well, nose to chin, since he has me by a few inches—with Cody. I open my mouth, not really sure what will come out, when to my surprise he pulls me close, dips his head, and plants a hot, delicious kiss right smack on me.

I should, of course, push him hard and stomp away, but since it would be difficult to pull that off in the pool and there's no door to slam or anything like that, I decide to give in to the kiss. For the moment, at least. I'll shove him away in a fit of anger as soon as I satisfy my curiosity as to whether he's a good kisser.

Ohmigod—is he *ever*.

His lips are wonderfully warm and supple. He gently coaxes my mouth open—well, okay, I open my mouth in invitation—*whatever*. Instead of pushing him away, I find myself fisting my hands in his wet T-shirt and kissing him back like it's my business.

Cody threads his long fingers through my tangled hair

and tilts my head back for better access. While slanting his mouth across mine he deepens the kiss, and when our tongues tangle, a hot tingle of desire slides down my spine. With a little moan I wind my arms around his neck and allow my body to lean against his.

I'd be embarrassed at my enthusiastic response except that I'm getting, um, the firm impression that he's having the same reaction. Mercy! When he eases back slightly I think he's ending the kiss, but instead, he slowly licks my bottom lip before capturing my mouth with his once more. I'm thinking that he's got to be the best kisser on the planet and that I could do this all day long, when he pulls away again.

With my eyes closed I'm hoping for another nice lick or maybe a nibble, but when nothing happens I raise my eyelids and blink up at him in the bright sunlight. It takes a moment, but I notice he's looking over my shoulder. "What's wrong?" My voice has turned breathless and husky, but can you blame me?

"We have an audience."

"Let me guess. Cordelia Crawford is standing on her deck watchin' us like a hawk."

"Yes." His usually smooth voice sounds irritated. Hmmm, so cool-as-a-cucumber Cody Dean is human after all.

"I told you—she thinks I'm her personal reality TV show." While wiggling my eyebrows I suggest, "Hey, how about let's give her somethin' to watch." I'm only half serious, but if I can get another amazing kiss out of it, I'm shamelessly game. "Okay?" I tilt my head up in a silent invitation.

"I don't think so." After glancing down at me, Cody shakes his head. I'm about to chuckle and tell him I wasn't really serious—well, one hundred percent anyway—but I don't like his expression. When he drops his hands and takes such a quick step away that he causes the water to ripple with waves, I suddenly understand.

Cody Dean doesn't want to be seen kissing me!

I just bet that if I were Marissa Clayton, he wouldn't care so much about a nosy, gossipy neighbor. Even though I don't know this for sure, I feel it in my bones. Of course, I'm hurt beyond all reason, not that I'm about to let him know it. "Oh, I was just kiddin', for goodness' sake." I wave my hand toward the pool house. "You can go and get your clothes. I'm sure they're dry by now."

"Jolie . . . ," Cody begins, and then looks at me as if he's about to say something more.

I hold my breath, hoping he'll dispute my line of thinking or maybe plant another kiss on me despite nosy old Cordelia. "Yes?" When he frowns but doesn't verbally respond, I hastily add, "This was a fun little diversion while waiting for your clothes to dry." I give a flip of my fingers, hoping for a flirty gesture but manage to splash him right in the face. "Oh, sorry!"

"That's okay." Cody wipes the water from his face with the back of his hand but doesn't look as if he believes me. I can't really blame him since I've just recently hosed him down and then pushed him into the pool. Both were accidents, but still . . .

I open my mouth to reiterate my apology, but then hesitate. Maybe I'm not so sorry. After all, the man basically came here to tell me that Daddy and I are single-handedly managing to bring down the property value of this god-almighty neighborhood. The kiss, I'm thinking, could have been some sort of ploy to throw me off track, but the kicker was that I really think he hated Cordelia seeing him kissing me. "Look, your clothes are probably dry. I'm sure you can see yourself out," I tell him in a pretty damned good haughty tone, when I suddenly want to cry. Since I'm not a crying kind of a girl, this wave of emotion is unexpected and catches me off guard.

"Jolie!" Cody begins, but I quickly turn away and wade toward the steps, blinking hard and not wanting him to witness my sudden weakness. The fact that he's the one causing my distress isn't lost on me and I clear my throat hard. Damn him anyway! Oh, how I wish I could stomp! "Jolie," he repeats softly, and to my surprise gently touches my arm just as I reach the steps.

I shake him off; well, I *want* to shake him off, but something compels me to turn around and face him. "What?" I try to sound exasperated, but my voice has gone soft and throaty. Since I'm on the first step we're nose to nose this time, and of course I have to notice how deep blue his eyes are. His eyelashes are dark and spiky from being wet and I know I'm supposed to be angry . . . but my gaze drops to his mouth and God help me, all I can think about is how amazing it was to feel his lips against mine.

"Why are you in such a hurry?" Cody finally asks, and I think he might actually kiss me again.

"I . . . ," I begin, and beg my befuddled brain to come up with something snarky, but then the thought occurs to me that I might be reading this entire situation wrong.

"Right," Cody says with a shake of his head. "I forgot about your dinner date."

"Date?"

Cody raises his eyebrows. "With Brett."

"Oh, yeah. My date with Brett." I put the heel of my hand to my forehead. "Slipped my mind there for a minute. Silly me. I'd better get ready," I add, and turn around so fast that I lose my footing on the step. I would have toppled sideways into the water, but Cody's arm encircles my waist and keeps me upright. "Thanks," I mumble, and try not to enjoy leaning back against him.

"You're welcome," Cody says low in my ear, and leaves his arm tucked around me just long enough to make my heart pound like a jackhammer. He feels warm and solid, making me wish for his strong arms to stay wrapped around me. The thought hits me from out of nowhere that it would be nice to have someone to lean on . . . someone to chase away my fears and hold me tight. I close my eyes but then swallow hard and remind myself that Cody Dean will never be that man.

When he clears his throat and releases me, I inhale deeply to clear my head. Although my knees are a little wobbly as I ascend the steps, I manage to turn around and say, "I'll read all those rules and whatnot." When Cody frowns at me I continue. "For the record, you didn't need to kiss me into submission." There, I can't believe I said that, but I'm glad I did.

"I—," he begins.

"Don't worry, Cody, I won't tell anyone." I glance over at Cordelia Crawford's deck and notice she's gone inside. "Hopefully she won't run her mouth either." Then, my back ramrod stiff, I walk over to the umbrella table and hand him his shoes. "Here you go."

Cody takes the shoes but has a confused expression on his face as if he doesn't know what to make of the situation. Well, join the club. He probably isn't rendered speechless often, and if I were in a better frame of mind I'd find it amusing. He clears his throat and appears decidedly uncomfortable. "It really wasn't my intention to offend you, Jolie. I just wanted to make you aware of the situation."

I shrug and pray that my voice remains steady. "I have a thick skin. Besides, I don't give a rip what those people think of me." Brave words, but neither statement is entirely true. Still, I raise my chin a notch and if I'm not mistaken, I see a measure of respect in Cody's expression. This makes me feel emotional again, but I don't want him to know that what he thinks matters to me. So, with a tight smile I turn on my heel and hurry into the house. I hear Cody call my name, but I refuse to turn back with tears in my eyes.

The air-conditioning makes me shiver as I head to the privacy of my bedroom. Closing the sturdy door, I lean against it and sigh. I can't believe the boy I once worshipped from afar just kissed me. Closing my eyes, I put trembling fingers to my lips and relive the moment. Admittedly I let my Russell pride get the best of me, leading me to wonder if the encounter could have ended quite differently. A hot rush of sadness washes over me, leaving an empty ache in its wake. With a loud sniff I blink back tears and try to smile when Rufus raises his head from his perch on my bed. I don't even have the heart to tell him to get down.

"It's for the best," I whisper firmly. "I might have money, but Cody and I are still worlds apart. Just like you and Misty."

Rufus whines.

"Yeah, well, you best get over her. You'll only cause yourself heartache," I warn him. Then, out of nowhere, a thought taps at the back of my brain like a persistent finger. Gritting my teeth, I ignore it and push away from the door. I know what I have to do. I really want to get out of my wet clothes, but before I can talk myself out of my decision I walk over to my nightstand and locate my phone. For a few heart-pounding moments I stare at the phone while I gather up the courage to make the call. Finally I use my thumb to dial the number.

5

Double Dog Dare Ya

"Yo, Jolie, what's up?" Brett asks in his deep voice, which is much like his brother's, only less formal.

"How'd you know it was me?"

"Caller ID."

"Right." I drag out the word with a shake of my head. "Daddy and I never had all of this newfangled stuff, as he calls it, until we moved here. It seems like there's a remote for just about everything. I even have one for my ceiling fan." I pick up the remote, push a button, and watch the fancy wicker blades turn in lazy circles. "In the farmhouse I had a box fan that sounded like a helicopter. We didn't even have city water, and now my water is softened and purified."

"So, that's why you called? To chat about new technology?" he asks with a touch of amusement.

"I guess I'm beatin' around the bush." I flop down on the big bed and smile. There's just something about Brett that makes me relax. "Oh, crap!"

"What?"

"I forgot that my clothes are sopping wet."

"Sopping wet? Okay, I'll bite."

"I fell into the pool. Actually, your brother sort of pulled me in." I purse my lips. "Or maybe I pushed him. Whatever." I get up from the champagne satin bedspread before I mess it up.

"Should I ask?"

"No, please don't. Let's just say it wasn't one of my finer moments. I've been havin' a lot of those lately." After a big sigh I say, "Okay, I'm gonna get down to brass tacks. I've decided that I'll do it."

"You mean you're willing to work with Abigail Marksberry?"

"Yes." I curl my hand around one of the smooth bedposts. "I'll let Ms. Abigail Marksberry make me over into a gentle Southern lady. Well, as close as she can get, anyway."

"You sound nervous."

"I am," I admit, even though I know he's teasing.

"Let me guess, my brother brought this on. Am I right?"

"Sorta . . . okay, yes." I try to sound matter-of-fact, but I can't quite keep the emotion from my voice.

"What did he say to you, Jolie?" Brett's tone becomes hard.

I shrug and then realize he can't see me through the phone. "Oh, nothin' much, just that Daddy and I are bringing down the property value in Copper Creek Estates."

"What? That sonofabitch . . . Sorry, that just royally pisses me off."

"He didn't intend to be mean," I say, defending Cody in a small voice. "Apparently Daddy and I break quite a few neighborhood rules as you mentioned earlier."

"Bullshit," he says through what sounds like clenched teeth. "Sorry for being so crude. This just blows me away."

I shrug again. "I suppose his complaints are warranted. Seems like Daddy and I were the topic of discussion at some HOA meetings or whatever." I walk over and stare out of the big picture window that overlooks the pool. When my gaze lands on the steps, I remember the long hot kiss and sigh. "Cody was only doing his job."

"He's an arrogant ass. Admit it."

Again I feel the urge to defend him. "Well, your friend Marissa Clayton had a hand in this whole thing too."

"I don't doubt it. And yet you're probably standing there thinking about Cody, just like I've been thinking about Marissa. What the hell is wrong with us?"

I have to laugh. "Damned if I know."

"Unrequited love sucks," Brett says.

"That's like lovin' somebody who doesn't return the favor, right?

"Yep."

I nod. "I have to agree with ya on that one."

"So, here's the plan."

"You have a plan?" I ask.

"Well, not entirely, but work with me here."

"Okay." He has me smiling again.

"First of all, Miss Abigail will teach you what you need to know. You'll make jaws drop at the Cottonwood Charity Ball."

I rest my head in my hands and groan.

"Trust me, okay? I know how these people operate, including my brother."

"And Marissa?"

"She's still a bit of a mystery, but yeah, I've pretty much got her number too."

"So, when do we begin?"

"Right away."

"I was afraid you were gonna say that."

Brett chuckles. "Hey, have you asked your father about working with Miss Abigail too?"

"No, he's been on a fishing trip for the past couple days. I'll talk to him tonight, but I'm thinkin' he'll be game. Oddly enough, in some ways Daddy has taken to this new lifestyle better than me."

"He hasn't been in the line of fire the way you have."

"I guess," I tell him while twirling my finger in a lock of damp hair. It's a nervous gesture, a habit I've had since I was little, and I can't seem to break myself of it. I suddenly envision big old mean Miss Abigail slapping my hand. "Oh, what am I gettin' myself into?" Oh crap, I said that out loud.

"Do you need some cheese with that whine?"

"Wine? I'm pretty much a beer drinker."

Brett laughs. "Whaa, whaaaaa, whaa."

"Oh *whine*. Sorry, Brett. I'm not usually such a wimpy thing." I stop twirling my hair and stand up a bit straighter. Then I wonder if I'll have to walk around with a book on my head.

"Jolie, this isn't going to be as painful as you think."

"I know," I answer brightly, even though I'm not so sure.

"I'll call you as soon as I firm things up with Miss Abigail," Brett says.

"Thanks. Listen, I really appreciate all of the trouble

you're going to on my account, especially since you barely know me."

"In an offbeat way, we have a lot in common," Brett replies. After a low chuckle he says, "Believe me, I'm going to love every minute of this."

"But why?"

"To prove a point." Brett hesitates but then explains. "I watched my father plow over people in his rise to the top. He took whatever he wanted without giving back, and he neglected my mother in the process."

"Oh, Brett, lung cancer took my mama. Daddy would give up everything to have one more day with her."

"Exactly. And although she is better now, it took my mother having heart trouble to make him see straight. But while Cody craved my father's attention and approval, well, I rebelled."

I'm beginning to understand. "But Cody is trying to change things at Dean Development, right?"

"Yeah, don't get me wrong. My brother is a good guy and he is trying to give back to Cottonwood. Like my father, he just needs to know there is more to life than work."

"Explain my role in this, Brett. I think there is more going on here than meets the eye." Since my clothes are still damp I sit down on the floor. Rufus hesitates since he is vertically challenged, but then leaps from the bed and whines to leave, likely in search of supper.

"The idea for Miss Abigail to work with you came from out of nowhere . . . oddly, as if someone whispered the idea in my ear."

Could it be Mama? The thought makes me shiver, but I swear she has a hand in things.

"And I thought to myself that you and your father

could help bridge the gap between the haves and the have-nots in this town. Oddly enough, not much has changed since we were attending Cottonwood High. Since there still isn't a private school available, you see kids pulling up in pickup trucks and Mercedes."

"And let me guess, they still don't mingle much."

Brett chuckles without humor. "It's almost as if Cottonwood has royalty and peasants."

"And you think Daddy and I can change the way people think? Brett, I don't know if I can make much of a difference," I answer, although I see his point.

"It would be a statement. A start. Give it some thought. I'm not exactly sure how, but something keeps telling me this is the beginning of change for the better."

"Oh geez, I hope I don't let you down." I shake my head. "I'm pretty much a redneck through and through."

"You're not going to let me down," he firmly assures me. "As a baseball coach I can spot talent that my players never knew they had. Jolie, you're going to surprise yourself and a lot of other people too, including my brother."

"I sure as hell hope so! Oh, wait, I mean, I certainly hope so," I say in a lower, more refined voice that sounds so silly, I laugh. "You have more faith in me than I have in myself."

Instead of laughing with me Brett says, "Well, it's time to change all that, Jolie. You need to believe in yourself too. Along with being the redneck ambassador for this town," he says with a chuckle.

"Redneck ambassador?" I have to laugh. "I kind of like that title. Wow, no wonder the Cottonwood Colonels win so many baseball games." I try to joke, but I'm a little choked up by his comment. "You sure know how to motivate."

Having lost my mama so young and with Daddy always so busy, I never really had anyone in my corner cheering me on. I tried to be the son that Daddy never had and at the same time provide home-cooked meals learned from Mama's handwritten recipes that I found tucked between the pages of her cookbooks. I cooked and cleaned, worked the farm, and then hunted and fished in my spare time. I did it all out of love and I'm glad I did.

But I never did really become, well . . . *me*.

"Jolie, you there? You're not going to back out on me, are you?"

A smile slowly spreads from ear to ear. "Not on your life!" I assure him.

"Now, that's the attitude! If I were there, I'd give you a high five."

"Ohmigod." I put the heel of my hand to my forehead.

"What's wrong?" His playful tone turns serious.

"Um, I have a little favor to ask of you," I reply.

"Shoot," he says without hesitation.

I start twirling my hair again. "Well, um, Cody might be under the assumption that we're havin' dinner together tonight."

"Really . . ." The long drawn-out word is heavy with amusement. "So, you were trying to make him jealous?"

A long sigh escapes me. "Making him jealous would mean I think he has an interest in me, Brett."

"You think he doesn't?"

"Come on," I scoff, but I suddenly recall the kiss and have to wonder. But then I remember his reaction after being seen by Cordelia Crawford. "If he did, he would fight it tooth and nail, believe me."

"I think there's something you're not telling me, but I'll get it out of you over a drink or two."

"A drink or two?"

"At dinner."

"Oh, you don't really have to *take* me . . . but if Cody asks, um, you might fib a bit." My face feels so warm that I lean my forehead against the cool windowpane.

"Are you kidding? That's the second part of our plan."

"You mean to make Cody and Marissa jealous?"

"Well . . ." I hear a shrug in his voice. "If we can't accomplish that, at least we'll have to make them wonder what they're missing, right?"

"Right," I reply firmly, even though I'm not completely convinced any of this harebrained scheme will work. "Where do you want to go? Pick a place where we'll be seen. It will be fun to have tongues wag."

After what happened with Cody, the irony isn't lost on me, but still I say, "I don't know . . . Don't you think I've made tongues wag enough today?"

"No way. I'm telling you, this town needs some shaking up. Some changes. How about the country club?"

"The country club?" My voice is so loud that I imagine Brett holding the phone away from his ear. "Tell me you are jokin'," I add in a nearly normal tone.

"Not a bit."

"B-but I haven't had my lessons yet!" I whine, drawing out the word *yet* for about a minute.

"Come on, where's your sense of adventure?"

"I've had enough adventure for one day, thank you very much. Besides, I'll surely screw something up, maybe fling food like Julia Roberts in *Pretty Woman*. Or

I'll use the wrong fork or drink from the wrong water glass. Oh, and I don't have anything fancy to wear. Wait, am I whining again?"

"Yeah, a little. Come on, surely you have something. A—what do you call it?—sundress and sandals will do. Jolie, you can't mess up eating dinner."

"Oh . . . ," I groan again, "yes, I could. Can't we just go for Chinese or pizza like normal folks?"

"Look, I'll ask for an out-of-the-way table," he responds, totally ignoring my plea. "Besides, Cody's likely to show up and you'd have all your bases covered."

Cody will show up? My heart pounds at the thought. "Wait, why do you even belong to the country club? I thought you steered clear of such things."

"What can I say? I like to golf and the food is excellent," he replies.

"Oh."

"Come on, Jolie. I *dare* you."

"You dare me? Ha, like that would work. What are we—ten?"

"I double dog dare you."

"Damn you, Brett Dean!"

He laughs. "I thought it would work. Was I right?"

"Ye-aa-us! I cannot resist a dare! How'd you guess?"

"We're a lot alike. I just knew tossing out a dare would work."

"Well, I hope you keep that bit of information to yourself. Knowledge like that could be dangerous in the wrong hands."

"Like mine?"

"Uh, I'm thinking yeah."

"I'll file it away for future blackmail," he responds

with a laugh. "See you at six o'clock, Jolie." He quickly ends the call before I can back out.

Closing my eyes, I fold my phone shut with a firm click. "What in the world have I gotten myself into?" I muse out loud. With a little shiver I walk over to my huge walk-in closet, which houses embarrassingly few clothes. "Great," I mutter while pushing through several pairs of jeans and a row of T-shirts. Finally I come to a meager display of dresses. Wrinkling my nose, I peer with a critical eye at each outdated dress. "Wow, these look like something women in compounds would wear. I just bet Miss Abigail would have a hissy fit and toss them all in the trash."

"Woof!"

"Hey!" I grin at Rufus. "How'd you get back in here?" The hum of the vacuum is my answer. "Carletta," I murmur with a fond shake of my head. "Those big sad eyes of yours get to her every time." Of course, I still can't quite get used to having a maid for pity's sake! In truth, Daddy and I didn't give it much consideration when we moved in. Sure, this is a big house, but compared to farm chores, cleaning was a piece of cake. But shortly after we settled in, Carletta showed up on our doorstep, asking if we were hiring. Daddy took an instant liking to her sweet demeanor and couldn't turn her away. She's forever getting after me for doing her chores, leaving her not much to do, but my hands aren't used to being idle and I just can't help myself. Plus, since Daddy is away fishing so often, I like having someone else around to talk to, so sometimes I jump right in and work along with her. She's got a great sense of humor when she lets herself relax around me, and I really hope we become friends.

"Whoof!" Rufus nudges my leg with his nose.

"Yeah, yeah, I know I've got you," I assure him with a scratch behind his ears, but then a big sigh escapes me. "But the truth is, Rufus, I just feel . . . lost. Ya know?" When Rufus flops down onto the carpet with a tired wheeze I add, "Yeah, you should be worn out after all the commotion you caused, you old mutt." A moment later he's snoring.

After a long sigh I go back to my task and pull out a yellow floral-patterned sundress. "You'll have to do," I mutter. Even I know that with big pearl buttons securing the straps and a thin satin sash at the waist, it's old-school, but nothing else even comes close to being wearable. I consider heading to the mall, but it's already getting late in the afternoon; I just know I'd wander around aimlessly and come home empty-handed. I'm thinking I need one of those personal shoppers.

After locating some chunky white sandals and a matching clutch purse I can't remember ever using, I lay it all on my big bed and head to the bathroom for a much-needed hot shower, but a soft knock at my door has me pausing to open it. "Carletta, what's up, girlie?" I ask.

She chuckles and waves a small hand at me. "You're always so funny."

"So I've been told. Problem is I don't always intend to be."

She chuckles again. "Hey, why are you all wet?"

"I fell into the pool."

She outright laughs this time. "See what I mean? You are too funny. You look like something the cat dragged in," she comments, but then covers her mouth with her hand. "Sorry! I shouldn't say that." When her brown eyes widen a bit, I realize she's really concerned that she's offended me.

"You know me better than that," I say lightly, and hate the thought that her employers might not always treat sweet Carletta in the nicest of ways. Of Hispanic decent, she's petite but curvy and pretty with doelike eyes, a full mouth, and a gorgeous head of rich brown hair. "Hey . . . ," I say slowly, "would you mind helpin' me out?"

"Anything you say, Ms. Russell."

"Call me Jolie, puh-lease! You're just a few years older than me, Carletta. We need to be on a first-name basis for goodness' sake."

"Anything, Jolie," she responds with a more relaxed smile.

"Would you mind assistin' me with my hair and makeup?"

She looks over her shoulder and then puts a hand to her chest. "Me?"

I nod eagerly. "If you don't mind?"

"Not at all," she says with a warm smile. "You have a hot date?"

"Mmmm, not really, but I want to put my best foot forward, you know what I mean?"

Carletta looks down at my feet and appears confused. "I thought you want me to fix your hair."

"I do. That's just a sayin'."

She shakes her head. "The English language is silly."

I have to laugh. "Especially the way I butcher it, but that's gonna change. I hope."

"Let me know when you're ready. I need to finish up sweeping."

"Thanks so much, Carletta," I tell her, then add, "You

know, you need to hang out by the pool with me. I think we could be friends."

Her eyes widen a fraction, but then she smiles again. "I would like that," she replies, but I don't believe she thinks I'm serious. I make a mental note to follow through and invite her soon. That ought to get Cordelia Crawford's tongue wagging faster than a dog's tail.

As I strip off my damp clothes I recall the crazy events of the day and I think to myself that Brett's right. "I need to show my Copper Creek neighbors a thing or two." That being said, I'm more than a little nervous about dining at the country club. I can't believe I actually agreed to do it, or any part of this insane scheme for that matter. One reason, I suppose, is that all of my life I've had chores to do and suddenly I have tons of free time and I don't always know what to do with it. Daddy has encouraged me to take some college courses and I've considered a job or even volunteer work, but the truth is I just feel so out of my element.

One nice thing is that I've had time to work on my children's books, my secret hobby that no one, not even Daddy, knows about. For several years now I've been doing sketches of the bedtime stories my mama used to tell me every night. We were too poor for picture books and the library was clear across town, so Mama made them up for me and I would beg her to repeat them over and over until I knew them by heart. But when the memories of her colorful barnyard characters were starting to fade, I panicked and began writing them down. The sketches just started to flow along with the words.

Drawing the pictures makes me feel as if Mama is sitting right there beside me while I work. I hear her soft and gentle voice in my head. The amazing thing is that when I ran out of the original stories, it was as if she began telling me new ones. When times had gotten tough, I did my research and had somehow mustered up the courage to send Mama's stories, along with my sketches, to children's publishers, and I had sparked some genuine interest. But when we sold the farm, my world became so topsy-turvy that I haven't thought much about it since. Now that we don't need the money, I'm not sure I want to share my memories of my mother with the world.

"Oh Mama," I murmur as I pick up a gold-framed picture of her from my dresser and slide my fingertip over the smooth glass. "It's hard to believe you've been gone for nearly fifteen years." It hits me rather hard that she isn't much older than me in the photograph . . . smiling, thinking she has the rest of her life ahead of her. She was the perfect mother, kind and caring, full of hugs and encouragement. When she was taken from us, Daddy and I were stunned. I never want to feel that kind of loss and pain ever again. With a jagged sigh I carefully place the photograph back on my dresser and head into the bathroom.

As I turn on the shower I wonder again if I should show the books to Daddy, but I know they would reduce him to tears. The only time I ever saw him weep was the day my mama died, and I don't think I could bear seeing him cry ever again.

The spacious, open marble two-headed shower is a far cry from the cramped little stall we had in our old farmhouse. The spray can be adjusted from a gentle rain to pulsating pelting blasts of water that soothe and massage sore muscles. Right now I opt for something in between and quickly wash my tangled hair. There's even a little built-in ledge to sit on while I shave my legs.

After the hot, soothing shower, I reach for a huge, snow-white warm and fluffy towel that soaks up the water beaded on my rosy skin. Everything in the bathroom gleams and shines. Soap scum would be embarrassed to show its smarmy face.

After inhaling a deep breath of the fragrant, humid air, I turn to gaze at my reflection in the mirror that spans the entire wall. My face is difficult to see in the misty, steam-covered glass and an odd thought enters my head. Peering closely I think, That's exactly how I feel: as if I'm *here* but not really myself, you know? "You need to find your place in this world, Jolie Russell," I say softly, but my voice sounds hollow in the silent room. A hot rush of loneliness washes over me and the unexpected image of Cody Dean seems to float before me in the mist and steam. Frowning, I reach over and wipe a dry circle on the mirror until I can see my reflection more clearly . . . but the image of Cody stubbornly remains.

"Just stop it, you fool," I chastise myself. "You'll never belong here. Never." Emotion clogs my throat; once again I feel dangerously close to crying, and it pisses me off. "And you were a means to an end for Cody Dean. Nothing more." I angrily swipe at a tear and then splash cold water on my warm face.

I'm considering calling Brett and canceling the whole doggone thing, when a soft knock on the door interrupts my thoughts. "You ready, Miss Jolie?" Carletta asks with so much enthusiasm that I clear my throat and force cheer into my voice.

"In a minute! I'm just dryin' off."

"All right. I'll wait here until you're ready."

Ready? I'm not nearly ready for any of this, but I take a deep breath, then blow it out. I tug on a fluffy robe, square my shoulders, and open the door. "Work your magic on me, baby cakes!" With my hands above my head I twirl in a circle.

"You're so funny!" Carletta's tinkling laughter is contagious. I'm not sure what she's going to do with me, but I make myself a promise that no matter how she styles my hair and makeup, I'll tell her it's beautiful and go with the flow. I do, however, utter a silent prayer . . .

6

Something Old, Something New

"So, what do you think?" Carletta asks.

"Oh! We've been jabbering so much that I haven't really been paying attention to my hair." I swivel around in the desk chair that I've been sitting on in the middle of the bathroom and check out my reflection in the mirror. "Holy cow."

"Okay, you have to explain if *holy cow* means a good thing or a bad thing. I know it can mean both."

"Um . . ." With wide eyes, I reach up and gingerly touch my hair.

When I don't immediately answer, Carletta fluffs it a bit. "You have great hair, Jolie. Thick and healthy. The lighter streaks in the dark brown are natural from the sun, aren't they?"

I nod. "I could never afford highlights or anything like that until recently."

"Amazing." She shakes her head. "So, what you think?"

"It's . . . I . . . uh . . ."

"I know it's big." She pats my shoulder.

I nod again and try for a smile.

"Jolie, you can pull this off." Carletta looks at me in the mirror. "I saw your yellow sundress and chunky sandals lying on your bed. Vintage clothing, am I right?"

"Vintage?" I frown for a second. "Oh, you mean, like, old-school?"

Carletta nods. "Very early seventies, right? That's why I went for the big hair."

"Well, no, couldn't be . . ." I angle my head while trying to remember when I last wore the sundress. Then I swallow hard and put a hand to my chest.

"Jolie, you okay? I can tone the hair down . . ."

"My goodness." I meet Carletta's eyes in the mirror. "You're right. That dress belonged to my mother." I swallow again and my heart thumps hard. "Ya know, I don't even recall how it ended up in my closet. I remember now that the shoes and purse were hers too."

"Well, I love it!"

"You do?"

"You must have put the dress there by mistake when you moved from your farm."

"I suppose," I tell her, but I'm not convinced. I might be one wrench short of a toolbox, but I sometimes believe my mother is my guardian angel. Crazy, I know, but still . . . "Daddy saved a few of her favorite things. I guess you're right and it ended up in my closet by mistake." I sit up straighter. "Oh, maybe I shouldn't wear it. Maybe it won't even fit!"

"It will. You have to wear it, Jolie. Seventies clothing is all over the catwalks."

"Catwalks?"

"Runways."

"Runways?"

"Fashion shows," Carletta explains with a grin as she waves a hand in the air. "Chickie, you'll turn heads at the country club and I'm sure your mama would be proud."

"You think? Oh, my goodness, I'm so nervous. Do you believe I can pull this off?"

She nods hard, puts both hands on my shoulders, and gazes at me in the mirror. "You know I moved here from LA, right?"

"I remember you saying that."

"I learned lots about hair, fashion, and makeup from rich skinny bitches." She puts one hand to her mouth. "Sorry. You are not a bitch."

"Or skinny."

"Nothing wrong with a few curves. Girl, you're built like a brick house."

I have to laugh. "Thanks, I think."

Carletta removes her hand from her mouth and waves it again. "Anyway, I learned from snooping through closets of designer clothes and shoes. I read fashion magazines. I observed. And you know what?" She arches one dark eyebrow and purses her lips while waiting for me to answer.

"What?"

Carletta leans close and whispers, "Rich bitches? They know how to fake it." She straightens up and smiles as if she's given me the answer to the universe. "It doesn't matter if it's rich LA bitches or snobby old money like here in Copper Creek. They're all the same."

I blink at her. "What do you mean?"

"They think they know it all, but they don't. When someone asks about your dress, you just say in a haughty tone, 'Why, it's vintage, of course!' And then flip your hair like this!" When she demonstrates, I laugh.

"I'll never be able to do the flip without laughing."

"Maybe that was over-the-top." She gives my shoulder a reassuring pat. "If you can round up a strand of pearls, you'll look very classy, Jolie. The vintage dress is a new trend. Now, let's do your makeup and nails, okay?"

"Okay." I still have this weird what-am-I-doing feeling in the pit of my stomach, but I slide open a drawer that's crammed full of cosmetics. Carletta looks at me in surprise. "I have all kinds of stuff," I explain. "I just don't know how to apply it."

"You just have to play around until you get the results you want."

"That's just it." I roll my eyes. "I've tried, but I always think I look like I need to be on a street corner after I'm finished."

She chuckles. "You need to apply with a light touch. You have great bone structure, by the way."

I touch my cheeks. "Really?"

She nods. "You don't give yourself nearly enough credit."

I nod but my heart thumps hard. "Carletta, I'll never be able to pull this off. How in the hell did I get my sorry ass into this, anyway?" I put my hand to my mouth. "I just know something like that is gonna fly out of my mouth. What if I drop the f-bomb? Heaven help me, I'm gonna be like a bull in a china shop."

"Jolie, you'll be fine! It's all in the attitude. Have some fun with this. Strut your stuff!" She snaps her fingers and wiggles her hips, and I laugh. I love that she's letting her guard down and being herself with me.

"Oh . . . I don't know how to strut my stuff."

"Sure you do," she says while applying eyeliner. "You just have to channel your inner diva."

"Yeah, but what about my outer redneck?"

Carletta laughs. "The two don't have to be, how do you say . . . mutually exclusive. Look at what's her name? You know, big boob chickie?"

"Oh, you mean Dolly Parton?"

"Yeah, her! She is what she is and doesn't make excuses. For me, my hero is Jennifer Lopez. She can be so elegant on the red carpet but is still Jenny from down the block, you know what I'm saying?"

I meet Carletta's eyes in the mirror and grin. "In other words, you're tellin' me to remember my roots and not become a rich bitch."

"That's exactly what I'm saying."

"How'd you get so smart?"

She wags a finger at me. "The power of observation. I have my foot in both worlds for a long time," she says, but then becomes a bit more serious. "Jolie, this I know for sure . . . money does not make a person happy. Believe me, I grew up dirt-poor and I was a lot happier than some of these people. Rich people worry all the time mostly about all the wrong things."

I nod slowly. "Sometimes I think Daddy and I made a big mistake."

Carletta clucks her tongue. "That doesn't have to be true. Enjoy the freedom that money gives you, Jolie, but use it wisely."

I nod. "I hope I will."

With a serious nod she squeezes my shoulders, but then her eyes twinkle. "Another thing I learned is that women are basically all alike. We just want to look good for our men." She winks at me.

"Oh, no, Brett is just a friend."

"He's not the hottie you were kissing in the pool?"

My eyes open wide. "You saw me?"

She purses her lips again. "I might have been peeking out the window."

"Carletta!" I feel heat creep into my cheeks.

"What? I was doing the windows, okay?"

"Likely story."

She smiles. "Yeah, and I'm sticking to it. So Mr. Cody Dean is the one you want, huh?"

"You know who he is?"

"Doesn't everyone around here?" She nudges my shoulder. "You go, girl!"

"Lot of good it will do me," I mutter. "I'm just a farm girl."

"You're funny and smart and beautiful. So there!"

"Thank you, but, come on, I'm rough around the edges. I could never be dainty and refined like Marissa Clayton."

Carletta wrinkles up her nose while smoothing foundation on my face. "Pffft! You don't want to be like her. That girl has . . . how do you say . . . issues."

"You know her?"

She nods slowly while applying blush with a fat brush. "Oh, yeah. I used to clean for her until she fired me." I want to ask more, but Carletta steps from in front of me and says, "What you think?"

My jaw drops. "Wow."

"You mean that in a good way, right?"

"Yes . . . Oh, yes!" My light blue eyes seem more intense and my cheekbones way more prominent. "You should do this for a living."

"Yeah, right," Carletta replies while rummaging through my drawer for lipstick. She wrinkles her nose at several tubes before selecting one. "This soft peach will be perfect with the yellow dress."

"Seriously, Carletta, you should be in fashion design or something of that sort."

A cloud passes over her face. "That would take education and a degree and besides, I'm already thirty years old, Jolie. I don't have the time or money." Her shoulders slump a little, but then she smiles. "Whatever. I like my life just fine."

While there's nothing wrong with the hard, honest work that she does, it suddenly dawns on me that I have the means to help her out. With that thought in mind, I beam at her.

"Now, there's the attitude I'm talking about!" Carletta says. "That pretty smile could light up a room." When our eyes meet in the mirror I get the feeling she wants to say something more.

"Whatever's on your mind, just go ahead and say it. You know I wasn't kiddin' when I said I needed a friend, Carletta. I need honesty. Don't hold anything back."

She pauses. "I don't want to overstep my bounds."

"Friends can't really do that, now can they?" I insist firmly.

The hesitation I noticed in her eyes vanishes. "I can tell you're a good-hearted, sweet-natured girl." She swings her hand in an arc. "Don't let all of this change that, okay?"

I nod.

"Good girl," Carletta says with a smile, but then points her finger at me. "But here's the thing. Don't let it hold you back either . . . You know what I mean, chickie?"

"I'm beginning to."

"That daddy of yours is a good man too. You'll do just fine after you adjust."

I raise my eyebrows at her. "Adjust? From being a dirt-poor farmer to . . . this?"

Carletta rolls her eyes. "Well, it's a tough job becoming rich," she says in a mock-sad tone. "Give it some time. You haven't even been in this house for a year."

"I need to quit whining, don't I?"

"Yes." Carletta gives my hair and makeup a critical once-over. While buffing my nails she says, "Just remember what I said and strut your stuff!"

"Gotcha!" I promise, and she leans down to give me a swift hug. "Thanks for everything, Carletta."

"No problem, chickie. Now get dressed and have some fun with this, okay?"

"Okay." I give her a brave smile. But after Carletta leaves and I'm sitting in the chair all alone while letting my nails dry, I struggle to keep my panic at bay. "You can do this, Jolie Russell," I proclaim to my reflection, even though I'm still considering backing out. The girl in the mirror doesn't look much like me, though, and I swear, gives me a challenging little glare. "Okay, okay! I'll do it!" I shout loud enough to wake Rufus, who comes lumbering into the bathroom with a what's-up? look on his long face. "I know. I'm crazy," I tell my dog. "But what else is new?"

Rufus blinks at me as if confused.

"It's me, silly dog. I'm just all prettied up."

"Whoof!" He seems relieved.

"I know. My hair is big. Your ears are long. So what?"

Rufus does that dog thing when one eyebrow goes up and then the other. When I laugh, some of my nervousness fades. But then I have to go and wonder whether Cody will indeed be at the country club, and a shiver of anticipation slides down my spine. His kiss woke up something in my body—a need . . . no, make that a hunger that I didn't know existed, at least not so strongly.

I never knew a kiss could be so intense, so exciting. Closing my eyes, I relive the moment again, going over the details until I'm feeling so warm that I force myself to stop.

"Get a grip," I whisper as I head into my bedroom to get dressed. I remind myself that Cody's kiss was a spur-of-the-moment thing, on his end anyway, and not likely to happen again. Plus, he was none too happy that Cordelia Crawford spotted our spontaneous lip-lock. I do have to wonder what prompted the kiss, but I guess I'll never know. He obviously regretted it. Trying to push disruptive thoughts of Cody from my mind, I decide to get down to the task at hand.

"Oh!" I put my hand to my chest when I look down at Mama's dress. I frown, trying to remember my mother wearing it, but I simply can't. I was the tender age of ten when she died, and was heading into those uncertain teen years when I needed her most. It frightens me when my memory of her becomes distant and foggy, making me want to run to my workshop and sketch so that she feels close . . . *near* me, at least in spirit. I promise myself to do so after dinner with Brett.

Realizing he'll be here soon, I slip into the dress and then hurry into the bathroom to look in the mirror. "Wow . . ." I exhale a breath of surprise when I view my reflection. Carletta was right. The floral dress makes me look softer, more feminine than I knew I could appear. A thin satin sash makes my waist seem tiny and the skirt flares at the hem, giving the dress grace and movement while the soft yellow color complements my hair and subtle makeup. The bodice shows off my golden tan and just enough cleavage to tease while remaining classy.

While the chunky sandals are a tad tight, they add a funky touch that keeps the outfit fresh instead of dated.

I do love it! I always wanted to be fashionable but didn't know how. Locating a bottle of rarely used perfume, I spray some on and then touch up my lipstick. With a contented smile I check out my nails for smudges and then take essential items from my big purse and place them in the clutch.

For the first time in a long while, I feel lighthearted, less unsure. "I feel like a girl!" I say to Rufus, who is snoring while lying on the cool tile. He opens one eye and then goes back to sleep.

But then the doorbell chimes and my confidence slips a notch. Thinking it's Brett, I hurry down the long, curved staircase that leads to the two-story open foyer. "I'll get it, Carletta," I shout, my sandals clicking on the shiny marble floor. Then, after smoothing my hair and dress, I take a deep breath and swing open the heavy front door.

7

Dust in the Wind

"Daddy! Why on earth did you ring the doorbell?"

He shakes his head while wiping his feet on the welcome rug. "Forgot the doggone code and didn't have my key on me."

"Oh, the numbers are your birthday, remember?"

"Yeah, but it wouldn't open."

"Did you press the star button?"

He chuckles. "No, I sure didn't. Jolie, I'll never master all these codes, remotes, and buttons a-blinkin' at me all the time. It's hard to teach an old dog like me new tricks, but I'm tryin'. You gotta give me that."

"You're doin' real good, Daddy. And for goodness' sake, you're not old!" I'm about to ask how his fishing trip went, when his eyes suddenly widen.

"Jolie . . . ," he says so softly, pauses, and then clears his throat. "You look beautiful. Like your mother."

My hand goes to my chest. "Do you mind that I'm wearin' her dress?"

He looks at me in surprise. "Of course not. She would love it. Oh, it would make her so happy."

I release the breath I've been holding. "Thank you, Daddy," I tell him, and then take a step closer so that we can hug. When he draws me close and holds me tight, it dawns on me that we don't embrace nearly enough. I suppose we've both learned to hold our emotions in check for so long that we need to learn how to live . . . how to love again without the fear of heartbreak and loss. I long to tell him so, but when he steps back I see tears swimming in his eyes and I don't want to make him cry. So instead, I decide to change the subject. "How was your trip?" I ask a little too brightly.

He doesn't answer right away, but his eyes meet mine, and although the words aren't spoken, *I love you* hangs in the air between us. Finally, he sniffs, clears his throat once more, and then smiles. "Caught me a string of bluegill."

"Any striper?"

"Nah, not biting much."

"Did Booker do any good?"

"Yeah, but I did better." He jams his thumb at his chest with a wink. Booker Brennan and Daddy have been best friends but fierce competitors since childhood. Their relationship became strained a bit when we sold the farm and built this big-ass house, but lately they've been hanging out again. "So, tell me why you're all gussied up, Jolie."

"Oh, um, I'm havin' dinner at the country club with Brett Dean."

Daddy's eyebrows shoot up. "Ya don't say . . ." He smiles while rubbing his chin. "I've always admired that boy for goin' his own way. Well, good for you, Jolie."

I feel heat creep into my cheeks. "We're just friends, Daddy." For some reason I feel the need to lower my voice an octave.

Daddy raises both palms in the air. "Okay, I hear ya."

"Um, Daddy, Brett and I were discussing the, uh, rather hard time we're havin' adjustin' to livin' in Copper Creek." I swallow and try to think of the best way to tell him the rest of the story. My daddy is a proud man, and I don't want him to take offense at what I'm about to ask of him. I decide to leave out the dog-chasing-cake-smashing incident that led up to the conversation with Brett.

"Jes say what's on your mind, child."

Taming the urge to twirl my hair I say, "Well, you know how Brett is a teacher at Cottonwood High School?" When Daddy nods I continue. "Well, it seems there is this teacher, a Ms. Abigail Marksberry, who also conducts etiquette classes on the side and, um well . . ."

"Let me guess. Brett offered to have her polish us up a bit?"

I give him a quick nod. "What do you think?"

Daddy shrugs his wide shoulders. "Why the hell not?" he declares in his big, booming voice. "I could use a bit of spit and polish."

"Me too." I let out a sigh of relief.

He tweaks my nose in the same way he has been doing since I was a little girl. "I think you're perfect."

"That's cuz you're my dad."

"Yeah," he says in a gruff tone, "and no matter how much of a young lady you become, you will always be my little girl." His light blue eyes mist over and he drags me back into his arms for a big bear hug this time. "I know that some boy is gonna come and whisk you away from me someday . . . ahh . . ." He backs up and swipes the back of his hand across his eyes in an uncharacteristic display of emotion. "Sorry for getting so mushy on ya, Jolie. I know this transition has been hard on ya. We was always so danged busy that it seems like you've grown up on me overnight, and then to see you lookin' so pretty . . . so much like Rosie." A tear slides down his cheek. "Damn." He turns away for a moment and gets himself together.

My own throat closes up, but I touch him on the shoulder. "I shouldn't have worn the dress, Daddy. I was afraid it would make you sad."

He turns around with wide eyes. "Sad? Oh no . . . seein' you lookin' so pretty makes my heart swell with pride." He clears his throat. "Now I'm gonna go get the smell of the lake off me. If Brett comes before I'm done cleaning up, tell him I plan on comin' to some Cottonwood Colonels games. Ya know I was a pretty darned good ballplayer myself."

"Better than Booker?"

"Course I was," he boasts with a deep chuckle. "Did you have to ask?" he says over his shoulder while clumping up the fancy staircase in his boots. I smile as I watch him, but when I see his elbow come up and his hand go to his face, I know he's swiping at tears, and my lips tremble. Although I haven't really thought about it, I suddenly realize how lonely for female companionship my daddy must get sometimes, and it claws at my heart. Here I am wearing Mama's dress, so it's an odd time to think this, but I suddenly wonder if Daddy will ever find love again. While my fingers trail over the silky ends of the satin sash, I realize that Daddy deserves a gentle touch, needs a tender kiss and a soft place to land at the end of the day.

Don't we all? The thought echoes in my head and brings my brain back to Cody's unexpected kiss. But before I can lapse back into the land of it-will-never-

happen-again, the doorbell chimes, making me jump.
Thinking it has to be Brett this time, I take a deep breath,
lick my lips, smooth everything again, and then open the
door.

My eyes widen and my big smile falters. "C-Cody?"
My brain sort of short-circuits, but I manage a polite,
"What brings you here?"

"I . . . ," he begins, but when his gaze sweeps over me
from my big hair to my pink-tipped toenails, he seems to
lose his train of thought. Something flickers in his eyes—
something that looks and feels like male appreciation.

My tummy flutters.

My heart thuds.

Cody clears his throat and begins again. "I'm sorry to
interrupt."

"Interrupt what?"

"Your date with Brett."

"Oh . . . right." I lick my bottom lip and wait, but Cody
seems unsure . . . distracted.

"I . . ." Cody threads his fingers through his hair. "You
look nice, Jolie."

Heat creeps up my neck to my face and I self-
consciously touch the ends of my hair. "Thank you. Oh,
um, would you like to come in?" I quickly take a step
back so he can enter, but one slippery leather-soled san-
dal slides forward on the marble floor. "Oh!" I grab for
the door before I do an embarrassing split, but Cody steps
forward and my hands clutch his arms instead.

"You okay?"

I nod. As if my hands on his forearms isn't enough to
get me flustered, he has to go and put his hand on the
small of my back. "This floor is slippery," I say in a silly,
.breathless voice. Damn, his hand feels so warm and firm

through the thin fabric of my dress. I swallow hard when his hand shifts just a tad, causing his fingertips to lightly graze my bare skin. Holy cow. It takes everything in me not to plaster myself to him and drag his head down for a long, hot kiss.

Because I'm suddenly nervous I start to jabber. "I keep making the mistake of coming in here in my sock feet and it's like bein' on ice. Just last week I was chasin' after Rufus cuz he was runnin' off with a Double Stuf Oreo, and let me tell you, what happens after he eats chocolate isn't pretty. I did a move that would make Scott Hamilton proud. I actually went airborne and spun around twice, I think, and it was so cool . . . well, until I smacked into the wall." I rub my shoulder at the painful memory. "But Rufus gets so sick when he eats chocolate! You know that dogs shouldn't eat chocolate, right?"

Cody nods and sort of smiles, but makes no move to remove his hand.

"I'd dearly hate to be a dog, then, wouldn't you? I mean, they have the life I guess, but still, who could exist without chocolate?" I shudder at the thought . . . or maybe I'm shuddering at the sensation of his fingers moving ever so lightly over my bare skin.

"I hear you." Cody's lips twitch with humor.

"Course, even if I were a dog, I'd say screw it and eat the chocolate anyway. Cuz who could live without Oreos, right?" I trail off when I realize I'm repeating myself. Oh, why can't I just shut up?

He nods politely. "You make a good point."

"Yeah." No, I don't. I'm babbling like an idiot, but his fingers are driving me to distraction. Any moment, I swear I'm going to melt like a marshmallow over a camp-fire. Common sense tells me to step away from his touch but logical thinking flew out the window the moment I saw him standing on my doorstep. I dig deep, trying to gather my scattered wits, and manage to ask, "What brings you here, Cody?" Wouldn't it be cool if he said that he couldn't bear the thought of his brother dating me and that he wanted to beat Brett to the punch and whisk me off to a romantic getaway?

"Oh, when I changed my clothes I must have left my watch in your pool house. Do you mind if we go look for it?"

"Oh." I try not to sound glum. *So much for that.* "Sure. We'll go out the back. Follow me." I walk quickly, trying to put some distance between us, but he matches my stride with those long legs of his.

"Lead the way." When his hand remains at the small of my back I firmly tell myself that this is simply a polite gesture on his part and not the desire to remain touching me. We walk down the long hallway past what Daddy calls the parlor, which neither of us ever ventures into. Then, on the right is a family room with a flat-screen television and dark brown leather furniture that's supposed to be more casual but still seems too fancy to me for kicking back and chilling.

"Very nice," Cody comments when we enter the huge state-of-the-art gourmet kitchen.

"It's my favorite room in the house," I tell him.

"So you like to cook?"

"Oh, yeah." I nod. "I always wanted Daddy to have a hearty supper after working the fields. I fixed, you know, basic meat-and-potato dishes handed down by my mama, but now I get to have fun and experiment. At first, I was intimidated just by the sheer size, but now it's like a playground for me."

"I can see why," Cody says, even though I'm guessing he has a similar kitchen where he lives.

"I can actually relax in this room." I wave my hand toward the forest green walls that offset the rich cherry cabinets. Stainless-steel appliances gleam in bright sunlight streaming in through an abundance of spotless windows that overlook the shimmering swimming pool. The white ceramic floor would be stark without the colorful braided throw rugs scattered here and there that were my personal touch. A gorgeous six-burner gas stove sits in the middle of the room, flanked by a tiered, granite center island.

"There're little nooks and crannies for everything," I explain, and to demonstrate I open the spice drawer. "Check this out." After Cody gives an appreciative nod I'm on a roll. "And this. The next cabinet holds all of my pots and pans. Look, it's all divided. There are even these narrow little slots for the lids! Somebody was thinkin'," I comment, and he grins.

My heels click on the tile as I head over to the other side of the room. "Is this not amazing?" I ask after throwing open double doors that hide a huge walk-in pantry. I turn around for his approval and then show it off like Vanna White. "I love that you can hide the garbage," I tell him, and then pull out the double-hung waste cans beneath the cabinets as if they are a work of art. "Oh, good lord, I must be boring you to tears. You can tell me to shut up anytime now."

"Not at all. I'm getting excited and I don't even know how to cook," Cody assures me with a smile that seems sincere.

"I could give you some cookin' lessons." The words roll off my tongue before I can stop them. "Oh, I'm sure you have a chef," I quickly add.

"No, I don't. I usually end up with takeout at my office or dining out, but I'd enjoy lessons, Jolie."

Although I realize he's probably just being polite, my heart beats a bit faster. "Well, I've rambled on long enough. I'm sure you have someplace to be."

Cody shrugs. "Actually, I don't," he admits. I know it's silly on my part, but I feel a little surge of joy that he doesn't have a date with Marissa. "But I guess Brett will be arriving soon, so I should locate my watch and get out of your hair."

At the mention of my hair, I self-consciously reach up to pat my teased tresses.

"Your hair looks pretty," Cody says as if reading my mind. He looks as if he might say something more but then clears his throat.

I'm about to thank him, but I glance at the digital clock on the microwave and frown. "Actually, Brett's late."

Cody's raises his eyebrows. "Really? It's unlike Brett not to be punctual," he says with a measure of concern. "How late is he?"

I shrug. "Only a few minutes. Maybe he's stuck in traffic."

Cody's frown remains. "Maybe, but I'm surprised he hasn't called."

As if on cue my phone rings and I hurry over to the answer it. "Hey, Brett," I answer, and glance over at Cody, who appears relieved. Although Brett had indicated there was some sibling rivalry between them, it's obvious that Cody cares about his brother.

"I tried to call you," Brett tells me, sounding a little upset.

"Oh, my cell phone must be upstairs in my purse. I'm sorry."

"That's okay," Brett says quickly, "but I have some bad news."

My eyes widen at Cody. "Really? What's wrong?"

"I had a player injure an ankle during baseball practice and I'm stuck here at the emergency room at the hospital. I'm sorry, but I'll have to cancel our dinner plans."

"Oh, it's no big deal. We can go another time."

"Would you mind calling and canceling the reservation? They're about to take Jordan back to X-ray and his parents haven't arrived yet."

"Sure, I'll call. Let me know the results, okay?"

"I will. Sorry about this, Jolie."

"Don't give it a second thought," I assure him before hanging up the phone.

"What's wrong?" Cody asks.

"Brett had to take a player to the emergency room. Apparently he injured his ankle during practice."

"Oh, that's too bad."

"You wouldn't happen to know the number of the country club off the top of your head, would you?"

"No, but I have it stored in my cell phone." He takes his BlackBerry out of his pocket but then pauses and looks over at me. "I don't have dinner plans. Would you mind if I joined you?"

"I . . . um," I stutter since I'm totally taken by surprise. "You don't have to do that."

"I know I'm a little underdressed," he says of his khaki pants and blue golf shirt, "but if you don't mind . . . ?"

"Well . . ." A little ball of panic settles in my stomach like a cold rock. I know it's only dinner, but it's at the country club! There will be all kinds of extra glasses, plates, and silverware that I won't know what to do with.

Brett was going to coach me through it. And then another thought slaps me in the face, making my spine stiffen.

"Jolie?" His voice is hesitant as if he senses something is bothering me.

"You don't have to be polite, Cody."

"Excuse me?" His eyebrows come together as he pockets his phone. "Is that what you think I'm doing?"

"Isn't it?"

"No," he protests a little too quickly.

"Look," I tell him quietly, "I know you don't want to be seen out and about with the likes of me. Thanks for the kind offer, but I'll pass."

His eyes widen slightly. "Now what in the world would make you think that, Jolie?"

"Maybe because it's true. When Miss Cordelia saw us . . . you know . . ." My face turns warm and I falter. "You seemed so upset."

Cody takes a step closer to me. "Wait, you think I was embarrassed to be seen kissing you?"

I nod. "Sure, you were." I flick a glance his way but then avert my eyes, wishing I had just kept my big mouth shut. "Look, it doesn't really matter. I understand." The smile I give him wavers just a little.

"Look, you've got it all wrong. I simply didn't like the idea of her gossiping. That's *all*. It had nothing to do with you personally," he insists firmly . . . maybe too firmly.

"If you say so."

"Hey, if I didn't want to be seen with you, why would I offer to take you to the most exclusive place in Cottonwood, frequented by people I know?" he sputters. I almost believe him except that something flickers in his eyes and he glances away, pauses, and then says, "Seriously, Jolie. Why?"

"Because you're so damned perfect," I tell him.

"I'm not following you."

I hesitate but then say, "You always do what's polite. What's expected of you. Instead of doin' the right thing, the politically correct thing, why don't you try doin' what you want for once?" I can't quite believe I'm saying this to him, but my chin juts out defiantly because I know I'm right and damn it, I want him to admit it to me. If he would, I could relax around him a bit more. "Do you even know how to relax?"

"Of course I do," he says so stiffly that I shake my head.

"Oh, Cody, you're so outta my league, it ain't, I mean *isn't* even funny."

"That's just plain silly." But when a muscle jumps in his clenched jaw, I know I've hit a nerve. Of course, I know I should leave well enough alone, but I just can't. I take another step closer until, with me in my heels, we're just about nose to nose. "Cody, there's not a hair out of place on your head. Your slacks are perfectly creased. I bet you iron your underwear."

"I don't iron my underwear." He disputes so seriously, it gives him a vulnerable edge that offsets his rigid sense of propriety.

"Yeah, I bet." I end up smiling in spite of my frustration and it ruins my little tirade. So help me, I have this huge urge to reach up and ruffle his hair and then drag those damned perfect lips to mine. "Have you ever just thrown caution to the wind, Cody?"

"I . . ." He looks at me as if he doesn't quite know what to make of my question and in truth, I'm not sure what I'm trying to prove. But when his gaze drops to my mouth, I wonder if he's about to call my bluff and kiss me senseless. I give him a challenging do-it look.

Cody holds my gaze while he slowly lowers his head. My heart pounds and I lean back against the countertop for support. I can feel the warmth of his breath on my cheek and smell the spice of his cologne. My eyes start to flutter shut in anticipation of a long, hot kiss, when through my eyelashes I hear the clump of footsteps.

Cody takes a quick step away from me and we turn at the unmistakable sound of . . .

A fart!

"Daddy!" Dear lord, please don't do that again, I silently pray, but he starts singing a George Strait tune so loudly that he must not have heard me. Not knowing that we have company, he heads this way, shirtless and in baggy boxers. He scratches his chest and then scratches, lord help me, *lower* and toots again, rapid-fire, like a machine gun!

"Speaking of wind . . . ," Cody mumbles with a grin.

"Daddy!" I shout, torn between laughter and mortification.

"Jolie-girl?" My daddy's booming voice rings out as he enters the room. I can tell he's ready to fart again and has to hold it in when he sees Cody standing beside me. "Oh, hello, Cody," he says with a sheepish grin. "Sorry 'bout that. Doggone baked beans are giving me fits." With a grimace, he rubs his tummy that even at his age is flat as a washboard from hard work. He might be rough around the edges, but I'm proud to say he's a handsome man.

"Mr. Russell," Cody says in a rather strained voice. I wonder what the problem is when I suddenly realize Cody is desperately trying to restrain laughter.

"Son, you need to call me Wyatt. *Mr. Russell* makes me feel too dammed old." When he extends his hand, Cody grabs it and, heaven help me, he passes the gas he's been holding in. It's not as loud, mind you, but it lingers in the air.

"Daddy!"

"Sorry," he apologizes after I glare at him. "Slipped out. How was I to know we had company?" he protests.

Trying not to be conspicuous, I reach back and turn on the overhead fan. I glance at Cody, whose face is turning red with suppressed laughter. When a chuckle escapes him, he tries to disguise it with a cough that sounds more like a high-pitched wheeze.

"You okay, son? Need a drink of water or somethin'?"

Cody looks at my daddy and gives him a negative shake of his head. His lips are clamped shut and he seems to be under control, but then his shoulders start to twitch. Even though I could box Daddy's ears for farting, I find the unflappable Cody's inability to control his laughter so funny that my own shoulders start to shake.

"Daddy!" I widen my eyes at him and shake my head, but one look in Cody's direction has me doubled over with laughter.

"You two haven't been smokin' any of that wacky to-backy, have you?"

"Daddy!" I stomp my foot but continue to laugh.

"Wait, aren't you supposed to be going out with the other brother?"

Cody clears his throat and swallows. Finally, after inhaling a deep breath he manages to say, "Brett had an injured player he had to attend to. I'm taking Jolie to dinner instead." He gives me a challenging look.

"Oh, well, have fun, you two. I just came down for a

soft drink." He opens the refrigerator and locates a can of Coke. He raises the red can in a salute and heads upstairs. "Sorry about—"

"Daddy, just go."

"All right, all right . . ."

I put my hand over my mouth and turn to Cody. When I shake my head, he grins and says, "You are coming to dinner with me, aren't you?"

Cody's challenging gaze is almost as good as a dare, so I find myself saying, "Yes, okay, yes." Of course, the moment the words are out of my mouth, I regret them. I open my mouth to ask if we can go for pizza or a burger but then clamp it shut. This is the world I'm living in. I might as well start trying to fit in. I had wanted a few etiquette lessons under my belt before venturing out into the world of the wealthy, but a little crash course might be of benefit. After all, what's the worst thing that could happen anyway?

8

Eat Your Heart Out

Cody, bless his heart, keeps up a steady stream of small talk while he drives to the Cottonwood Country Club in his snazzy, little black Audi TT Roadster. He politely leaves out mention of Daddy's recent flatulence display and I do believe we chat about every subject he can come up with. I know he's trying to keep me relaxed, and it pretty much works. But then we turn down the oak tree–lined road that leads up to the country club and my nerves start tap dancing in my tummy once again.

"This sure is pretty," I comment, and Cody nods his head. An antebellum plantation house that serves as the country club is classic white with a red gabled roof. Stately Greek pillars offset the wraparound covered porch and second-story balcony. I've often admired the boxy, yet grand symmetrical style that oozes Southern charm. The front lawn is green and lush, making the deep pink azaleas in front of the porch pop with color.

After Cody pulls around the circular driveway and stops for valet parking, I subconsciously put a hand to the butterflies in my stomach. When Cody notices my trepidation, he reaches over, places his warm hand over mine, and gently squeezes. "You'll do fine."

My smile trembles a little, but I'm touched by his concern. "Yeah, well, you'd feel just about as comfortable at a Russell family reunion pig roast."

"I'm sure I would feel right at home," he gibes.

"Right. Last summer Uncle Will spiked the lemonade with white lightning. By the end of the day everybody was showing their hiney."

"Including you?"

With one eyebrow raised, I give him a deadpan look and let him wonder.

After a brief chuckle and what I hope is a fond shake of his head, Cody firmly cups my elbow while we walk down the long sidewalk leading to the entrance. As we ascend the front steps I admire the many hanging baskets with leafy Boston ferns that creak and swing in the cool evening breeze. White wicker furniture is filled with chattering patrons clinking glasses while sipping cocktails. Many of them turn with eyebrow-raising interest when we reach the porch landing. When I inhale a deep, steadying breath, the pungent aroma of expensive cigars mixes with the sweet sent of flowers. Cody nods and waves while I paste a petrified, but what I hope passes for dignified, smile on my face.

While Carletta might know the current fashion trends, it dawns on me as I look around that these people with old Southern money cling to classic country club attire. Men in sport coats in yellow and green-blue are abundant, along with cable cardigans and argyle V-neck sweaters. My outfit, I notice as I let out my breath with relief, blends in with an array of pastel sundresses and floppy hats. Big hair never went out of style here in this ageless, timeless society, and although my dress and shoes have a bit of a funky flair, I don't stand out as much as I had feared.

"Why, I declare, Cody Dean!" breathes a white-haired ethereal wisp of a woman. She all but floats over to us and holds her birdlike hand up for Cody to kiss.

"Audrey Rose." Cody lightly kisses her hand and then turns to me. "I'd like you to meet Jolie Russell. Jolie, Audrey Rose Mitchell. She and my grandmother go way back."

"That we do. We spent many a summer evening on this very porch. Ahhhh, sometimes I think I hear her vivacious laughter and turn to greet her, but of course she isn't there." When her smile trembles a bit at the corners, Cody reaches over and lightly pats her on the shoulder.

"Nice to meet you, Ms. Mitchell." I shake her blue-veined hand with a measure of caution, hoping I don't crush it.

"A pleasure, I'm sure." Her return handshake is much firmer than I had anticipated. Although elderly and more refined, she reminds me of my mother, who was beautiful and delicate on the outside but made of steel on the inside. "I don't believe I've met you, child. Are you new to these parts?" Her voice is hushed, soft but with an authority that holds my attention.

"You could say that," I answer with a small smile, and manage to give Cody the slightest of nudges with my elbow. If I could just relax, this could turn out to be fun.

"Hmmm, well." She gives me a measuring look and then nods to Cody as if giving him her approval. "I hope you two have a lovely evening. I must be off to dinner. Noreen Ballard and Ruth Montgomery went in a while ago, but I wanted to finish my whiskey sour. They'll get all huffy with me if I linger much longer, but it was nice to meet you, Jolie." She places a cool hand on my arm.

"Likewise." I draw out the word and dip my head in what I hope is a genteel manner.

"And always nice to see you, Cody. Don't be a stranger, you hear me?"

"I hear you," Cody answers with a gentle smile, and then leans over to place a kiss on her cheek.

I'm watching her float away, pausing here and there to greet people, when Cody presses a cold glass into my hand.

"Pinot Grigio, okay?"

Peee-no what-e-o? I want to ask, but I can see that it's some sort of white wine. "Sure, why not . . . um, I mean, why yes, thank you very much." Hoping that it won't make my nose scrunch up, I give him a polite nod and accept the glass.

"It's crisp and light bodied," he explains. "I thought you might like it."

"Oh, definitely," I tell him, and wonder if I should flutter my eyelashes the way Audrey Rose did. No way, I could never pull that off.

"I had hoped it would be your choice."

"Of course. Perfect for um . . . a warm, sultry night such as this," I bluff in such a snooty voice that he grins. I wish I knew how to do the swirling-around thing where you stick you nose in the glass, but I'm certain I would snort it.

"It was between that and the Chardonnay."

"Well, you're a damned good guesser, Cody Dean. Musta read my mind." I say this a little too loudly because a few heads turn my way. I feel like sticking out my tongue but then remind myself I'm supposed to act refined.

"Really?"

I give him another deadpan stare and he shakes his head and grins. Well, if nothing else I'm good for a laugh. I arch one eyebrow and take a delicate sip. "Hmmm, although I'd rather have a longneck bottle of beer, this isn't as bad as I anticipated." I close my eyes and make a soft humming sound.

"What are you doing?" Cody asks.

"Channeling my inner Southern diva."

Cody grins. "You're something else, you know that?"

"You mean that in a good way, right?" I take another swallow, bigger this time, and actually enjoy the cold wine sliding down my throat. "Yep, not bad at all." I glance around to make sure I'm holding the glass right and force myself to take small, feminine sips because I don't think peeno whatever-e-o is supposed to be gulped. "Course I'd rather have that bourbon you're drinkin'." I take the glass from him and inhale an appreciative sniff. "Let me guess, Wild Turkey, single barrel?"

"Right," he says with a surprised but impressed look.

"Thought so." While pursing my lips, I nod, even though it was a damned lucky guess. "Vanilla and spice nose with a delicate fruity accent? Slightly sweet with no hard edges?" Of course, I read this in a magazine, but he doesn't have to know that.

A deep voice from behind us says, "Now there's a Kentucky girl who knows her bourbon." The tall man slaps Cody on the back. "Where've you been hiding this pretty young thing?"

"Dad, this is Jolie Russell," Cody says. "Jolie, my father, Carl Dean."

"Oh . . . yes, the Russells from Copper Creek Estates," he says with an odd look of surprise on his face that he quickly masks. Oh mercy, I wonder if he was in attendance at the Worthington anniversary party. "Nice to meet you, Jolie," he booms, and engulfs my hand in his big grasp. If he was witness to my dog-chasing-cake-smashing incident, he is polite enough not to mention it. "Now that I'm retired and Cody has taken over the reins, I'm not as up on things as I once was."

"Semiretired," Cody amends, "and not much gets past you."

"Yeah, well, your mother has been keeping me so busy that I might as well be retired." He shakes his head. "Not that I'm complaining. I'm falling in love with her all over again and trying my best to make up for lost time."

Cody's eyes widen in what seems like surprise at his father's admission.

Carl Dean looks me in the eye as he gives my hand a hard squeeze. He angles his head toward Cody but says to me, "This here boy needs to learn how to kick back and relax some too. You seem like the type who could help him do that. Am I right?"

"Dad!" Cody says, but his father ignores him and keeps his focus on me.

"It's a pleasure, Jolie Russell."

"Same here," I tell him, and he seems impressed by my firm handshake. He's a big, robust man, slightly overweight but handsome in a less refined way than Cody. He has an engaging smile, but I know a brilliant businessman lurks behind that good-old-boy persona. I can definitely see how he could make you relax and say yes to something without even knowing it.

Cody watches the exchange with interest and then says, "Are you here for cocktail hour or dinner with Mother?"

"Cocktails with clients." He glances at his watch. "I'd better get a move on before your mother has a fit. I was supposed to be home for dinner fifteen minutes ago."

Cody grins. "I'd hurry if I were you."

Carl grimaces when his cell phone rings. He fishes it out of his pocket and says, "I can't decide if these things are the best invention or the worst." He squints down at the small screen. "I'm in for it now," he complains but in a good-natured way that tells me their marriage is on solid ground. "Miranda, I'm on my way, sugar," he croons in a soothing tone, but then shrugs and gives me a wink.

I widen my eyes and make a shooing motion with my hands and then take a sip of wine to hide my smile. After he hurries off I turn to Cody. "So, does your mama wear the pants in the family?" Of course, I'm joking, but Cody's eyes turn serious.

"You could say that, but it wasn't always the case." Cody swirls the ice in his glass. "My mother had some serious heart problems this past year. It was a wake-up call for my father, who had always taken her for granted. I jumped in and took over the company before I was really prepared so that he could spend time with her and nurse her back to health."

"Oh, Cody," I say, and put a hand on his forearm. "I'm sorry for bein' such a smart-ass. I truly thought it was sweet of him to jump when she called." I remember now that Brett has said his father neglected his mother, and I wish I had kept my mouth shut. "Is she okay ?"

He nods. "She gave us a scare, but yes, she is in better health and better spirits than I've ever seen her. My father dotes on her now," he says, and then smiles. "By the way, I think you charmed my father."

"Was he at the Worthington anniversary brunch this morning?" I ask casually, and then hold my breath.

Cody gives me a reassuring smile. "No, he and Mother had previous commitments and couldn't attend."

I release my breath and then roll my eyes. "Oh, well, thank God for small favors."

Cody laughs and I swear he looks as if he wants to hug me. "You really don't know how engaging and refreshingly charming you truly are, Jolie. I could tell that my father was quite taken with you."

"When he found out who I was, I think he was expecting bare feet and missing teeth," I scoff, but feel a warm blush steal into my cheeks. "I sure wish my feet were bare." My shoes are starting to squeeze my toes, so I wiggle them to get the circulation going.

When Cody looks down at my feet I'm grateful to Carletta for my pink-tipped toenails. But when he leans in close and says low in my ear, "You need to sit down?" I completely forget about my aching feet. He smells like single-barrel bourbon and sultry citrus cologne, and I'm thinking it would be lovely to have him suck my earlobe into his warm mouth. The memory of Cody's mouth against mine filters into my brain and then oozes like warm honey through my veins.

"These shoes are squishing my toes," I admit in a husky voice. Embarrassed, I take a sip of wine and clear my throat as if I had something stuck there.

"Well, maybe it's about time we headed into the dining room." Cody glances down for his watch, which of course isn't there. "Get you off your feet."

"Oh, sorry, we forgot about your watch in all of the commotion."

"That's okay. We can get it after dinner," he says casually, as if we're a couple and are heading home together. I give myself a mental shake, knowing that Cody's heading home with me will never be a reality and I shouldn't even go there. He pulls out his cell phone and checks the time. "We should head on in and at least tell the hostess we've arrived."

"Okay," I answer, and take my last sip of wine.

"Would you like another?" he asks as he hands my empty glass to a passing waiter.

"Sure." The wine might be the reason that I'm just starting to relax a little bit more, when I spot Marissa Clayton heading our way. I dearly wish I were drinking bourbon on the rocks like Cody.

"Well, hello there," she sweetly croons at Cody, then turns to me. "Jolie," she says in a fake-friendly tone that makes me cringe as if it's fingernails on a chalkboard. When she gives my dress a once-over I try not to fidget.

"Vintage," I tell her, remembering Carletta's instructions. "Seventies sundresses are all the rage on the catwalks." I widen my eyes and toss her a little finger wave. I wish I could give Cody an elbow nudge without her noticing, but then I think he might not take my poking fun at Marissa lightly. I don't quite know how he feels about her, but it's clear she isn't happy I'm here with Cody.

"So, are you two having a little business meeting?" she asks sweetly, as if saying that Cody couldn't possibly be with me on a date.

I wonder if Cody will explain that he's filling in for Brett, when he says, "No, just dinner."

"Oh." Marissa's eyes narrow ever so slightly. "How nice of you, Cody," she remarks smugly, and lightly touches his shoulder before giving me a look that shouts that Cody is doing this out of sympathy. "Well, I must be off. I'm meeting some friends for happy hour." She blows a stupid kiss in the air and flits away, stopping here and there like a hummingbird in search of nectar.

Cody thoughtfully watches her walk away and then looks at me as if he's going to say something but then thinks better of it. Finally, he says next to my ear once more, "Don't let her get to you."

At the feel of his warm breath tickling my skin, a delicious little shiver of pleasure travels slowly down my spine. It must look as if he's saying something suggestive in my ear and I experience another shot of heat, but the fact that he thinks I'm so insecure that I would let the likes of Marissa Clayton bother me makes me inhale sharply. Of course, he's somewhat right, but I would rather walk barefoot through a cow pasture than let him know it. With a slight lift of my shoulders I say, "I find her sadly amusing."

"I bet you do," he replies with a crooked smile. "I'm glad you're relaxing and not letting this setting intimidate you."

"Pffft." I wave my hand and give him a twist of my lips. Hopefully I'm convincing.

"Good for you." His steady gaze is filled with admiration. "This isn't so painful, is it? Are you ready for dinner?"

"Sure." I am such a liar. Having a glass of wine on the porch is one thing. Now I have to go into the chamber of tortures and fake my way through dinner.

With his warm hand at the small of my back and his

firm fingers guiding me, we head inside the plantation house. The foyer is filled with antiques and gold-framed paintings of various landscapes. A majestic staircase curves around to the second story, where I believe is a grand ballroom for weddings and other social events, including the charity ball that Brett wants me to attend. Holy cow.

The aroma of food blends with the lemon wax that makes the woodwork gleam and shine. A chandelier glitters above our heads, sending shards of light dancing on the paisley wallpaper. I'm taking all of this in while Cody speaks to the hostess.

"Follow me," she says with a polite smile at me before turning an adoring gaze at Cody.

Cody remains at my side as we enter the large dining room. White linen adorns round tables with centerpieces of lively fresh flowers. Glasses and china clink and tinkle in an almost musical accompaniment to soft music that I think is piped in, until I spot the baby grand piano at the far end of the room. Conversation hums, interjected by muted laughter.

Cody nods here and there as we weave our way to our table tucked, as Brett had promised, in a private corner. Except for a few familiar faces from Copper Creek Estates, no one notices or seems to know who I am. When we pass Mason Worthington, he smiles and nods to Cody, but his eyes widen when he does a double take and realizes it's me. He looks to the floor and angles his Colonel Sanders head as if worrying that Rufus might be hightailing in after me. I give him a sheepish smile and a fluttery wave as I hurry on past him and his wife.

Cody holds my chair for me and I slide in pretty as you please. I'm thinking that this won't be too difficult until I look at the stack of plates, millions of pieces of silverware, and several glasses of various sizes. Holy cow. I swallow hard and suppress a shudder. At least I won't be taking someone else's something or other since it's a table for two. I take a deep breath and tell myself to simply watch what Cody does. How hard can that be? Thank goodness another glass of wine appears. Willing my fingers not to tremble, I reach for the delicate stem and take a deep drink.

A waiter appears with menus and a long-winded explanation of chef's specials, most of which is meaningless to me, but I frown, nod, and even throw in a word or two of appreciation. After a smile he hands us each a leather-bound menu and hurries off.

"What sounds good?"

I peek over the menu at him and decide to come clean. "A lot of it *sounds* good . . . I just have no idea what in the world most of this stuff is. Who is Oscar and why is a steak named after him?"

Cody has just taken a swallow of his drink and almost chokes with laughter. He holds up one finger while he gets control of himself. "It's a fillet topped with lump crab meat and asparagus and drizzled with béarnaise sauce."

"Oh, good. That's as clear as mud."

Amusement flashes in his eyes. "Your honesty is refreshing."

"It's better than ordering something I'll regret." I look over some of the choices and shake my head. "Chicken picatta?"

"It's an Italian dish. Chicken in a lemon butter sauce with capers."

"Capers . . . okay . . . What do you recommend?"

"Well, the steak Oscar happens to be one of my favorite dinners here. They make it for two . . . ," he says, and raises his eyebrows.

"Good. Order it up."

"Seriously?"

"Yes, why wouldn't I mean it?" I'd eat snails if it kept that smile on his handsome face. Okay, maybe not.

He shrugs his wide shoulders. "I'm never quite sure when to take you seriously."

I smile back. "I get it from my daddy. We needed humor to get us through the hard times."

Cody regards me a bit thoughtfully. "That's a good attitude to have."

I peer at him over the rim of my wineglass. "Well, high school teachers weren't always so appreciative of my attitude." I lean forward and say in a hushed tone, "I can sometimes be a . . . smart-ass."

Cody laughs. "Um, I've been on the receiving end, remember?"

"Well, I guess I keep you on your toes then, don't I?"

His smile is slow, sexy. "That you do, Jolie." He takes a sip of his drink. "And you know what?"

My heart beats faster. "What?"

"I can't remember the last time I had this much fun on a date."

A date?

"Remind me to thank Brett."

It's my turn to smile. "I will."

His smile falters a bit as he rubs his fingertip over the rim of his glass. Finally, he looks over at me. "You and my brother . . ."

"We're just friends," I quickly interject.

Cody nods. "Good, then I can tell you without feeling guilty that you look amazing in the candlelight."

"Yes, you can." Am I really flirting with Cody Dean? Who knew this would be so easy?

"I'm sorry if that sounded like a line."

"Don't be sorry. Say it again . . . or you know, something equally nice."

Cody laughs and is about to say something more, but the waiter comes and takes our order. "We'll have the steak Oscar dinner for two."

"Excellent choice." The waiter turns to me. "Salad dressing?"

"Um . . ."

"The house dressing here is good," Cody assures me. "It's a raspberry vinaigrette."

"Um, I think I'll stick with ranch." I'm not sure what the raspberry stuff will taste like. And I guess I want to show Cody I can think for myself.

"How would you like your steak?"

When Cody looks as if he will answer for me again, I say, "Medium, please."

"Baked potato or rice pilaf"?

I'm not certain what the pilaf part is, but is doesn't sound like something I'd eat. "Potato with butter and sour cream."

"Thank you very much. Sir?"

Cody rattles off his choices with practiced ease and then smiles across the table at me. "I know I talked you into this, but I hope you are enjoying yourself."

"I am, thank you." My heart thuds and my return smile trembles just a bit.

"Good, I'm glad."

Somewhere in the distance I hear the piano playing a

soothing love song. The candlelight flickers, casting a soft glow against the muted lighting of the room and we fall silent, lost in our thoughts and perhaps in each other. Glasses clink, china clatters, and conversation buzzes; yet something warm and intimate seems to pass between us . . .

The memory of a kiss? The hope of another? Of course, it might just be me. Cody might be planning his grocery list or thinking about the stock market.

A moment later a wicker basket of fragrant rolls arrives along with a plate filled with fancy balls of butter. I have to wonder why time is spent on such nonsense, but whatever; they are kind of cute. I just hope they don't fall off my knife, but I take Cody's lead and stab one with the little fork.

"These smell delicious." I break open a warm, crusty roll and slather it with a marble-sized ball that melts into the delicate dough. After I take a generous bite of the sweet, yeasty goodness, a sigh escapes me. I lick some melted remains off my thumb and then glance Cody's way. When his gaze lingers on me, I wonder if that was a totally uncountry club thing to do and make a mental note to make good use of my huge cloth napkin. I reach up and dab at the corners of my mouth just to show him I do have some manners. "Mmmm, yummy," I declare after devouring that last morsel, but then wish I had used a more dignified word. "The butter tastes a little bit like honey."

"You're right," Cody agrees just before sliding a bite past his lips. Why I find this supersexy I don't really know, but my gaze is riveted to his mouth. I watch him chew before I catch myself and take a quick sip from my water goblet.

It might be my imagination or maybe the mellow mood resulting from a couple glasses of wine, but I feel as if this is going well. Cody seems at ease too, relaxed, instead of on his usual uptight-businessman edge. Even his blue golf shirt, although no doubt expensive, gives him a casual appearance, which in turn makes me feel more comfortable.

"Thank you," I murmur politely when our entrées arrive. The food is artfully arranged and the rice that Cody has on his plate looks totally edible, so I make a mental note that pilaf is okay to order. "This looks amazing." I remember that Brett has stayed a member because of the food and now I know why. From the crisp tossed salad to the tender steak topped with succulent crab, crisp asparagus, and smooth sauce, the meal is magnificent.

I tuck into the meal with gusto and I'm almost finished when I wonder if I should have picked at it in a daintier, feminine fashion. I swallow a bite of potato and decide that maybe I should apologize. "Um, sorry. I'm a farm girl and we can put away some food."

Cody seems amused by my heartfelt admission. "You don't know how refreshing it is to dine with a woman who isn't afraid to eat."

"Really?"

He nods. "Definitely."

"So I shouldn't feel like a big fat cow if I order dessert?"

"No way. I would love it. That way I can order too. The crème brûlée is to die for."

"I was thinking chocolate, but we can share."

"Now there's a plan." When the waiter pauses at our table, Cody orders our dessert. He smiles at me. Although I know I shouldn't get my hopes up, I do think

Cody Dean is becoming rather fond of me. I'm thinking this is a fairy-tale night and I'm really starting to feel like Cinderella.

And then out of the corner of my eye I see Marissa Clayton heading our way. My heart sinks. This can't be good.

9

A Night to Remember

As Marissa sashays across the room, I remind myself that the evening has been a success and that I should feel nothing less than confident. Her progress is slow, however, since she has to pause and chat with just about everyone. Her demeanor is so animated as she flings her hands through the air and tosses her head that I wonder why people don't see right through her fakery. Although she's reed thin and impeccably groomed, there seems to be a quiet desperation lurking behind her polished exterior. Even her laughter seems forced.

"Well . . ." Marissa draws out the word in several syllables and octaves and gives us—well, make that Cody—a dazzling smile. "There y'all are tucked away in the corner where you can't be seen." Her smile turns smug as she seems to say, *Smart move.* She glances down at my empty plate and presses her lips together as if suppressing laughter. "Why . . . I'd ask if you enjoyed your dinner, but it's evident that you surely did."

"The food was delicious," I quietly reply, but I can feel heat creep into my cheeks. My fingers tighten around my napkin and I try not to feel big and clunky next to her tiny figure.

Her eyes widen a fraction and she gives Cody an amused glance. "Obviously." She places a delicate hand to her chest. "I do envy your hearty appetite. I can never finish more that a little bit since the portions are so generous here, aren't they, Cody?"

Cody appears uncomfortable but nods. "I suppose."

Of course, the waiter chooses that very moment to arrive with our desserts and Marissa's hand rises from her chest to her cheek. "Oh *my*. Cody, it's not like you to indulge in dessert," she says in a hushed tone, as if we're doing something illegal.

Cody merely shrugs his shoulders and doesn't appear concerned.

I realize that Marissa's making it clear to me that she and Cody have dined here together often. I know I don't have any real reason to be jealous since this isn't a real date, but I kind of feel that way, which is why I open my big mouth and say, "I suppose he was in the mood for something sweet for a change."

Her eyes harden. "Oh, I suppose the temptation for the forbidden makes it all the more enticing." She wrinkles her nose. "But the guilt and regret afterward just flat-out aren't worth it. You know what I'm saying?" she asks, but directs her comment to Cody.

Cody's eyes narrow at her in warning and while I'm somewhat glad, it galls me that he feels the need to come to my defense as if I'm no match . . . not that I'd want to be a viper like her, but still, if I want to survive in this new environment, I need to learn to hold my own. Hopefully Abigail Marksberry will teach me how to deal with the Marissa Claytons of the world.

"Well, I must be off," Marissa says with a breezy wave of her hand, causing her thin gold bracelets to jangle. "Enjoy your dessert. Oh, by the way, Cody, I have some urgent business we need to attend to."

"Really?" Cody frowns. "About what?"

Marissa gives him a sassy little head bop that makes me want to roll my eyes, but I politely refrain. "The charity ball, silly boy."

"Marissa, the ball isn't until the end of the summer."

She inhales sharply and strikes a pose with her hands on her hips. "These things don't happen overnight and I *am* the chairperson, you know."

"Yes . . . I know." When he says this in a tired, how-can-I-forget tone, she visibly bristles.

"Have you forgotten that Dean Construction is the main sponsor?"

"No, I haven't."

"Good! Well, I'll be calling you first thing tomorrow," she snaps, and with a flip of her hair walks off with her nose so high in the air, I'm surprised it doesn't bleed.

"Well, all righty, then." I remember what Brett said about Marissa being after Cody and have to bite my tongue so I don't say something snarky. Instead, I watch her stomp off before I turn my attention to Cody. "You could have put her out of her misery by telling her this isn't a real date. Not that she has any reason to be threatened by me."

"Why would you say that?" he asks from across the flickering candlelight.

"Well, because you're simply filling in for your brother."

Cody shakes his head. "No, I mean, why shouldn't she feel threatened by you?"

I'm taken by surprise. "Oh, come on, Cody. We're not exactly cut from the same cloth and she knows it."

"No, you're not," he says slowly, and I swear it feels as if he's looking at me . . . differently. "And I know it."

To hide my blush, my confusion, I stare down at the slice of cake and study the plump raspberry that tops a generous swirl of whipped cream. Deep red sauce is art-fully drizzled over the gold plate in festive figure eights.

"Don't you even consider not eating your dessert."

Startled that he's read into my thoughts, I look up. "Not on your life." To prove my point I sink my fork into the soft cake and take a healthy bite. Moist and rich, it's topped with fudge icing and has mocha mousse between the layers. "Oh, this is heaven. What's it called?"

"Death by chocolate."

"What a way to die." I try to joke, but my laughter is breathless and my heart is pounding like a big bass drum.

Cody scoops up a spoonful of his crème brûlée, but in-stead of putting it up to his mouth, he extends his long arm across the table. "Here, try this."

While nodding, I swallow my cake and then lick my lips before complying. Watching me intently, Cody slides the spoon between my lips. I almost moan as the velvety custard melts into my mouth and finishes with the slight crunch of the caramelized sugar.

"Good?"

"Mmmm . . . mercy yes." I nod and then, willing my fingers not to tremble, I slide my fork into my cake. "It's your turn. But be forewarned about the whole dying part."

"I thought you'd never ask," he says, and puts his hand over mine in order to guide the fork to his mouth.

"I wasn't going to offer but . . ." I try to joke, but when his warm hand remains on mine I forget the rest of my line. I have to come from my chair a little and lean forward. I know I'm giving him a good look at my cleavage, but with the wine eviedntly lowering my inhibitions, instead of being embarrassed, I hope he likes what he sees.

"Marissa was dead wrong," he comments while licking frosting from the corner of his mouth.

"About what?" My voice is husky . . . sexy? Me?

"This is definitely worth it." His warm gaze makes me melt more quickly than the whipped cream on my tongue and although the room is crowded with people, this moment feels intimate, romantic, and my heart thuds. Can this really be happening?

The lights dim a fraction and a lounge singer, sounding similar to Frank Sinatra, joins the piano player and starts crooning "Embraceable You." Couples soon head for the hardwood dance floor at the far end of the room.

"Would you like to dance?" Cody asks.

"Oh . . . I'm not much of a dancer."

"Me neither, but I want to anyway," he implores, and before I can protest he stands up and offers his hand.

"Cody . . ."

He nods his dark head toward the dance floor. "Come on, Jolie."

Unable to refuse his warm smile, I stand up and put my cool hand in his warm grasp even though my heart is skittering in my chest. Dance? When was the last time I slow danced? I'm thinking it was a high school dance with Jimmy Baker, who was a good five inches shorter than me. This . . . I know is going to be quite a different experience. When we reach the dance floor Cody draws me into his arms. Not knowing if I should wrap my arms around his neck or what to do, I sneak a peek at the other couples. Oh . . . one hand in his and the other one on his shoulder. And then, just sway a little. I can do that. Of course, it would be easier if my knees weren't knocking.

"Just follow my lead," Cody says in my ear while he gives my hand a reassuring squeeze.

"Okay, but if I mangle your toes, this is all your fault. Don't say I didn't warn you."

Cody pulls back his head to grin at me just as I turn my face, causing our lips to brush ever so slightly, but I swear it's as if a lightning bolt shoots all the way to my pinched toes. It's a wonder my hair isn't standing on end. When his eyes widen a fraction I wonder if he felt the same sizzle. Oh no, maybe his eyes rounded because he thought I meant to kiss him.

"That was an accident," I explain with a nervous little laugh.

"Really?"

While nibbling on the inside of my cheek I nod vigorously.

"Well, just so you know . . . this isn't." Cody gently tilts my chin upward and enchants me with a brief but tender kiss. "And in case you're wondering, I don't care who saw us," he says in my ear.

At this point I'm not dancing . . . I'm floating on air. This is a night that dreams are made of; almost too good to be true. We dance cheek to cheek until "Embraceable You" blends into "New York, New York" and Cody has me laughing when he starts singing along in my ear. "These vagabond shoes . . ." His voice is surprisingly pleasant and he's lighter on his feet than he led me to believe, but I'm not surprised. He has me gliding and twirling until I'm out of breath. Praise the lord, I don't stomp on his feet even once. We clap at the end of the song and head back to our table, hand in hand and laughing all the way.

"Whew!" I exclaim as I slide into my chair and take a long drink of water. "That was a workout!" I fan my face with my napkin.

"Yes, I think we worked off our dessert."

I glance down at the crumbs on my plate and purse my lips. "I do believe that's wishful thinking on your part, Cody."

He lifts his shoulders. "Nothing wrong with a little wishful thinking, don't you agree?"

If only he knew . . .

Cody takes a long swig of his water, then continues. "Well, Jolie, we'll just have to dance the night away."

"I'm game," I assure him, "but first I have to freshen up in the ladies' room."

"It's out the doorway and to the left."

"Thanks. Excuse me," I remember to add, thinking I've retained more of my mother's manners than I thought. "I'll be back in a few minutes." I pick up my purse and walk away with my head held high. For the first time I believe I might be able to ease my way in this upper-crust society.

The ladies' room has a lounge area with fresh cut flowers, wingback chairs, and a Queen Anne sofa. The sweet floral scent mingles with spicy potpourri and hair spray. When I catch a glimpse of my reflection in the wall-length mirror, I pause to stare. My cheeks are flushed and my smile is wide, making me feel pretty and feminine in the yellow sundress. I've waited a long time for this feeling to emerge, so I stop to savor it.

"Hello there." I nod politely at a couple of women fussing with their hair and then breeze past them into a stall. While softly humming "New York, New York," I place my purse on the small shelf and proceed to take care of business. I'm about ready to open the door, when Marissa's voice makes my hand pause on the latch.

"Dear lord, Katie, you should have seen it. Not one morsel of food was left on her plate."

"Maybe she licked it clean," Katie answers with a snort.

"I was waiting for her to pick her teeth. I truly don't know how Cody kept a straight face."

With a pounding heart I peek through the crack between the door and the side of the stall. Katie, an equally slim but taller redhead, applies lipstick and then turns to Marissa. "People are still buzzing about the incident at Mason Worthington's brunch this morning."

"I know! I wish I had it on camera."

Katie giggles. "We could send it to *Country Fried Home Videos.*"

I swallow my gasp.

"You watch that show?" Marissa sneers.

"Of course not. I've just, you know, heard of it," Katie replies.

Marissa rolls her eyes. "Why on earth is Cody with her? Has he taken leave of his senses?" With a little pout Marissa fluffs her hair, then answers her own question. "It's simple. Cody is trying to civilize her. At the last Copper Creek HOA meeting, Jolie and Wyatt Russell were actually typed on the agenda. Their redneck antics are keeping people from purchasing property in Copper Creek Estates."

Katie puts a hand to her chest. "Shut up!"

Marissa checks her perfectly white teeth in the mirror and nods. "Oh, believe it. It's like having Jed Clampett and Ellie Mae living in the neighborhood." She hums the theme from *The Beverly Hillbillies*, then tosses her head back and laughs.

Katie gives Marissa a playful shove. "You are so very bad."

Marissa shrugs her narrow shoulders. "It's the truth and Cody knows it. If he thinks he can tame her wild ways and introduce her into polite society, he has another think coming, even though he assured the committee he'd take the matter into his own hands. What a joke!"

I narrow my eyes and wonder if I should open the door and kick both their bony butts. I actually start to slide the latch, thinking I could just pick them both up and knock their heads together. But instead, I silently count to ten. A huge lump forms in my throat and I find myself in real danger of crying. But then I stiffen my Russell backbone, knowing that either option would just play into their hands. And neither option is acceptable. Maybe I'll just burst into the bathroom and give each of them a wet willie. A wedgie would be good but not doable in a dress. Oh dear lord, what am I reduced to thinking?

"They looked pretty cozy on the dance floor," Katie says a little tentatively, and slides Marissa a curious glance. Wow, they are mean even to each other.

Thank you, Katie, I mouth, and then shift my eyes to Marissa.

Her lips twist as she fingers a single strand of hair that had the nerve to stray. "Oh puh-lease. They looked ridiculous. I had to press my lips together to keep from peals of laughter. Are you insane? I can't wait for Cody to tell me all about his so-called date."

Katie lifts one shoulder. "I'm just saying . . ."

"Well, I think those two mojitos are clouding your judgment."

Katie laughs. "I guess you're right. Jolie does sort of look like Jessica Simpson playing Daisy Duke."

Nothing wrong with that, I think to myself.

"Uh-uh. More like Ellie Mae."

Katie snaps her fingers. "How about Joy on *My Name Is Earl?*"

"Too pretty," Marissa snaps.

While the two of them argue, I narrow my eyes and fist my hands. I count to ten.

But it's no use.

I've had enough. Somebody's gonna get an ass whoopin'.

10

Rock My World, Little Country Girl

Okay, opening up a can of Whoop Ass sounded good in my head, but since I've never really been in a fight or even thrown a punch, it's likely I'd get my own butt kicked. After all, those two are mean. I just bet they would pull hair, poke at eyes, and fight dirty. I'm thinking I should just wait for them to leave, but these two are taking primping to a whole new level. Dear lord, come on!

While I know I shouldn't let the likes of Marissa Clayton get to me, I have to question whether she was right. Was Cody bringing me here for some etiquette lessons? Was he trying to put local fear to rest by showing up in public with me? Was he laughing at me and not with me, filing away little anecdotes to share with her later? Oh, surely not. Suppressing a groan, I lean my forehead against the cool metal door and try to think straight while keeping my emotions in check. Up until lately I've been an expert at doing just that, but right now

I have to swallow hard and rub my throbbing temples. Okay, so what Marissa said makes sense, except that Brett was supposed to come here with me in the first place. So she must have it all wrong . . . right? Well, regardless, I have to return to the table before Cody comes looking for me.

Why don't they just leave?

"Mercy, Katie," Marissa says, uncapping her lipstick and leaning close to the mirror, "when Jolie Russell plopped her big butt into that cake, I laughed so hard I thought I might dribble in my panties! I had to grab Cody's arm for support!"

Big butt? I narrow my eyes—okay, my one eye— through the crack between the door and the side of the stall.

"If I were her, I wouldn't be able to show my face or my butt ever again!" Marissa's tinkling laughter echoes in the bathroom and she starts applying lipstick to her bottom lip.

Well, horse pucky! Enough is enough. I slide the latch over and fling open the door. "You mean this face?" I jab my thumb at my nose for good measure. I really don't know where I'm going with this, so I'll just have to wing it. I don't think I've ever been this angry in all my born days and it must show, because Marissa's eyes widen and she drags her red lipstick from the middle of her lip clear up the side of her cheek. "And this big butt?" I turn sideways and point to my left cheek.

"I don't think your butt is big, Jolie," Katie says in a high, squeaky voice. Ha, I guess they're not so big and bad after all. This gives me a boost of bravado. Katie swallows hard and tries to smile. When I don't reciprocate she quickly adds, "And—and I like your shoes."

"Thank you," I respond tightly, you know, because it's the polite thing to do, and then I turn my attention to Marissa. "Um, you might not want to show your face right about now." I point to the red slash on her cheek, which I'm sure will be difficult to remove. Too bad.

Marissa juts her chin in the air and makes no effort to apologize, but I'm not surprised. But instead of getting even angrier, I simply feel sorry for her. Of course, not sorry enough to tell her that she has toilet paper stuck to her pointy heel. While she fusses with her face, I step over to the sink and quickly wash and dry my hands. With my head held high I exit the ladies' room while experiencing a measure of satisfaction that I confronted mean and meaner, but as I walk back to the table I'm dragging my feet instead of walking on air. So much for my perfect, fairy-tale evening. Now all I want to do is go home, get into my jeans, and hang out with Daddy and Rufus.

Of course, I'm a big fat liar.

I want to rewind and go back to where I was before going to the ladies' room.

It sure sucks to be swept off your feet, only to land with a big splat. This is precisely what I text message Carletta just because I have to tell someone. It makes me feel a little bit better when she texts back that we will talk tomorrow. Her next text message reads: *We will plan our revenge*. I text back: *What?*

Carletta answers: *Looking good is the best revenge. We have only just begun to show those skinny hussies!*

I text back a smiley face and then slowly make my return. When I pass the front entrance I consider bolting, but what would I do? Walk? I remind myself that this isn't Cody's doing and running would be cowardly and rude.

"Hey, I was getting worried," Cody comments with a slight frown. "Are you okay?"

No! "Sure. Sorry, I was on the phone."

He looks at me while toying with the stem of his glass. I can tell he's unconvinced. "What do you say we get out of here?"

I give him an eager nod and that stupid lump in my throat returns. While he settles up the bill, I take a drink of my water and it helps a little.

Once we're in his Audi he says, "Brett called."

"Oh?"

"His player's ankle is just sprained, not broken."

"That's good news," I tell him. Where before I was becoming comfortable, now I'm nervous and it doesn't help that in this two-seater car we're very close. When he shifts, his arm comes close to brushing against my thigh and of course he makes driving the sexiest thing ever. His hand covers the gearshift and the muscles in his tanned forearm flex with every move he makes; so help me I just want to jump into that little bucket seat with him and kiss him senseless. Now how stupid of me is that?

When we stop at a red light Cody angles his body toward mine. "I thanked him."

"Who?" I ask, but I know what he's going to say and my heart pounds.

"Brett." He gives me a half grin. "You know what I like about you, Jolie?"

"My bodacious butt?"

He tosses back his head and laughs before shifting into first gear. "Well, now that you mention it, as a matter of fact, yes."

Thank you God and Daddy for my infallible sense of humor.

"I like your inability to lie."

"Pfft." I wave my hand. "That's what all the boys tell me," I say drolly, adding a roll of my eyes. "I do declare, it gets old," I continue to coo, and give my hair a flip.

"Jolie," Cody chuckles, but then shakes his head as he pulls up my driveway. He kills the engine and twists in the seat to face me. "Something is suddenly bothering you. Would you mind telling me what it is?"

"Nothin'," I scoff, trying so very hard to be convincing. Of course, I fail miserably. "I'm fine." I try again while I toy with the clasp on my purse.

He looks at the dashboard and then back at me.

"Right, that annoying inability to lie." I put the heel of my hand to my forehead. "No seriously, I'm fine. Tonight was just . . ." I shrug when I don't really know how to describe it.

"Hey, Jolie, why don't we get out of the car and sit by the pool for a while?" When I don't immediately respond he says, "It's a nice night." After another slight pause he adds, "Unless you want me to go."

"I really . . . I mean it would be *best* if . . . we didn't," I say.

"Okay," he responds with a silent nod, although he appears confused. But ever the gentleman, he comes over to my door and opens it, offering his assistance. When I slip my hand into his grasp I try to ignore the sweet tingle of awareness. And so help me, as he helps me to my feet, the close proximity of our bodies invokes a need, a longing that I don't fully understand, only that I want to be in his embrace . . . held close. Oh, how I want to lean on him with my head resting on his shoulder.

He wouldn't have to say a word; just hold me.

Flustered, since strength all these years has been my

friend, I decide to take a step backward and put some much-needed distance between us. But instead of letting me go, Cody pulls me into his arms, lowers his head, and kisses me softly. Startled, I put my hands on his chest, thinking that I should push away, but he gently coaxes my lips apart and continues to kiss me until the icy ball of fear in my gut starts to melt.

I can feel the heat of his skin beneath my palms, the beat of his heart. He threads his long fingers through my hair and moves his mouth to the tender spot on my neck where my pulse is racing. When his tongue touches my skin a breathy sigh escapes me.

"Let me stay for a while." His voice is low, husky, and feels like a warm caress. "We can sit by the pool, go for a night swim . . . talk. Whatever. I don't care." He pulls back and tucks a lock of hair behind my ear and, while gazing down at me, says, "I just don't want to leave."

The pool glows invitingly in the background. The thought of gliding through the warm water with him is so enticing that the logical part of my brain, which should be screaming that I'm just going to get hurt, short-circuits, and I find myself nodding my head. "A swim would be nice."

Cody lets out a sigh of what I guess must be relief, but then I wonder if it's just wishful thinking on my part. A smile tugs at the corners of my mouth when I remember his earlier comments about wishful thinking.

"That's better."

"What?" I ask.

"Your smile is back."

"Well, Daddy always said that a smile don't cost a thing." I shake my head. "Smiles got us through some tough times." I wave my hand toward the stately house, the pool, the lush landscaping. "You're well aware I didn't grow up with these trappings. While I don't want to sound like the poor little rich girl, I don't feel as if I belong here."

He tucks his thumb beneath my chin and tilts my face up. "You didn't seem to have any problem at the country club tonight, Jolie."

"I was with you, so that made me acceptable." I wonder what he would make of the conversation I overheard between Katie and Marissa. Right now it's difficult to believe there is a shred of truth to anything she said, but then again, standing here in the moonlight with Cody could be clouding my judgment. "Look, let's round up some swimsuits and hit the pool and forget about all that other stuff for now." When he arches one eyebrow but doesn't answer, I have to ask, "What?"

Cody lifts his shoulders. "Are swimsuits necessary?"

My eyes widen and all I can do is stutter. "Cordelia Crawford would have a field day with that . . . and so would the god-almighty HOA."

"To hell with Cordelia Crawford and screw the HOA," Cody says forcefully.

"Oh my! I'm shocked at such language!" I press my hands against his chest and give him a small shove. "Oh, I get it. This is a test. Okay then, how about this?" I put my hands to my cheeks and say in a soft, high-pitched voice, "Why, Cody Dean, I would nevva, evaa do such a thang. Shame on you." I bat my eyes for good measure and then say in a normal tone, "Okay, do I pass?"

Cody looks at me for a long enough moment for me to wonder if he had been serious, but then he seems to tap into his reasonable side and shakes his head. "You pass with flying colors. Too bad for me, I guess." He laughs but looks uncertain, as if taking a walk on the wild side has some appeal.

Knowing I should leave well enough alone but simply unable to, I tap his chest and say, "Yeah, too bad. It would have been fun."

He blinks at me for a minute as if skinny-dipping holds such sensual appeal that he might suggest it again. "Your father might have seen us." He seems happy that he's found a reason to ditch the idea.

"Mmmm, no." I shake my head. "The farmer in Daddy makes him early to bed and early to rise. He's sound asleep by now." I look toward Miss Cordelia's house. "I've never seen her out past ten either." I purse my lips and pause. "But you know, rules are rules." I flip my palms upward and shrug. "Indecent exposure and all that . . ."

"It's not indecent exposure if nobody sees you." Cody rubs his chin, a chin that's sporting a delicious five o'clock shadow. "You know, I don't think there's any mention of skinny-dipping in the HOA bylaws. I mean, this is your own backyard."

"True." I purse my lips. "But since I'm already in hot water, I need to keep things on the down low. Start conducting myself in a proper manner." With that I turn and head toward the pool house. Cody swallows, then nods. What he doesn't know is that he could easily talk me into it. I've always loved a dare, a challenge, or a practical joke. There aren't too many guys who can best me on a dirt bike or a four-wheeler, simply because I'm willing to keep going when others stop, and I have the scars to prove it. I'll dive off a cliff or ski down a mountain or stare down a bear . . . okay, I made that last part up, but still, I'm game for just about any challenge, and I think it's rather amusing that I've rocked Mr. Conservative-Follow-the-Rules Cody Dean's world. Ha!

When I don't hear footsteps, I pause and turn around. "Coming?"

11

Wet and Wild

Now that I'm back on my home turf—well, sort of—and away from Marissa and her sidekick, some of my earlier good humor returns. Calling Cody's bluff was way too much fun and suddenly the rest of the night is looking up, not that I'm expecting anything more than a relaxing swim in the pool. With that in mind I slip into a hot pink bikini, grab a towel, and then open the door to inform Cody that a pair of swim trunks is on the bed.

"Cody?" I look around the main room of the pool house, but he's nowhere to be seen. With a stab of disappointment I wonder if he decided to cut his losses and go home. "Well, I might as well go for a swim anyway," I mutter darkly as I wrap a fluffy towel around me and then head outside.

The night air has turned a bit cooler, making the heated pool all the more enticing. I hope to spot Cody lounging by the pool, but the chairs are empty and except for the slight lapping sound of the water and hum of nocturnal nature, all is silent. I push back the pang of longing, telling myself I have no real right to be sad or angry;

yet I toss the towel onto a chair with more force than needed.

While trailing my toe on the surface of the water I think about doing a pretty little dive, but the mood I'm in calls for an angry splash, so I do a big cannonball into the deep end. I never have been one of those ease-into-the-pool types. The water feels warm and silky against my cool skin. My hair fans out and I let myself sink, and then I push up from the bottom like a rocket. I've been doing the same thing since I was a kid but never in my own pool. As I pop to the surface like a dolphin I decide I should swim a few laps to work off my death by chocolate.

"That was impressive. I'll give you a nine point five."

"What!" I squeal, and flop around like a bluegill just reeled into a bass boat.

"Do you always have to splash me directly in the face?"

"Do you always have to scare the pants off me?" I shoot back, and then my eyes widen. "Speaking of pants . . ."

"What?" His slow grin confirms my suspicion.

"No, you . . . *didn't*," I sputter at him while treading water just a few feet away.

Cody slicks his hair back from his face and then hooks his arms over the edge of the pool, drawing my attention to a ripple of muscle and his tanned bare chest. "There's only one way to find out." His white teeth flash in the semidark glow of the underwater lighting.

I shake my head. "I'm not coming over there."

"Why not?"

"Because . . ." I start to backpedal while searching for solid ground and cognitive thinking.

"Because, why?"

Because you're dangerously sexy and I won't be able to resist you. Because one kiss and I'll be putty in your hands. "Because . . . be-*cau-zaaa* I need to swim some laps to work off my dinner." There, that was as good an answer as any.

He arches one dark eyebrow and I know what's coming, so I press my lips together and brace myself. "Jolie . . ." His voice is low and laced with a hint of a challenge.

"Don't," I mutter out loud when I should have kept my mouth shut.

"Don't what?" he asks innocently, making me want to splash him. Or kiss him. Kiss him and then splash him. Before I do either one, his teeth flash again and he whispers, "Chicken."

Oh why do people always dare me? Resist, Jolie, be strong! But I don't want to resist. I can't resist. Plus, my arms are getting tired. But swimming over to wet and naked Cody Dean could lead to . . .

My heart pumps hard and for a second I forget to move my arms. I sink briefly and when I come bopping back up, Cody is gone. What? I look left and right, but then all of a sudden I feel something graze my leg and he surfaces next to me, sleek, wet, and sexy as hell.

We tread water for a long, steamy moment while he looks at me with a challenge in his deep blue eyes. I try to distract myself, you know, think about the price of gas, world peace or something, *anything*, but all my brain will process is the fact that he is naked . . . and mere inches away.

"You want to join me?" he asks.

"Noooo! You're breaking the rules, you know."

"It feels great." He grins and I have a very hard time not grinning back.

"The water or breaking the rules?"

"Both."

"What's gotten into you, Cody?" I suddenly have to ask, since this seems so out of character.

His broad shoulders lift, making the water ripple. "You."

"Really?" I ask softly, and my heart thuds. I want to tell him not to toy with me. I'm not sophisticated and if this is a game we're playing, I'm way over my head—and I don't mean the water.

"I guess it was about time I did what I wanted to do and not . . . what people expect of me," he quietly explains. I'm somehow moved that he remembered what I said to him. But then I look into his eyes, trying to assure myself that he's sincere and not mocking me. When his gaze is level and true, I breathe a sigh of relief.

"Good move, because I surely didn't expect you to be skinny-dippin' when I did my lovely cannonball." I try to joke, but my voice is breathless and well, I can't help it, but I'm staring at his mouth.

"Well, I seem to be underdressed for the second time tonight," he says.

"I'm sure that's a record for you."

"Yeah, probably," he answers.

"So . . ."

He inches closer. My arms are getting really tired. I might have to wrap myself around him to keep from drowning. Something brushes against my thigh . . . My eyes widen.

"That was my hand."

"Likely story."

"You're something else, you know that?" he says.

"So I've been told."

Cody laughs and then without warning snakes his long arm around me and draws me close. With his other arm, he slices through the water until we are in a totally secluded corner of the pool, away from the underwater lights. We both know where this is leading and his eyes search my face as if in question.

"Jolie . . ."

While there are logical reasons why I shouldn't do this, the sensation of smooth, wet skin sliding against mine is all I can process. He brushes his lips lightly against mine, and then with a sexy growl he captures my mouth in a deep, delicious kiss. His mouth is so warm, his lips are firm, full, and when his tongue tangles with mine I wrap my arms around his neck and rub my breasts ever so slightly against his chest.

"You taste amazing." He runs the tip of his tongue along my bottom lip. "Sweet." He kisses me again. "But hot." He nibbles, licks, and kisses me once more, until I can't resist reaching up and untying the knot at my neck. Hot pink triangles flutter downward to the surface of the water and my breasts tumble free. Cody sucks in a breath while my breasts play a teasing game of peekaboo in the water. When my nipples graze against his chest I gasp at the sheer pleasure that begins to tighten into a ball and then slowly unravels.

When Cody dips his head and tugs a sensitive nipple into his mouth, a moan escapes me. I arch backward, allowing him to look, touch, caress, and then, ohmigod, lick, nibble . . . *suck*. My body feels weightless, liquid, and when he hooks his thumbs into the sides of my bikini bottoms, I allow him to slide them down to my ankles. I impatiently kick them off and let them slither away, not caring where they end up. While I am not innocent in the ways of a man and a woman, I've been longing for a hot, delicious moment like this to happen.

When his hands glide over my breasts and then down to my navel, I shudder with anticipation. Then, tugging me upward, he brings me flush against the hard length of his body. The sensation is like sliding next to hot silk and it takes my breath away.

Emotion, passion, raw and intense, takes over.

This is spinning out of control and I don't care. No man has ever made me feel this way. Oh, this is what I've been wanting, missing . . . needing. I don't think Cody planned this and I sure didn't expect it, but it's happening. And I don't want it to end.

Cody brushes my wet hair from my neck, then nuzzles and kisses me in that sweet spot until I can't see straight. "I didn't plan this," he says, echoing my thoughts in a husky voice that sends a hot shiver down my spine. "I want you to know that."

I pull back and gaze at him. "I didn't think you did." He looks down, shuttering his eyes with wet, spiky eyelashes. I wonder if he's trying to talk himself out of making love to me based on some misguided sense of propriety. While rubbing my fingertip over his bottom lip I say, "Cody, if I didn't want this, I wouldn't allow it."

He raises his eyes to meet mine. "This is . . ."

"Unexpected?"

He nods and gives me a small smile.

"Look, I won't, that is, I realize I'm not . . ." I falter and look away.

He gently nudges my face toward him. "If you say

anything remotely like *good enough*, I'll dunk you," he jokes, but we both know I'm close enough to the truth.

"I was going to say *your type*."

Both eyebrows shoot up. "Really, now? So gorgeous, spunky, funny, and smart isn't my type?"

I try to smile, but my lips tremble at the corners. "Cody, you of all people know what's bein' said about Daddy and me."

"Yeah well, I'm seeing things from a different perspective now," he insists, and then lowers his head and kisses me softly. In the back of my mind I realize that he's trying to prove something to me and perhaps to himself. And just maybe he is seeing things from a different angle . . . my angle.

"Daddy and I might come from humble roots, but we're good people with much more worth than the stereotypical laughing stock that my illustrious neighbors make us out to be."

When Cody raises his head he looks searchingly at me. "I don't doubt that." But I see something like guilt flash in his eyes and I'm not quite sure I totally buy what he's selling. I think he *wants* to believe it, but that's not the same thing. Still, I want him, need him, crave his touch on my body, but when my hands grip his shoulders and I slide against his skin, I feel the muscles tense beneath my fingers, so I pull back.

"Cody, you don't have to fight this." I pause, then add, "And whatever happens between us will stay between us."

"Do you still think I'm worried about that?" he asks.

My shoulders lift slightly and I glance away.

"Ahhh, Jolie . . ." Cody says. I want to be wrapped in his arms so badly, but the logical part of my brain has the

nerve to shift into gear right now and good sense rears its
ugly head.

"Cody, now just how in the world did we end up naked
in my pool?" I try to lighten the moment that has to come,
because as much as I want him, I know I'm likely to get
hurt.

"Spontaneity."

"You don't seem the spontaneous type," I say.

"I wasn't." He presses his warm lips to my shoulder,
not making this any easier. "At least not until now." *Until
you* hangs unspoken in the sultry night air. He begins a
trail of kisses over my collarbone and even though I long
to wrap my legs around his waist and make love to him,
I suddenly realize I don't want to be a spontaneous walk
on the wild side that Cody will regret later. If and when I
do make love to him I want him to be sure . . . and I want
it to mean something special with the hope of something
lasting. I don't think that can happen until Abigail Marksberry works her magic on me.

"Cody . . . ," I say softly. He looks at me with disappointment, but he's too much a gentleman to push.

"Okay." Something else flashes in his eyes and I think
it's respect. "I'm sorry things got out of hand," he says.

"Don't be. I egged you on. I should have warned you
I'm good at that," I tell him.

A slow smile spreads across his face. "I'll be better
prepared in the future."

The future? Does this mean he wants to see me again?
But instead of elaborating, he dives deep and comes back
with my bathing suit. "Thanks." A warm blush steals into
my cheeks as I take the hot pink pieces from him. My
eyes widen and I should, but can't, look away as he hefts
himself up and out of the pool. Water sluices down his

body and I can't help but notice that he has an amazing butt. I watch until he disappears into the shadows. I hear the rustle of clothing and can't quell a pang of disappointment even though I sternly tell my sorry self that I'm doing the right thing for a wide variety of reasons.

Still . . . I sigh and then half drown myself as I struggle into my swimsuit. Cody comes to the edge of the pool and squats down. "Coming out?" he asks.

I shrug. "I think I'll swim for a while."

His eyebrows come together. "I don't like the idea of your swimming alone."

"Cody, I'll be fine. Unlike Rufus, I'm a strong swimmer."

When his frown remains I try not to feel glad he's concerned about me. "Please?"

"Oh, okay." When he offers a hand, I decide to take it. He hoists me up with little effort, but then I stumble forward from the momentum. He catches me around the waist and takes his sweet time removing his hands. "Sorry, I've made you wet again. It's becoming a habit."

"I don't mind." He looks down at me and I think he might kiss me, but after a moment's hesitation he takes a step backward, as if he needs to put some distance between us.

"Thanks for dinner," I tell him, and pray my smile doesn't wobble. For some reason, I'm suddenly emotional again. Maybe I'm ready to start my girl period, I think to myself, but I know better.

"It was truly my pleasure, Jolie."

My heart pounds when I hope that he'll mention calling me or seeing me again, but he threads his fingers through his wet hair and remains silent. "Good night," I say.

"Good night." When he stands there a moment longer my hope swells again, but he turns and starts walking away.

"Drive safely," I call out softly. He pauses and turns around.

"I will."

I smile and nod, and when a cool breeze kicks up, I reach down to retrieve the towel. After wrapping it snuggly around me, I sink down into a lounge chair and sit there for a minute or two, listening to the soft ripple of water and sounds of night. I relive the evening in my mind, amazed at the chain of events that led to skinny-dipping. I'd be lying if I didn't harbor a measure of regret that I'm not making love to Cody Dean right this very minute. "Well, damn it all to hell and back."

Rufus suddenly comes lumbering up the driveway. Seeing me, he picks up speed and hurries over to me as fast as his short legs will carry him.

"Now, just where did you sneak off to?" I ask when he flops down at my feet. I narrow my eyes and say, "Did you hunt down that hussy, Misty?"

At the sound of her name, Rufus looks at me and then sighs with what I think sounds like satisfaction. "You lucky dog, you."

But then I put my hand over my mouth. "Holy cow, Rufus, I hope she's been fixed or you and I will be in a heap of trouble." I reach down and scratch him between his ears. "I wonder what tomorrow will bring. But it would surely take something amazin' to beat tonight."

12

Makeover Madness

"So, what's this with you and that Dean boy?" Daddy asks while we're having coffee and Danish by the pool. "Or should I say *boys*?" He teases with a wink.

"Daddy!" I push my sunglasses up on my nose and try to act casual. "Brett and I hit it off when he helped me get Rufus back home after my unfortunate cake incident at the Worthingtons' anniversary party."

"Cake incident?"

"Don't ask." I lick some cherry filling from my thumb and continue. "Cody was just stepping in when Brett had to cancel our dinner plans."

Daddy adjusts the bill of his John Deere baseball cap, which for some reason always shifts to the left. He's wearing faded swim trunks and a Hawaiian shirt he's owned ever since I can remember. I'm thinking we really do need help, especially in the fashion department. "So, are you sweet on either of them?"

I feel heat creep up my neck and I hide my blush behind the rim of my coffee mug. "I don't really know ei-

ther one all that well, now do I?" I try to cop an attitude
but can never quite pull it off.

"Fair enough. But ya know I'm here for you to talk to
whenever you need an ear to bend, for what it's worth,"
he says.

"It's worth the world to me." I watch him stretch his
long legs and look out over the pool; my chest tightens
with emotion. I know it's surreal for him to believe that
this is ours, but I know he would trade it all in an instant
to have my mother back. After last night, I understand
even more how he must feel. "Daddy?" I ask softly, and
he turns his attention to me.

"Yeah, baby doll?" His hat shades his expressive blue
eyes, but I sense that his thoughts were going in the same
direction as mine.

"Have you thought any more about doin' our little
makeover?"

"Makeover?" He uncrosses his ankles and sits up
straight in the lounge chair. "Isn't that the sorta thing
women do?"

I pick a cherry off my Danish and pop it into my
mouth. "I was referring to our etiquette sessions with
Abigail Marksberry that we talked about."

"Oh . . . right."

"Well, are you still willin'?"

He purses his lips and adjusts his hat but then nods.
"Sure."

I grin. "Thank you, Daddy!"

"So when do we begin these little lessons?" he asks.

"Well, Brett said Miss Abigail could head our
way . . ." I bite my bottom lip and wince. "Sometime this
morning?" I look over at him to be sure he is okay with
this. "Unless you're not ready."

Daddy shrugs his wide shoulders. "Now's as good a time as any." He purses his lips and then says, " I guess she'll be some mean old biddy smackin' my hand and pointing out my lack of good breeding."

My chin comes up. "There's nothin' wrong with your breeding. We're Russells and I'm proud of it."

"Whoa there, little girl."

I take a deep breath and calm myself down. "I'm just sayin'. This isn't about who we are but knowing the ins and outs of how to conduct ourselves in certain social situations we're not accustomed to."

Daddy reaches over and pats my hand. "I know. I was just jokin'. Believe me, I don't think for a minute that money makes the man, Jolie Rae Russell. But a little lesson or two in good manners couldn't hurt a person."

I'm pretty sure that it will take more than a lesson or two, but I keep that bit of information to myself. "Good. I'll call Brett and let him know you're ready and willing, and to send Miss Abigail on over."

Daddy nods and ironically looks a lot more relaxed about this whole thing than I am, but I take a deep breath and make the call.

An hour later Daddy and I are anxiously awaiting the arrival of Abigail Marksberry. Well, actually I'm peeking out the window and wringing my hands, and Daddy's relaxed on the sofa reading the newspaper. Finally, he looks over his reading glasses at me and says, "Girlie, you need to sit down and just *chill* as you call it."

"You're right, but I keep thinkin' I'll be like Julie Andrews and Anne Hathaway in *The Princess Diaries*." I remember the dinner party scene and cringe. Note to self, don't put your name card next to a candle. Of course, I'm not a princess, but then again the way life has been going lately, I don't discount anything.

"Who and what?"

"Nothin'. Ohmigod, here she comes!" I glance over my shoulder at Daddy and then back out the window. With a grimace I tug on my T-shirt and smooth my palms over my jeans. I wish I had worn something a bit nicer, but the problem is I don't have anything nicer. The shirt is a plain pale blue, free of any beer logos or anything, and my jeans are without holes, but even that was hard to find in my giant closet chock-full of nothing to wear. This is why she's coming here, I firmly remind myself. Just let her work her magic.

"Does she have a bun on top of her head and a big wart on the end of her nose?" Daddy jokes and doesn't look apprehensive in the least. In fact, he appears a little amused by this whole scenario.

When Abigail Marksberry parks her white sedan in the circular driveway, I turn to Daddy and shrug. "Well, let's see . . . We'll soon find out."

"Give me fair warning."

"Okay. Oh, wow." Although she's wearing a conservative, light green summer suit, she swings shapely legs from her car. Instead of being gathered in a bun, her deep auburn hair is cut in a sleek bob angling slightly toward her chin. She's tall and graceful and I know she's close to fifty, but she sure doesn't look it.

"Was that a good wow or a we're-in-for-it wow?"

"Well . . ." I hide my grin and finish, "I'll let you decide.

The sun glints off lighter red highlights as she walks toward the front door. When she gets closer I notice that her face is attractive and she appears nice.

Of course, appearances are sometimes misleading, so I could be way off the mark in the friendly department. She might be as mean as a wet old hen. When she rings the doorbell I glance back at Daddy, who smiles and gives me an encouraging nod. He too is fresh out of the shower and putting his best foot forward. While Daddy might be a little rough around the edges, he's fit and trim and I must say handsome in a blond-haired, blue-eyed John Schneider kind of way. Even with the heartache he's had to endure he's managed to hold up pretty darned well, if I do say so myself.

"Jolie, you have to open the door, sugar," Daddy says in a gently amused tone. I didn't realize I'd been standing there with my hand squeezing the doorknob, until his deep voice brings me back from my wandering thoughts.

While smoothing my hair in place, I nod. "Right." Then curling my lips into a smile, I open the door.

"Hello," Abigail says in a smooth, cultured voice. "I'm Abigail Marksberry. I trust you're expecting me?"

"Oh, yes." I wonder why she said that last part, but it might have something to do with my wide-eyed expression. For the life of me I don't know why this has gotten me so uptight, but for some reason high diving off a cliff, which by the way, I've done, seems easy in comparison. Silly, I know, but that's the way my brain operates.

"Excellent. May I come in?" She tips her head to the side, making her smooth hair brush the top of her left shoulder. I think once again that she looks a lot younger than I expected.

"Oh yes. Where are my manners?" I ask, and she laughs softly, because of course that's why she's here. So she has a sense of humor. Sweet. "Come on in," I offer a little too loudly. I then step back for her to enter, noting that she smells like expensive perfume. I recall that Brett said she was from old money but had fallen on some tough times, although you'd never know it to look at her. *Impeccable* is the word that comes to mind. "I'm Jolie Russell, by the way," I tell her, and then extend my hand.

"Nice to meet you. Brett Dean has said some flattering things about you, Jolie." Her skin is cool and soft, but her grip is firm and sure. She then turns her attention to Daddy, who seems a bit stunned for a second. "Mr. Russell?"

"Um . . ." Daddy seems to have forgotten his own name and fusses with his reading glasses. The newspaper ends up fluttering to the floor, forgotten. When he stands up from the sofa and walks our way, Abigail's eyes, a pretty shade of mossy green, widen just a fraction. I have to wonder if she'd been expecting a big beer belly and a chaw of tobacco protruding from Daddy's jaw.

Full lips, a deep shade of classic red, curve upward in a demure smile. She extends her hand to my father, who I notice still seems a bit flustered. "Mr. Russell?" she repeats, even though she has to know he's my father since right now we're acting like dumb and his daughter, dumber.

"Uh . . . yes." Daddy engulfs her slim hand in his big grasp. "Please, call me Wyatt," he corrects with a warm smile, and I do think Miss Abigail is blushing a little. I don't think either of them is anywhere near what the other had anticipated.

"Abigail or Ms. Marksberry. Never Abby," she primly informs him. I shoot him a glance of warning since I know he wants to call her Abby in the worst way. Daddy also thinks that everyone should have a nickname, but

Miss Abigail doesn't look as if she wants to be called anything other than her full given name.

"Abigail, then," Daddy says, and I shoot him a grateful look. "Welcome, and I suppose I should say good luck."

My eyes narrow at him and I mouth, *Daddy, be good.*

Of course, I might as well have been whistling Dixie, but Miss Abigail's green eyes flash with amusement and perhaps a bit of female appreciation.

"I've learned never to rely on luck," she replies while raising one perfectly plucked eyebrow.

"I hear ya there," Daddy agrees.

"Good. Well then, shall we get started?" she continues in a brisk, no-nonsense tone that tells me she's tougher than she appears and means business.

"I always say there's no time like the present," Daddy responds with a nod.

"Marvelous. We continue to be on the same page." She clasps her hands together and gives us both a brief smile along with one sharp nod of her head. "Then by all means, let's begin."

"Where would you like to go?" I ask her. "The family room?"

She taps the side of her cheek. "The kitchen would be a better place. I need to take some notes."

I notice her monogrammed leather briefcase and think this is going to be some serious stuff. "Okay, right this way."

Miss Abigail follows me down the hallway with Daddy bringing up the rear. Rufus, who must have heard our voices, finally musters up the energy to lumber in and satisfy his doggy curiosity. A watchdog, he isn't.

When he blinks his sad eyes up at her, she smiles.

"Well, hello there." She actually bends down and scratches him behind his ears and of course Rufus rolls over and begs for a belly rub.

"Rufus! Up!" Daddy commands. With a little whine of protest Rufus rolls over and gives Daddy a she-was-going-to-do-it look. "He might need a lesson or two as well."

"I'm afraid that might be a little out of my realm of expertise. Although I do love dogs."

Daddy seems pleased that Abigail's an animal lover, but when I think he might comment, she goes right back into teacher mode and clicks her heels with authority across the tile floor. She places her briefcase on the kitchen table and opens the little latches that spring open with let's-get-going enthusiasm. She studies the neatly stacked sheets of paper and rubs her hands together before turning to Daddy and me. Gesturing to the round breakfast nook table she says, "Please, have a seat."

While Daddy and I are sliding into the chairs, Carletta enters the room. I give her a slight grin, knowing full well she's just being nosy.

"Hello," Miss Abigail says in her clipped but polite tone. She extends her hand. "Abigail Marksberry."

"Nice to meet you," Carletta responds. "May I get you anything? Drinks? Snacks?"

"We're fine for now, thank you," Miss Abigail answers for us. "Perhaps we'll need refreshment in a while."

"I'll check back later," Carletta promises, and widens her eyes at me. I have to press my lips together so that I don't chuckle.

"Okay, then." Miss Abigail takes some paper from her neat stack and hands Daddy and me a sheet. I notice that it's some sort of survey or something. She places a pen in front of us and gives us a tight, businesslike smile. When Daddy picks his paper up and slouches back in his chair with his ankle resting on his bent knee, her red lips come together in a disapproving pucker. After Daddy fails to notice, she clears her throat, drawing his attention. She doesn't say a word but merely gives him a frown and a slightly raised eyebrow. To my surprise Daddy seems to understand her silent message to put his feet on the floor and to sit up straight.

When Daddy's feet come down with a thump and he scoots up in the chair, I happen to find this unreasonably funny. A giggle bubbles up in my throat and even though I try to disguise it, Miss Abigail turns her raised eyebrow on me, quickly quelling my mirth. Daddy, who knows me all too well, gives me a slight grin that has me dying to laugh all over again. I control myself, however, until Carletta secretly peeks her head around the doorway and rolls her eyes. The suppressed laughter erupts, but since I've had the laughing-at-times-that-will-land-you-in-hot-water problem all of my life, I'm an expert at disguising it with a cough that sounds pretty authentic.

Or so I think.

I've forgotten that Miss Abigail is also a schoolteacher and therefore has eyes in the back of her head, mental telepathy, and the ability to sniff out a lie quicker than a bloodhound on the scent of a rabbit.

"Do you find something amusing, Jolie?"

Yes, the fact that you can make my six foot four daddy squirm with a mere look is hilarious. "No, ma'am."

She gives me a deadpan stare that says she knows exactly what I find funny. "Good. I turned down a corporate account simply because Brett Dean speaks so highly of you and your father. I hope you'll take this seriously or it will all be for naught."

Guilt washes over me and I nod. "I will." Of course, I remember that Brett let me know Miss Abigail had a bit of a bone to pick with the upper-crust members of this town, but I'd never let on that I know any of her personal business. Remembering the snotty comments by Marissa and Katie and knowing the hurt that rejection can cause, I nod and redouble my efforts to be good.

"Excellent," she says in a more gentle yet firm tone. "This survey tells me about your background and where you feel in need of improvement. This will be a tool for us all and help us set our goals. Jolie, I know Brett wants to escort you to the Cottonwood Charity Ball at summer's end. Am I correct?"

I nod and Daddy looks at me with some surprise.

"I think that's an excellent goal." She turns her attention to my father, who is already answering the survey. But then again, Daddy had learned from running a farm to always get a chore done so that you can move on to other things. On the farm this basically meant other chores. "Wyatt?" She angles her head and waits for Daddy to respond.

"Excuse me?" Daddy raises his gaze to meet hers. Now, before my incident with Cody, it would have gone over my head that something is crackling between my father and Miss Abigail. But I sense some attraction that seems to surprise and intrigue them both.

"What do you think your ultimate goal should be, Wyatt?"

"I haven't gotten to that question yet. I'm too busy filling out my biggest weaknesses," he tells her with a bit of a grin. "Give me a minute to finish since it might take me a while for that one."

"No doubt," she shoots back, and her lips twitch as if she's holding back a smile. "Take your time." She nods and purses her lips while giving him a once-over as if measuring him up. Seemingly lost in thought, she nibbles on her inner cheek. Daddy's wearing a faded blue T-shirt that I'm certain he doesn't realize shows off his wide shoulders and ample biceps. His hair, in need of a trim, curls over his forehead, and at the nape of his neck it is bleached light golden from constant outdoor activity.

The brackets of fatigue around his mouth are gone and for the first time Daddy looks ten years younger than his age rather than ten years older. His deep tan offsets his blue eyes, and it suddenly hits me that my daddy is . . . a hottie—you know, in an older-guy way, but still. I wonder if she's picturing my father in a tuxedo. He would, in fact, turn female heads.

"I think the Cottonwood ball would be the appropriate ending for you as well," Abigail suddenly announces. "A graduation of sorts for you both, don't you agree?"

"I . . . um . . ." My sure-footed, quick-witted daddy seems at a loss for words. "That's a mighty lofty goal."

"The question is: Are you up for it?"

Frowning, he glances down at his sheet, but he stops writing. Just as it is for me, it's difficult for Daddy to turn down a challenge.

"Of course, I would be your . . . companion for the event."

Daddy looks up in surprise and then glances at me.

"To ensure your success," she hastily explains, but there are spots of color in her cheeks, making me wonder if there is another hidden motive.

Daddy's never been anywhere with anyone other than my mother. I give him a slight nod, letting him know that I get it and it's all right, but he hesitates, and it clutches at my heart. As I sit here looking at my handsome, vital father, I truly believe it's about time he starts living again. "Daddy, I think we need to set Cottonwood on its ear. Show them just what the Russells are made of."

Miss Abigail smiles her agreement. I think this was her personal goal all along and the fact that Daddy is a looker makes it all the more doable.

Daddy looks at me for a long moment and seems uncertain. "I didn't know this was goin' to be this . . . intense."

Miss Abigail gives him a slight lift of her shoulders. "I understand it would be a bit of a challenge. You would need to learn to dance . . ."

"I know how to dance," he says, and something flickers in his eyes. Pain? And then it hits me. I remember now that Mama loved to dance and they would go often—barn dances mostly, but sometimes to the city.

Suddenly I'm certain that Daddy needs to do this. Never, ever do I want him to forget how much he loves my mother, but I know in my heart of hearts that Mama would want my father to live his life to the fullest. I've been too blind to realize that he hasn't been. With a lump in my throat, I reach across the table and put my hand over his. "Daddy, you should do this."

"Do you really think so, Jolie?"

I nod. "Yes." And my eyes tell him that Mama would too.

"All righty, then, Abigail. You got yourself a deal." He hands her his questionnaire. "As you can see, you've got your work cut out for you." His blue eyes sparkle with humor.

"Failure is not in my nature, Wyatt. If you agree to this, I want your word you'll give it your all."

"I don't know how to do things any other way."

She extends her hand once again. "Excellent." They shake and it might be my imagination, but I do believe the contact lasts slightly longer than necessary before Abigail pulls her hand away and appears a bit flustered, even though she tries to appear businesslike. I wonder if her heart is pounding and if her legs feel a little weak in the knees.

I hide my smile by bending my head over my questionnaire, but I think to myself that our adventure is destined to continue and it will be interesting to see how it all plays out.

13

Making a Splash

"I'm plum tuckered out, Jolie-girl," Daddy complains after our first full week of etiquette classes. We're sitting outside taking a break by the pool. "That woman is relentless," he continues, but his expression softens as if he's thinking about Abigail. While she and Daddy have been making steady progress, I don't seem to catch on nearly as well.

"You're doing a fine job, though, Daddy. I'm the one who keeps messin' up."

"You just get too uptight. Learn to relax."

"I'm tryin'."

"You know, I think it's because I have Abby to practice with. You need a guy."

"So you call her Abby?" I tease.

Daddy appears a little embarrassed at what I imagine was a slip of the tongue. He fidgets and adjusts his hat. "Abigail sounds too danged old. She needs to be called Abby, if you ask me."

"I dare you to call her that."

He snorts. "Right. I'm scared to death of that woman."

I think what he's scared of is his growing attraction to her, but I don't think he's ready to admit it, so I remain silent.

"I do think you need a boy to practice with," Daddy suggests again.

I shrug. "Who? Daddy, all my rowdy guy friends are just as rough as me and then some." I shake my head. "It would be a joke.

"True." Daddy scratches his chin. "Hey, how about one of them Dean boys?"

My heart skitters in my chest at the mere thought. "Brett is too busy with baseball."

"And Cody?"

I push up my sunglasses. "Are you kiddin'? He's even busier than Brett." That's what I've been telling myself is the reason he hasn't called me since our date. Not that I've been thinking of him constantly or anything. Okay, I have.

"You sure 'bout that? Why don't you ask him?"

"I'll think about it," I say in a calm oh-whatever tone, but I know I'd never muster up the nerve to call Cody.

Daddy takes a long pull from his frosty iced tea and looks out over the pool. "I was gonna swim some laps, but I think I might flop down on a float and be lazy."

"Sounds like a plan," I agree, glad to change the subject, but in truth, I don't think my father knows how to be lazy. I give him ten minutes and he'll either be swimming laps or doing yard work that he could hire out but insists that he and only he can do it right. Not that I blame him, because I feel the same way about my truck. I could buy a fancy new one, but I love my old F-150.

"You comin' in?" he calls from the center of the pool.

"I'm gonna finish my tea first and catch some sun. It's

Carletta's day off and she's comin' over in a bit. I'll be ready to cool off by then."

"Suit yourself. But it feels great."

"Okay, just give me a few minutes."

I have to smile when Daddy seems to fall asleep while trailing one foot and one hand in the water. Maybe Miss Abigail really did wear him out. I know I've been wearing *her* out. I plug my iPod into my ears and find some Rascal Flatts, then untie my bikini top. Lying back in the lounge chair, I let the strings hang down so as not to get tan lines up around my neck. When I close my eyes, though, I daydream about Cody, who hasn't called me even once since last week and does not deserve to be occupying my thoughts, not that my brain is listening.

Not that I care that he didn't call. In fact, it's better this way. "Oh, who am I kiddin'?" I grumble under my breath. I'm hurt. No, I'm pissed. Okay, I'm hurt and I'm pissed, and I wouldn't give him the time of day even if he showed up right here and now. With that thought in mind I take a deep breath and sing along with the music. "Seems like toda-a-a-a-ay . . . ," I croon, drawing out the word like Gary LeVox from Rascal Flatts. "Seems like—"

"Hey there," says a deep voice that at first I think is in my head or part of the song, but when I open my eyes, Cody Dean is standing right next to my lounge chair, casting a shadow over me and looking too doggone delicious for words. The song dies in my throat and I blink up at him, thinking the man has a knack for arriving just in time for me to do something embarrassing. Of course, I find myself in a lot of embarrassing situations, so the odds are in his favor, but still . . .

"Oh, hey . . ." I tug the earplugs out so hard that they

pop sideways and I sit up so quickly that I get light-headed.

"Uh . . . Jolie?" When his eyes widen I suddenly remember I had untied my bikini top. Great, so, I don't give him the time of day but rather an eyeful of bare breasts.

"Oh shit!" I curse, adding to my embarrassment, and flap around for the strings. My sunglasses slide to the tip of my nose and of course my fingers refuse to cooperate. I find one string and manage to cover one breast and hide the other one with my hand, which makes it impossible to finish my task. Then, I realize I'm sitting on the other string. When I swiftly lean my butt cheek up, the lounge chair tips, and I roll directly to the concrete with a painful thump in front of Cody's fancy loafers, which are either new or survived the previous soaking. My sunglasses are now on my chin and my bare breasts are staring up at him.

"I didn't mean to do that," I tell him from my prone position, and quickly cross my hands over my chest.

"I didn't mean to look."

"One of us is lying."

He laughs and offers his hand, but of course that won't work.

"Nice try."

"Can you blame a guy?" He laughs harder while I sit up and then he kneels down behind me. "Here, let me help." His fingers brush against my skin while he locates my lime green bikini strings, tugs them up, and ties them securely around my neck.

"Well, I can tell my etiquette teacher I've mastered the art of a warm welcome," I say dryly while pushing my sunglasses up in place.

Cody continues to chuckle and I decide I like the low, rich rumble. "May I help you up now?"

"Sure." When he extends his hand again, I take it. His hold is firm and he easily pulls me to my feet. I glance toward the pool; thank goodness Daddy's hat is covering half his face and he seems to be sound asleep.

"Would you like a glass of sweet tea?" I offer in the soft voice Miss Abigail makes me use, and try to act as if nothing out of the ordinary just happened . . . which is sort of true, for me, anyway.

"Sure, I could definitely use some cooling off," he answers in a voice laced with humor.

"Where's that garden hose when I need it?" I manage to joke, but I hope he thinks the heat in my face is due to the sun and not my total embarrassment. I should be acting snotty because he hasn't called me, but after the breast-baring incident I don't think I could pull it off.

"You could always push me into the pool again."

"I didn't push you in." I put a finger in the middle of his chest and try not to notice how hard and firm it feels. "You pulled *me* in."

"If you say so," he says lightly. Of course, I don't think he looks attractive at all in a forest green Copper Creek logo golf shirt and Dockers. And his stubble and silver Oakleys aren't one bit sexy. No way.

"What brings you here?" I ask in what I hope is a casual voice as I walk over to the umbrella table, where a pitcher of iced tea and glasses are sitting. I try not to think about the fact that he's fully clothed while I'm once again nearly naked in my tiny swimsuit. The lime green color probably makes my butt look like a bouncing beach ball, but at least my top is secure.

The ice clunks into the tall glass, but I manage to pour

without splashing more than a little. "Thanks." He accepts the tea from me and takes a long swallow. "Do you mind if I sit down?"

"Oh, I should have offered." I join him at the round, glass-topped table and sit in the shade of the big umbrella while trying to act casual and not as if I just showed him my breasts. Of course, he's seen them before and that thought brings additional heat to my cheeks. I take a long drink of my cold tea, hoping to cool off a bit. The ice cubes fall forward and hit me in the mouth, and I manage to spill tea down my chin. Cody, ever the gentleman, hands me a paper napkin. "Well, maybe I should just go back to bed and stay there all day," I joke, but mentioning being in bed, with Cody sitting across from me, warms my cheeks up all over again.

Although I can't see his eyes behind his mirrored sunglasses, his hand seems to tighten around his tea and he swallows hard, making me wonder if his thoughts are going down the same dangerous path. He clears his throat and starts to say something, but stops and takes another swallow of his tea. When he sets down the glass, I watch his long fingers slide up and down the condensation and can't stop the memory of his hands on my bare, wet skin from flooding into my brain.

"More tea?" I ask, trying to make my train of thought switch tracks.

"I'm fine." He answers a bit distantly, as if something is on his mind, prompting me to wonder just what brought him here in the first place. Well, the only way to find out is to ask.

"Cody?"

"Hmmm?"

"Is there a particular reason for this visit?' "

Cody sits up straighter in his chair and says, "Actually, there are a couple of things."

"Oh?"

He nods. "Abigail called Brett and asked if he would, um, assist, I suppose you could call it, you in your lessons. Take you out to places and events. While I know Brett is supposed to escort you to the Cottonwood Charity Ball, Abigail thinks you need to ease your way up to that particular event. But Brett called me and said that with baseball in full swing he's just too busy."

"So he's tossed the ball in your court?" I'm going to have to kick Brett's butt.

"You could say that." Cody nods, but it feels as if he wants to explain something more to me but is holding back.

When he seems to be fumbling for words I have to surmise he's trying to gracefully bow out of doing this, so I decide to let him off the hook. "Cody, you certainly don't have to step in. Your time is too valuable to be stuck parading me around town." I roll my eyes for good measure.

"Jolie, believe me, it's not that," he insists, but his failure to elaborate makes me wish I could see his eyes and try to determine just what's going on here.

But then I get it and it hits me like a sucker punch to the gut. "Oh, listen, if this is about what happened . . . ," I begin softly, but then look toward the pool to make sure Daddy is still sleeping. Both hands and both feet are trailing in the water, so I guess he's dead to the world.

"Well, yes, I've been meaning to call and talk to you about that evening," Cody says. My heart thuds low and hard in an almost painful way. "I've been thinking—"

"Oh, don't give it another thought. I wasn't expecting

you to call." No, just hoping and praying. I'm such a dumbass. "It was kind of you," I tell him in my best polite voice, "to stop by to apologize. But not at all necessary."

"Jolie, I've been swamped with work and every time I wanted to call I was interrupted." He seems sincere and I notice he appears exhausted. I suddenly want to stand up and give him an old-fashioned neck rub to ease his stress. The realization hits me that my feelings for Cody already run deep. I care about him and his well-being, and for some reason this causes a cold shot of fear in my gut that I don't even begin to understand.

"Really, don't give it another thought. As you said, you're swamped and don't need to parade me around town," I assure him, because I know what will happen. I'll fall harder for him and after the charity ball he'll go on his merry way. "Seriously, it's kind of you to offer but not necessary."

"But I have given it thought and I realize that—"

"Mercy," I say, fanning my face. "It's getting hot out here. I think I'll take a refreshing dip."

"Speaking of dip, that reminds me," Cody says firmly. When I start to get up from my chair he puts one hand over mine. "I want to take you to an old-fashioned ice cream social on Friday at Cottonwood Park in the center of town. Copper Creek Estates is one of the sponsors raising money for the proposed arboretum and botanical gardens. We built an enlarged gazebo that will enable Cottonwood to hold concerts in the park."

"I know all about it. Daddy bought us a brick paver in honor of my mother."

"Then you know the importance of the project."

"Yes, but—"

"So you'll come?"

I would have been able to resist the temptation even though his hand still covered mine, but then he had to go and lift up his silver glasses, revealing those intense eyes that I can't help but get lost in. Once again I'm like putty in his hands and find myself nodding. "Okay." I relent against my better judgment. "But this doesn't mean you need to be a stand-in for Brett."

His slow smile is another lethal weapon that I need to learn to steel myself against. "We'll discuss that part later. I'll pick you up around five o'clock."

I find myself nodding again. "I'll try not to have another wardrobe malfunction, but I can't promise."

Cody laughs and then squeezes my hand before standing up. "There's never a dull moment with you, is there, Jolie Russell?"

"Now, where would be the fun in that?" I ask, and grin as if I'm confident, when really I could just kick myself for agreeing to go with him. To Cody Dean, I'm merely another project that needs to be completed, but I suppose that as long as I remember that, my heart won't get crushed too hard.

"Okay, then," he says, and after a moment's hesitation, as if he wants to say something more, he leans in and gives me a quick kiss on the cheek. "Enjoy your swim."

"Thank you. I will," I assure him, and look toward the pool, where Daddy's still sawing logs. But just then a bee or fly or something buzzes beneath his nose. He swipes at it, relaxes briefly, and then swipes harder, rocking the raft so hard that he flips it and lands in the water with a big splash. He comes up sputtering and cursing. He tries to get back onto the raft but flips it over again. Finally he manages to wiggle his way back. Knowing he has an audience, he tips his soggy John Deere hat at us and then smacks it back on his head.

I have to grin as I turn to Cody. "What can I say? I'm a chip off the old block."

"And that's a good thing," Cody assures me with a smile. "See you Friday."

"Okay," I answer softly, but I can't help noticing again that he seems tired. As he pushes up from the lawn chair I can't stop myself from saying, "Cody, you take care of yourself and get some rest, you hear me?"

"I hear you," he says a bit gruffly as if he's a little moved by my concern. He leans over and gently rubs the pad of his thumb over my cheek in a gesture that feels so tender that I long to tilt my cheek into his palm. It occurs to me that he might seem older than his years but has much more on his plate than most people his age. "I'll take care."

"Promise?"

He nods and then brushes his mouth briefly to mine. It's a butterfly, a barely there kiss, but by God I feel it to my bare toes. "See you soon."

I nod mutely and watch while he walks away. The man needs more than a neck rub. He needs a home-cooked meal and a night of tender lovemaking to ease every last drop of tension from his body. Holy moly, the image of me doing just that makes me break out into a sweat. I put a hand to my chest and take a deep breath. I'm torn between the excitement of going to the ice cream social with Cody and the apprehension that goes along with it. In dire need of cooling off, I run to the deep end of the pool and with a little whoop, do a fantastic cannonball that causes Daddy to have to hang on for dear life.

"I don't know how an itty-bitty thing like you can

make such a big splash," Daddy comments with a deep chuckle.

Thinking of Katie and Marissa I say, "I'm not itty-bitty, but I guess making a big splash is just in my nature. Can it be that I take after you?"

"Nothin' wrong with that, girlie."

I laugh as I grab a purple noodle and hold on while kicking my feet. Out of the corner of my eye I see Carletta heading toward the pool in a colorful cover-up, so I lift one hand up and wave. "Come on in!"

"I'm coming! Hi there, Mr. Russell."

"Now you know you can call me Wyatt," Daddy says. "*Mr. Russell* makes me feel too doggone old, little princess."

"Okay." Carletta gives Daddy a wide smile. He's been telling her from day one that she's as pretty as a princess, and Carletta still blushes every time he repeats himself. He says it in a teasing, good-natured way and truly means it. He hates having her wait on him and treats her more like a daughter than an employee. I've been meaning to talk to him about funding her education.

Carletta quickly sheds her cover-up and tosses it onto a lounge chair. Her swimsuit is a lemon yellow tankini that hides her extra curves while showing off her assets. Her rich, chestnut brown hair is pulled up in a stylish ponytail, and oversized sunglasses, which give her an appearance of glamour, shade her expressive eyes. It occurs to me that she really does know fashion and when she slips into the water I pounce on her.

"Carletta, I need your help."

Her tinkling laughter sounds like cheerful wind chimes. "You got it. What?"

"You need to take me shoppin'."

She grabs a green noodle and kicks toward me. "Oh, a special occasion?"

"Not really." I try to sound casual. "Just an ice cream social with Cody."

Carletta stops kicking and lets her legs dangle in the water. "Shut up!"

"I know, I'm ca-ra-zeeee," I say in a low voice so that Daddy doesn't hear.

"He must be into you or he wouldn't ask you out."

I shrug, making the water ripple. "I dunno. I think I'm more like a project for him. Like a house that needs renovation." I try to joke.

"Oh, Jolie, I think you're dead wrong. But having said that, we're going to have you dressed to kill, sista. You're gonna kick some, how you say . . . upper-crust butt." She gives me a high five. "So after we work on our tans, let's hit the Galleria. It will be so much fun shopping with someone with money."

Her laughter is infectious. "I haven't mastered the art of spending," I tell her.

Carletta snags a float and scoots up on it. "Not to worry. I teach you. I'm a rich chick in a poor girl's body. It's a curse, I tell you."

I high-five her again. "I can relate in an opposite kind of way."

"Okay then, lie back and chill, and in a little while we'll have to eat a power-packed lunch because, girl, you're gonna need your stamina."

14

Shop 'Til You Drop

"Carletta, this purse is three hundred twenty-five dollars!" I tell her in a stage whisper. The snooty little clerk who has been eyeing us with suspicion all along looks our way. I guess I should have worn something other than my favorite Kid Rock T-shirt and faded Levi's.

"It's an investment," Carletta assures me. "A Coach purse shouts class and refinement."

"Well, the price tag shouts highway robbery. Come on. It's a danged purse!"

"Use your indoor voice," Carletta reminds me with a grin when the clerk narrows her eyes at my outburst.

"That *was* my indoor voice." When I return the purse to the display table, Carletta picks it back up and shoves it into my hands.

"You need this. It's a must-buy and essential to your wardrobe."

"That's what you said about all the other stuff. The cargo storage in my truck is almost full, Carletta. Besides, my feet are killin' me."

She fists her hands on her hips. "You gotta toughen up, chickie! Quit whining."

"But I'm hungry."

Carletta rolls her eyes. "You had a giant pretzel in the food court an hour ago."

I'm about to say . . . okay, make that I'm about to whine that I'm thirsty, but Carletta shoots me a look that makes me clamp my mouth shut. She's like a drill sergeant when it comes to shopping. I clutch the purse closer to my chest and let out a sigh. Out of the corner of my eye I see that clerk heading our way. Her high heels click with authority on the marble floor.

"Excuse me, but are you planning on purchasing that purse?" She arches a you've-got-to-be-joking eyebrow at me. I wasn't until now. She eyes me up and down from my ponytail to my cowboy boots and actually sneers. "There is a Payless on the other side of the mall." She holds out her hand for me to give her the purse and suddenly I feel like Julia Roberts in the movie *Pretty Woman*.

"I do believe I will take this purse." I turn to Carletta and say, "Pick one out for yourself."

"Jolie . . ." Understanding, she grins but shakes her head. "You've bought enough for me today."

"You just said it's a must. Pick one out. I insist." I know I'm being childish, but damn it's fun. "Come on, let's shop." While the clerk watches with wide eyes, we pick out wallets, something called a Mini Skinny, and key chains with our initials.

"Oh, would you look at these!" When Carletta squeals over the colorful ponytail scarves, I tell her to pick out several, and when she looks totally cute in an itty-bitty hat called a Karee, I add it to our growing pile.

"Here you go," I say in a cheerful voice when I hand

the clerk my American Express. I try not to cringe when she tells me the total, but I remind myself I can afford the purchases. I try not to wonder why the little logo makes it all so expensive, but then again, what do I know?

"Thank you," coos the little clerk, suddenly all smiles. I want to tell her that she should treat everyone who enters the store with respect, but maybe she already learned a valuable lesson.

"That was so much fun!" After we exit the store Carletta laughs so hard that she has to hold on to my arm for support.

"Yeah, it was." I start rattling off prices and end with, "And the amazed look on the snippy little clerk's face?"

"Priceless," Carletta finishes, and then gives me a knuckle bump.

"Are we done now?" I ask with such hope in my voice that Carletta nods.

"For today." After dragging armloads of shopping bags to my room, Carletta and I flop down onto the bed and stare up at the ceiling fan. She sighs. I groan. "Carletta, I've helped my daddy plow fields, picked tobacco, mucked out stalls, fed the animals, you name it, but for the life of me, nothing has ever exhausted me like this."

"That's where the phrase 'shop 'til you drop' comes from."

"Well, I've dropped."

"It requires much more stamina, skill, and speed than most people realize, especially men. I personally think it should be an Olympic event."

I muster up a weak laugh, but I think she might be serious. "You'd win the gold, I'm certain."

"I think you're right." Carletta comes up on her elbows and looks over at me. "By the way, thank you for the clothes and accessories you bought for me, Jolie. You and your daddy already pay me more money than I've ever made in my life. You shouldn't have done that."

I don't have the energy to push up to my elbows, but I look up at her and say, "Are you kiddin'? Watchin' you try on clothes and squeal in pleasure was the most fun I've had in a long time. Besides, Carletta, we have more money than we know what to do with. And your help and fashion sense were invaluable. Without your assistance I'd be wanderin' around like those people on *What Not to Wear*. Buyin' all the wrong stuff."

"You watch that?"

I grin. "Well, yeah, I should be on that show! But if Stacy and Clinton tried to throw away my stuff, there would be an ass whoopin'."

Carletta leans back her head and laughs. "Well, you got me now. But oh I do love that show! We'll have to have a girls' night slumber party when they do one of their back-to-back marathons. I'll make us some kick-ass mojitos . . . fresh, not from a bottle, let me tell ya."

"That would be fun." I realize how much I've missed having a girlfriend. "I never had much time to do girl stuff before now. Growing up with Daddy made me into a tomboy and it's been nice to discover my feminine side."

Carletta rolls over to her stomach and puts a hand on my arm. "My mother lives in Florida and I miss her terribly. It must have been hard for you, chickie."

"What about your daddy?"

While plucking on the bedspread she says, "He was some rich man I never knew."

"He never helped your mama out?"

"I don't think she knew how to go about doing that." She shrugs. "I guess we weren't good enough for him."

"That's just plain stupid," I sputter, and Carletta laughs.

"You are so fun to be with. I'm glad I knocked on your door and you weren't some skinny rich bitch," she said.

I shove her arm while laughing. "I tried to be one at the mall."

"Yes, but still . . . you didn't need to buy me all of those clothes and shoes."

"Well, there is a catch, though, you know."

"Really?" She doesn't seem concerned. "What might that be?"

"Well, now that we have the fancy-ass clothes, we have to hang out in fancy-ass places."

Her eyebrows arch toward her forehead. "We?"

"Yeah, we." I nod slowly and then giggle. "We'll be like Paris Hilton and Nicole Richie on *The Simple Life* . . . only the opposite. We'll be poor chicks invading rich-people territory."

"Um, okay, except that you're not poor, Jolie. You always seem to forget that part."

I laugh harder. "Yeah, well, that's the fun twist in the whole thing. Dang, we should have our own reality show, don't ya think?"

"Yeah, we would rock," she answers. "Shake this stuffy old neighborhood up, that's for sure."

"I've kind of already done that."

"Good for you. Keep doin' it."

"Whew . . . I'd suggest goin' for a swim, but I'm too pooped to move."

"I'll whip you into shopping shape in no time," Carletta promises. Judging by the look on her face, she's serious. "That's okay. I should get on home anyway. I've got a pile of laundry to do. And of course, I want to try on all my cool stuff."

"You're kiddin'? I couldn't try on one more piece of clothing if my life depended on it."

"Wimp." She gives my shoulder a shove. "Seriously though, Jolie, I had a blast shopping."

"Me too," I reiterate.

"Yeah, right. You whined like a baby."

"Nuh-uh."

She gives me a deadpan stare.

"Only the last four hours or so . . . ," I protest.

Carletta rolls her eyes. "We only shopped for five."

"Then I think I did pretty darned good."

Carletta laughs. "Well, consider today conditioning. You'll toughen up." My eyes widen and my jaw drops, but she keeps on talking as if I'm not in shopping shock. "Now, you're going to wear the turquoise stretch-cotton sateen sheath to the ice cream social, right?"

"You think it's the best choice? It kinda hugs my butt."

"And that's a good thing with your butt. The sleeveless scoop neck is perfect . . . just a little bit sexy and it shows off your toned arms. I also *adore* that high-waisted belt. Now remember," she says, and then pauses to make sure I'm really listening, so I look at her with all the attention my tired brain can muster. "Wear silver accessories. I'm thinking the crystal silver hoop earrings. Amazing with the turquoise! And use the Coach Soho Signature purse with the laced pocket flap. It's classic but just a little bit chunky and modern." Attempting to talk with her hands while perched up on her elbows, Carletta looks kind of comical, but I keep a straight face and add a bit of a frown to let her know I'm concentrating. "Finally, go with the

Kate Spade open-toed slingbacks." She sighs again as if in total bliss. "Damn, I'm good."

I nod in a serious manner as if I comprehend all of this jargon while I'm trying to remember what a slingback is. "I might need this all written down, and add footnotes."

She grins as if this delights her. "No problem-o. I'll send it in an e-mail along with some other notes too. If you want, I can stay late tomorrow and help with your hair and makeup."

"I was hopin' you'd say that."

"Good." She sits up and makes a dusting motion with her hands. "Well, I think you're all set. You're gonna knock 'em dead, Jolie."

"Oh, I'm sure I'll do something memorable." I roll my eyes toward the ceiling. "That's a given." When my cell phone rings I manage to push up to a sitting position. "Who can that be?" When I look down at the little screen I say to Carletta, "Oh, it's Brett."

"Hey there," I answer cheerfully. "What's up?"

"I wanted to apologize for being so busy," Brett says, and I can hear the sincerity in his voice. "Baseball has been consuming me. Normally, we have a few rainouts, but the weather has been amazing, so I've been at a game or practice every day."

"No problem. I understand. Daddy's been wanting to attend some games." When Carletta flops down on the bed with every intention of listening, I grin and mouth, *Nosy*.

She shrugs her shoulders but whispers, "Do you want me to leave?"

Nah, I mouth back, and then turn my attention to Brett. "But I do have a bone to pick with you. You asked Cody to step in? Brett Dean!"

"Go run some laps," he yells, and I realize he's at practice right now. "Sorry. Listen, Ms. Marksberry mentioned to me that you need someone to work with you and you know I would, but I'm just too swamped. Besides, Cody needs to get his ass out of the office and have some fun, and I had a brilliant moment and decided to ask him to help you out."

"Killin' two birds with one stone?"

"Let me tell you, he jumped all over it, Jolie. The botanical garden is going to be an asset to the science department at school, so I thought I should attend after my game on Friday. I was going to ask you, but I hear my brother beat me to the punch. Um, I think Cody might be . . . into you, Jolie."

Overhearing this, Carletta silently claps her hands together toward the ceiling, then falls back to kick her legs up in the air. When I roll my eyes at her she mouths, *Don't deny it.*

"He sure likes to talk about you."

"Yeah?" I try to sound casual. "Well, it seems like I'm the topic of conversation a lot around here," I respond. "I provide comic relief for the rich and the bored."

Brett laughs. "Do me a favor and don't ever change," he says in a more serious tone, and Carletta nods her agreement.

"I won't." I hope.

"I won't let you," Carletta says, and then clamps her hand over her mouth.

"Who is that with you?" Brett asks.

"My friend Carletta. We're back from a marathon shopping excursion."

"Oh, well, tell her I said hi."

"Brett says hi."

"Right back at ya," Carletta says loud enough for him to hear, but then whispers to me, "He sounds cute."

He is, I mouth back to her.

"Okay, I guess I'll have to go alone," Brett says with a long sigh. "Hey wait, unless your friend is interested? I'm not a fan of these things and I absolutely hate going alone."

I raise my eyebrows at Carletta, who puts her hand to her chest and mouths, *No*. I ignore her answer. "I'll ask her. Carletta?"

She shakes her head so hard that she almost falls off the bed and has to catch herself.

"Here, I'll let you ask her."

Carletta looks at the phone as if it will bite her and then looks at me as if she'll bite *me*, but I push it into her hand and force it up to her ear.

"Hello? Carletta?"

"Yes," she says without her usual feistiness. I hope I haven't overstepped my bounds.

"Hey, I know this is spur-of-the-moment and you don't even know me, but would you be willing to go with me? Hopefully, Jolie will vouch for my being a nice guy."

"Oh, that might be stretching it," I joke, but nod to Carletta.

When Carletta hesitates Brett says, "Well, there might be a few umpires who don't like me, but other than that . . . So whad'ya say? Are you game?"

She gulps.

I narrow my eyes in challenge.

"S-sure," she finally answers, and I bounce up and down on the bed like a little kid.

"Awesome. Can I get directions to your house?"

I shake my head. "Carletta, you have to help me get ready. Is it okay if he picks you up here?"

Carletta looks relieved and after a minute I understand why. "Sure. That's fine."

"Great, see you tomorrow."

"Me too. Bye," Carletta says, but then flips the phone shut and shakes her head. "Jolie!"

"What?" I ask innocently. "Brett really is a nice guy. Oh, and did I mention, hot?"

"I'm sure he is. But he's Brett Dean."

"So?"

Carletta angles her head at me and braces her hands on her thighs. "He's filthy rich. And I'm a maid. I feel like Jennifer Lopez in *Maid in Manhattan*."

"Brett is a schoolteacher and baseball coach at Cottonwood High School. He's as down to earth as they come." I cross my legs on the bed. "And I hate the word *maid*." I wrinkle my nose and then sit up straight. "Hey!" I shout when an amazing thought hits me. Once in a while it happens.

"What?"

"No more of this maid crap. No more uniforms and all that stuff. From now on, you're my personal assistant."

"Personal assistant?"

I nod my head. "Yeah, God knows I need one."

"Well then, who will do the cleaning?"

I shrug. "I don't know. Me?"

"Jolie!"

"Okay . . . okay. I don't know. I'll hire someone."

Carletta grins. "No, I'll hire someone. That's my job now."

I laugh. "You're right."

"What else will I do?"

I shrug again. "Assist me. Just like you've been doin'. You're now officially a part of the makeover team. So tomorrow, come dressed however you wish." When Carletta looks at me as if she might protest, I shake my head. "Trust me, you'll earn your salary," I assure her with a playful shove. "It will be a part time job because you'll need to go back to school."

"And school will be fun!"

I know what pride is, and I want her to feel comfortable with this new position, which if I'm honest, is totally legitimate. I need help in a lot of areas. "You know, if you really think about it, you've been doing the job as a personal assistant anyway. This just makes it official."

"Yeah, okay. I'll do it." Carletta gives me a return shove. "I'm outta here, girlie. Get your beauty sleep."

"I will." I give her a swift hug, thinking that it's so great to have a friend in my life. "You're not mad at me about the whole Brett thing, are you?"

Carletta shakes her head. "I was all talk before, but now I know how intimidated you must feel. I get it now."

"My daddy said to me just recently that money doesn't make the man. Let's just have fun with it, okay?"

She nods and gives me a high five, but we both know we're nervous wrecks about the whole thing. "See you tomorrow."

I smile thinking that Carletta is so much like me . . . brave on the outside. "Together we can pull this off, you know."

"I know," she says over her shoulder as she leaves the room. "What doesn't kill us will make us stronger."

I laugh and thank God she's in my life. I did have fun shopping in spite of my constant whining. My heart thumps hard when I look across the room at the array of shiny, colorful shopping bags and think about how much money I spent. "Holy . . . shit." Part of me wants to take it all back and head to Wal-Mart, but then I take a deep breath and try to steady my racing pulse. I know I need these things in order to fit in to this new lifestyle.

I'm just not sure if I want this new lifestyle.

Still, I have to do this for Daddy's sake. I encouraged this move and now I'm going to have to make the best of it.

Funny, when you're dirt-poor you always dream of being filthy rich. But now that I have all of this money, I find I'm not comfortable with it . . . and then a sudden thought slams into my brain. I need to make the money matter. Do good things.

Now if only I could figure out how to go about accomplishing that, I'd be able to find peace with this windfall. First, I need to learn how to fit in. And then I plan on making a difference.

Somehow.

With a huge yawn I stretch my limbs and then smile as a sense of peace settles over me. I know I'm on the right track. I just have to figure out how to go full speed ahead.

15

Some Like It Hot

"We're so hot the ice cream is going to melt before it ever gets to our mouth," Carletta declares, and then strikes a pose in front of the bathroom mirror.

"Yeah, baby. I sure don't look like a farm girl," I agree, and strike a pose of my own but snort because I think I look silly.

"Because you're not . . . even though it is something to be proud of. The farmers feed the world."

"You got that right!" I nod and give her another high five. "Well, girl, you don't look like a maid."

"Um . . . hello! That's because I'm your official personal assistant, or PA as I prefer to call it. I've been telling everybody. Did a bulletin on my MySpace." She does a little head bop, but her carefully arranged tresses don't budge due to a liberal amount of hair spray. "I feel like Turtle on *Entourage*."

I have to laugh. Now that I have HBO, I get it. "You're not like Turtle," I scoff. "Vince sure is hot though."

"I'm into Drama."

"What? You're kiddin' me. He's so smarmy."

Carletta gives her hair a pat and then laughs. "Yeah, but Kevin Dillon cracks me up."

"I've just now gotten to see some episodes. Before, I never had the time to watch much television. Early to bed and early to rise and all that."

"We'll have to rent the first seasons for you to catch up. Another girls' night." She taps her cheek. "Hmmm, I think pitchers of margaritas are in order for that one."

I laugh again but then say, "We're yackin' about a bunch of nothin' to keep our minds off the fact Cody and Brett will be here soon. You know that, right?"

She groans. "Yeah. Do you think Brett will like me?" she asks, but then raises her hands up in the air. "Oh God, what am I—ten? Maybe I'll just pass a note to you to give to him. Do you like me? Check yes or no," she says in a childlike singsong voice that makes me laugh. "God!" She takes a deep breath and adds a little bit more eyeliner.

"No, you're not ten. You're a funny, smart, and gorgeous woman. Brett will have a blast with you, Carletta."

"You think so? Speaking of age, I'm a few years older than Brett, right? Isn't he your age? Holy crap, what am I doing, Jolie?"

"You're not exactly robbing the cradle." I roll my eyes. "Stop worrying," I advise her, even though I have the market cornered on worry. "We said we're just going to have fun, remember?"

"We *say* a lot of things."

"Well, it's time to put our money where our mouth is . . . whatever that really means, but Daddy is fond of sayin' it."

"How about—how you say—put up or shut up?" Carletta suggests, and then laughs. "Okay, enough of that. We've got to shift into classy mode." She smooths the slightly flared skirt of her navy blue dress and with narrowed eyes looks in the mirror. "Does this empire waist work for me?"

"It's perfect."

She wrinkles her nose. "Is the yellow bow over-the-top?"

"Carletta, it's the reason you loved the dress in the first place, remember?"

"Yeah . . ." She draws out the word before turning around and checking out her butt. "I need to lose twenty stinking pounds."

"Oh, you do not!" I pivot and point to my butt. "I have a little junk in the trunk too. Better than being skinny bitches, don't ya think? You gotta shake what God gave ya." When I do a little demonstration Carletta laughs.

"Well, you look stunning in the turquoise sheath. And your hair is amazing. Rich brown with streaks of gold. I like it up, too. Shows off the delicate curve of your neck." She peers at her handiwork with pride.

"Delicate? Not usually the word used to describe me." I try to joke, but in truth I feel out of my element. Although, in the classy dress with my hair swept up, I have to admit I feel downright pretty. The silver earrings dangle and glint when the crystals catch the light. My sexy sandals show off my pink-tipped toes and with Carletta's help, my makeup is subtle yet also has a smoky hint of drama. "We're gonna kick some ice cream social butt," I proclaim with a glossy-pink smile that echoes the color of my toes.

"Yeah, baby!" She turns toward me and we do a modified chest bump that's sort of like an air kiss so as not to mess up our dresses. Then we laugh so hard that we have to touch up our mascara.

And then the doorbell rings.

Our wide eyes meet in the mirror.

"It must be *them*. Are you ready for this?" For some reason I feel the need to whisper.

"Hell yeah," Carletta whispers back, and adds a wave of her hand. But instead of moving, we stare at each other until the doorbell chimes again.

Rufus, who had been sleeping on the tile floor, looks up at me with an aren't-you-going-to-get-that? expression. "Yes, I am," I tell him, looking down. "Give me a minute."

"Wait, did you just read your dog's mind?"

"Yes, well actually I read his expression," I explain to her as we head toward the stairs and then carefully descend in our heels.

"But his expression is always the same." She glances back at Rufus, who is trailing behind us since he has trouble on the steps with his little legs.

"It's in his eyes," I tell her. Again we're jabbering about nonsense in order not to think about answering the door. "Do you think they're both here?" I feel the need to whisper again while we stand in the foyer.

Carletta bites her botom lip for a second and then shrugs. "Well, let's find out."

"Okay." I hold my fists out for a knuckle bump and then with a smile on my face, I swing the heavy door open. "Holy cow," comes to mind once again. "Oh wait, I said that out loud, didn't I?"

Brett grins, "Uh, yeah. You meant it in a good way I hope?"

"Mmmm, I *guess* you could say that," I tell him while I give Carletta a visible nudge with my elbow. "Ya think we should be seen with these guys?"

Carletta's eyes widen at me as if she's not quite sure whether I'm kidding or serious. I'm trying to break the ice with some humor, but I'm not so sure her brain can handle it. Finally, she simply nods.

Both Cody and Brett are standing there in dress shirts and Dockers, looking as handsome as sin. In casual blue stripes, Brett has his shirtsleeves folded back to reveal tanned forearms and a leather-banded Fossil watch. A five o'clock shadow and silver aviator sunglasses make him look bad-boy dangerous, but his easy smile seems to put Carletta at ease.

Cody, on the other hand, is wearing a solid white shirt and, peeking out from the cuff, a gold watch that probably cost the earth. His cheeks are smooth-shaven, and rimless Ray Bans shade his baby blues, making him appear aloof; yet he's been showing me a different, more relaxed side to his personality that has me intrigued in spite of myself. Both men are tall and athletically built and sure to turn every female head, young and old.

When Carletta gives me a slight nudge I realize I need to quit gawking and invite them in. "Well, come on in, boys." Wait, did I just sound like Mae West? Clearing my voice, I step back and rephrase my greeting in my refined, Miss Abigail tone. "Please, come in." When Brett looks as if he might snicker, I quell his laughter with a slight narrowing of my eyes and then say, "Cody, Brett, I'd like you to meet Carletta Arce."

Cody extends his hand first. "It's very nice to meet you, Carletta."

"Same here," she responds with a bright smile, but when she accepts Brett's extended hand, she seems a bit flustered.

"Hello, Carletta," Brett says with a deep voice and a

warm smile. He removes his sunglasses and his gaze lingers on her long enough to let me know he likes what he sees. "I hope I didn't strong-arm you into this."

Carletta waves her hand with a delicate gesture. "Oh, not at all. I'm looking forward to it. Such a beautiful summer evening for an ice cream social, don't you agree?" She responds so smoothly that I want to take notes. Apparently fashion wasn't the only thing she learned over the years. She doesn't even realize that she's beautiful in a luminous, Jennifer Lopez kind of way, gorgeous but with a don't-mess-with-me attitude that's softened by an underlying vulnerability.

"I totally agree," Brett answers. If I'm not mistaken, he's immediately smitten. Good. Maybe Carletta will make him forget about Marissa. I almost shake my head just thinking about it.

"Whoof!" Rufus hates to be ignored and makes himself known.

"Hey there, Rufus." To my surprise, Cody kneels down and scratches him behind the ears. "Been swimming lately?"

"Don't you mean sinking?" I joke, but the memory of *my* swim that night makes me want to fan my face. When Cody looks up at me I hope I'm not beet red. I really need to learn to control this blushing thing.

"Yeah, I guess sinking is more like it," Cody agrees as he rises to his feet. Rufus whines in protest and flops over on his back, hoping for a belly rub.

"Rufus!" I scold, but I know just how he feels, I think while grinning at my shameless dog.

"Oh, he's okay," Cody assures me, but when Rufus gives me a sad-eyed, oh-come-on-*please* look, I shake my head.

"Uh-uh, get up. And don't you dare go chasing after Misty while I'm gone." I wag my finger at him as if he understands English, even though my warning might have come too late.

Rufus moans in protest but dutifully rolls to his big paws. With a doleful look at us over his shoulder, he lumbers off to the kitchen, probably in search of dog chow.

"Are we ready?" Cody asks everybody in general. We all nod. "Let's go then."

When we step outside, Carletta and I slip on our oversized designer sunglasses, another purchase from our marathon shopping excursion. She made me try on about a thousand pairs, but I have to admit they are very cool.

"By the way, you both look amazing," Cody comments as we walk across the driveway.

"I'll second that," Brett agrees with an admiring glance at Carletta that brings color to her cheeks.

"Thanks for sayin' so, because it sure took a lot of work to look this good, and my feet will be killin' me in these fancy little shoes," I answer. Carletta clears her throat, and I can tell she's rolling her eyes at me from behind her bodacious sunglasses.

Cody, however, seems to appreciate my humor. "Well, it was worth it." When he chuckles I start to relax a little.

"I'll be good at the event," I promise Carletta, but I'm not sure she believes me. "I wouldn't want the wrath of Miss Abigail," I add under my breath, and then suddenly wonder where she and Daddy are. They left for lunch hours ago and I haven't seen hide nor hair of them since. I still manage to get into hot water with her even though I like her a lot. Daddy, however, has become the teacher's pet.

"We'll meet you two over there," Brett says as he

opens the door of his SUV for Carletta. "Sorry about the baseball equipment stacked in the back," he apologizes to her. "I wanted to get this dirty thing washed for you, but I ran out of time."

"Don't give it another thought," Carletta assures him as she steps up into the vehicle. I can't hear Brett's response, but Carletta's laugh floats my way and I have to smile, thinking they just might hit it off.

Cody opens the door of his Audi TT and I slide onto the smooth leather seat. After he folds his long legs into the driver's side, he says, "I'd put the top down, but it would mess up your hair. Maybe afterward when we leave and the sun sets, we can go for a spin?"

I'm taken by surprise that he's treating this as if it's a real date. "That would be nice. Normally I love the wind in my hair."

"I thought as much," he says with a smile.

"Well, you thought right." I try to sound matter-of-fact, but whenever I'm with him, my voice takes on a breathless quality I can't seem to control. It doesn't help to be in the close confines of the two-seater car. I can feel the heat of his body sitting next to me. His cologne is woodsy but with a citrus edge that smells clean, yet sexy. I'd love to lean over and bury my face in the crook of his neck and fill my head with his masculine scent—maybe even sneak a taste of warm skin—but I don't come close to having the nerve.

Still, the mere thought has me feeling warm and tingly. To distract myself from my wayward thoughts, I say, "Mind if we listen to some music?"

"Not at all." We both reach for the radio at the same time. The backs of our hands brush together, turning my warm tingle into a hot flash of awareness that shoots like a firecracker to my toes. "Sorry," he says. His long finger presses the button and he flicks a glance in my direction. Carrie Underwood's silky voice fills the air. "This station okay?"

"Sure." I nod. Is it my imagination or is his tone a little bit husky? But then I think it's probably just wishful thinking on my part again. I try to concentrate on the song, but all I can think about is the man sitting next to me. When he returns his hand to the gearshift, his forearm lightly touches mine and like an idiot I jump as if startled.

"Hey," he says in a deep but soothing voice, "don't be nervous about this ice cream social thing."

Angling my head, I nod, glad he mistook my jumpiness for nerves and not the reaction to his touch. "Oh, I'm fine."

"Good," he says as we stop for a red light. Then just when I get my heartbeat back under control, Cody leans and kisses me on the lips. It's brief, soft, and achingly sweet.

Damn, there goes my heart again.

Thank goodness for the cool air blowing through the vents or I might have slid into a puddle onto the floor mats. I'm trying to think of something clever or funny to hide the fact that he's making me melt, but my sense of humor fails me at the moment. Think, Jolie . . . *think*!

Oh, I'm thinking, all right. Thinking about grabbing him and kissing him a good one, but then the light turns green and he shifts into first gear. Not that I would have done it anyway.

Even though my tongue is perfectly tied in a big old knot, I'm going to have to think of something just to break the silence. I'm about to ask him something lame like what his favorite ice cream is, when he turns off the radio and says, "I have a confession to make."

Well, so much for small talk. With a this-can't-be-good feeling in the pit of my stomach I turn my head his way. "Okay, Cody . . . shoot."

16

Hope Floats

"I had been wanting to do that since you opened your front door."

I frown at him. "To do what?"

There is a moment of silence as if he's not sure he wants to tell me. "Kiss you," he finally responds in his deep, husky voice that would make reading a grocery list sound erotic—*tomatoes, toilet paper, chicken* . . . Mercy, take me now! Not knowing how to respond, I remain silent, but my heart beats so hard that I think he must surely hear it. When we stop for another red light, he turns his full attention to me. "I wasn't handing you a cheesy line, you know. I really enjoy your company, Jolie."

"Thank you," I finally manage. He smiles as if my answer amuses him just a bit. "I seem to be entertaining even when I don't mean to be. I'm not sure if it's a talent or a curse." I try to joke, but I have to wonder if I'm nothing more to him than redneck comic relief wrapped in a designer package. I can't see his eyes, but his lips draw together as if he's trying to understand what I'm getting at. How can I tell him I don't want to be just an amusing little diversion or a walk on the wild side for him before he goes back to his own high-society circle?

It's been hard because I've heard of some pig roasts and parties I would have been invited to, and now my old friends seem to have forgotten about me. It's as if I'm caught between two worlds and don't really fit in either one.

Cody seems confused by my sudden silence. After he slides the car into a parking space he kills the engine and turns to me again. "Are you sure you're okay?"

While nodding I have to tamp down a hot rush of emotion that washes over me. "You know, Cody," I tell him while fiddling with the clasp on my fancy purse, "while these clothes are certainly beautiful, I don't really feel like myself. I'm much more comfortable barefoot and in jeans. But on the other hand, my old life is gone . . . so where does that leave me?"

Cody looks at me thoughtfully for a moment. "Maybe you've yet to discover that." He takes my hand from my purse and gives it a gentle squeeze.

I inhale a shaky breath. "I know, I keep sounding like the poor little rich girl. Annoying, huh? I should be grateful instead of whining." I shrug my shoulders and then slide my sunglasses down to look over the rims at him. "Let's go eat some ice cream, shall we?" I ask in my very best refined voice.

"Yes, let's do," Cody responds in the same snooty tone that makes me laugh, and I start to relax again. With a smile still in place, he looks as if he's going to say more, but instead he pulls my hand to his mouth and lightly kisses it. While I know it's a simple gesture on his part, for some reason the sweetness of it moves me beyond measure. When he comes around to the passenger side of the car he assists me out and then says, "You really do look beautiful, Jolie. I'll be the envy of every man here."

"Oh, it's getting deep in here," I tell him, and act as if I'm stepping over cow pies.

After a short laugh Cody shakes his head. "You know you're going to have to let me compliment you once in a while."

"Yeah, but that one was over-the-top. Admit it." I give him a nudge with my elbow.

"Can't do it because it wasn't. You just watch and tell me if I'm not right. Deal?"

"Okay . . . deal." I laugh while holding out my fists for a knuckle bump. He looks at my hands for a questioning second, then grins when he understands and gives my knuckles a firm tap. This tender side of Cody tugs at my heartstrings and I remind myself not to get my hopes up, but I don't always listen to reason . . . well never really.

"Hey, there're Brett and Carletta." Cody points across Main Street to the town square and even though there is a gathering crowd milling around, I spot them near the new gazebo. Carletta's skirt is fluttering in the breeze and she looks up and smiles at something Brett says close to her ear.

"Let's catch up with them."

"Okay." I'm surprised when he takes my hand as we cross the street, but I tell myself it's a polite gesture and not to read too much into it. Oh, but his hand feels warm and somehow gives me a sense of confidence and security. He doesn't let go when we reach the sidewalk on the other side.

The evening breeze carries the tantalizing aroma of funnel cakes, cotton candy, and buttered popcorn. A barbershop quartet sings "A Bicycle Built for Two" from the center of the pristine white gazebo. Bright red geraniums line the brick-paved sidewalk, and big planters overflow with multicolored petunias and dark green ivy that spills over the sides. Conversations buzz, babies cry, and there is a festive feeling in the air that's both relaxing and energizing.

"The gazebo is a nice addition to the park," I comment as we approach Brett and Carletta. "If I didn't see cell phones and iPods, this could be a scene out of the past."

Cody nods. "I hope it breathes life back into the town square. City council has a nice lineup of events that hopefully will be well attended and gather support for the botanical gardens."

"If tonight is any indication, I'm sure it will be a big success."

"I hope you're right," he says. I can tell by his tone that he's sincere.

"I usually am," I answer with a cheeky grin, even though at that very moment I think to myself that I've been wrong about a whole lot of things. I remember when Daddy and I were of the opinion that Cody and his father were money-hungry developers with no concern for Cottonwood and its residents. I'm beginning to see we were mistaken. While I've complained about being judged, I suddenly realize I've done my fair share of it as well. People shouldn't be measured by what they have or don't have, but by their character. Daddy was right that money doesn't make the man, but lack of it doesn't either.

"Just what are you pondering so seriously?" Cody asks as we weave our way through the swelling crowd.

"What makes you think I'm doin' some serious thinkin'?"

"Your brows are drawn together above your sunglasses as if you're deep in thought."

"I'm trying to decide whether I want a big dip of chocolate chip or a funnel cake."

"You could always have both."

"Yeah right. Pretty soon my butt will have its own zip code."

Cody chuckles, but I don't think he's really buying my answer. I don't have to elaborate since we've finally made our way to Brett and Carletta.

"This place is packed," Brett comments. "I realize it's a good thing, but geez . . ."

"Let's round up some ice cream," Cody suggests and then gives me a questioning look.

"Ice cream it is," I answer.

"I'd rather have a cold beer, but okay," Brett says with a good-natured grin in Carletta's direction. She smiles back and I suppose she knows I was right when I said Brett is as down-to-earth as they come.

"I think you'll have to settle for a *root beer* float," I tell him, and point to a sign on a booth not far away.

"I guess a Budweiser float wouldn't work."

"Ew!" Carletta and I answer simultaneously.

"Hey, don't knock it until you've tried it," Brett says, and smacks his lips.

"Tell me you didn't ever really put a scoop of ice cream into a mug of beer?" Carletta asks.

"He's pulling your leg," Cody says, and gives Brett's shoulder a shove. "I think, anyway."

Brett laughs and shoves Cody back. "Come on, man. I'm not that crazy."

Cody gives him a deadpan look.

Brett shrugs. "Okay, so I've thought about it," he says,

although we all know he's kidding. It's nice to see that even with Cody's and Brett's lives having gone in separate directions, they still seem fairly close. I can't count the number of times I wished for a brother or sister.

"Jolie?" Cody asks.

"Actually a root beer float sounds pretty refreshing," I admit as we stroll past a face-painting booth with a long line of children waiting for a work of art on their cheeks. I kind of want one, but I guess it would mess with my classy outfit.

"I agree," Cody says. "Brett? Carletta?"

"Carletta says she needs a hit of chocolate," Brett answers. "We'll meet you back here in a few minutes."

"Okay," Cody says, then guides me over to the root beer booth. Although the sun is sinking lower in the blue sky, the evening air has a hint of humidity. When Cody hands me my cold cup, I gladly take a long sip from my straw. "Good?" he asks after we take shelter beneath a maple tree away from the crowd.

"Mmmm." I nod and then take a generous bite of homemade vanilla ice cream. "Hits the spot. Daddy used to make me one of these after a hard day in the fields, but I haven't had—" I pause and put my hand on Cody's arm. "Oh my goodness!"

"What?" He stops sipping and looks in the direction of my gaze.

"It's Daddy and Miss Abigail over at that booth and I do believe they are selling my daddy's wood carvings!" I look up at Cody. "Did you know about this?"

He shakes his head.

"Well, that explains where he's been all day."

"Let's go check it out," Cody offers, and I nod.

"Daddy!" I say when we finally get close enough. His carvings are selling like crazy.

"Hello, baby cakes," he booms with a big smile.

I swing my hand in an arc. "When did this all come about?"

Abigail waves in my direction after she hands a delicate wooden angel to an elderly lady and then takes her money. "This is my doing, Jolie. I was in charge of a stuffed animal booth and they got lost in shipping. Your father graciously donated his lovely carvings to the cause. I had no idea he was so talented!" She gives him a big smile and I swear my big, strong farmer daddy seems to get flustered. "It was last-minute and we've been rushing around all day!" She seems a bit breathless and I wonder if my daddy is the cause.

"I was happy to help," he gushes with a sidelong glance at Abigail. "Whatcha got there?" he asks, nodding at my cup.

"A root beer float."

Daddy grins. "Haven't had one of those in a while, have we?"

"Would you like one, Wyatt, Abigail?" Cody asks.

Miss Abigail shakes her head, making her silky-looking auburn hair graze her shoulders. "We'll probably sell out within the hour at this pace. Then we're going to chow down."

Chow down? I swallow my laughter since it's one of Daddy's favorite expressions and sounds funny coming from her. And although not a hair is out of place and a bead of sweat wouldn't dare show its face, Miss Abigail is dressed fairly casually in white slacks and a light green sleeveless blouse. Daddy's wearing a Polo golf shirt in soft blue, and black dress shorts that I've never seen before, making me guess they've been shopping. A tiny twinge of regret that it's not my mother standing at his side unexpectedly slides into my brain, but I quickly shake it off. Daddy seems to glow with happiness. He deserves it.

"Perhaps we'll catch up with you later," I tell them. "We have to go and find Brett and Carletta."

Daddy's eyebrows shoot up and then he smiles as if thinking, *Why not?* He's standing there with his etiquette teacher and I'm with Cody Dean. Could life get any crazier?

Then out of the corner of my eye I see Marissa Clayton sashaying our way . . .

And judging by the determined look on her face, apparently the answer to my question is a great big *yes*.

17

Count Me In

"Why, there you arrrrre," Marissa coos, of course, to Cody. She turns and widens her eyes as if to say, *He's with you again*? and affords me a tiny, pinched smile before whipping her head back around so fast that her sleek blond ponytail smacks my cheek like a horse's tail going after an annoying fly. "Did you *not* get my calls?"

From the guilty look on Cody's face I'm guessing that, yes, he did. "I suppose I couldn't hear my phone over the noise," he responds, ever the gentleman.

Marissa appears relieved. "Understandable," she says in a hushed voice, and flicks me a frown as if I were somehow the reason for the missed calls. In a way I suppose I was. She quickly curves her pink pouting lips back into a smile and returns her attention to Cody.

She appears so fresh and innocent in a Reese Witherspoon kind of way that it's hard for me to imagine how her personality fails to match. "May I steal him away for a few?" she asks sweetly, but then turns away before I can respond, as if I really didn't matter anyway. "Cody, would you come with me to the VIP tent over by the lake?" She leans in and says behind her hand, "You know, the one for the *large* contributors, like you. I have a teensy-weensy favor to ask of you and Brett, if he's around." She holds her index finger and thumb to illustrate how small her favor is, but I have my doubts.

"He's here," Cody reluctantly responds.

"Oh, I thought I saw him a little while ago with some dark-haired girl I didn't quite recognize." She frowns as if trying to place Carletta. My heart pounds when I remember Carletta had briefly worked for Marissa. I dearly hope she doesn't remember Carletta and then say something snarky to embarrass her. While I'm certain Brett doesn't give a rip that she is, well, *was* a maid, I'm not so sure Marissa wouldn't find a way to be mean about it. "Well?" she persists.

"I'll go, but is there a reason why Jolie can't come with me?"

Marissa moves her shoulders side to side in an agitated manner before she catches herself and then fans a hand and a false smile in my general direction. "Why no, of course not." She puts her palm to her cheek as if she had a brain fart or something. "Follow me and keep a lookout for Brett and that"—she flicks her fingers—"*girl*."

I'm confused at Marissa's reaction to Brett having a date since she still seems to be after Cody. Then I remember Brett saying there was something between them, but she doesn't consider his schoolteacher and coach position worthy of her attention. *What an idiot*, I think to myself. Her tiny butt sways back and forth as she leads us to the special tent for so-called important people, where I really don't want to hang out . . . but whatever.

By now we're at the outskirts of the ice-cream crowd and away from the festival atmosphere. As Marissa said, there's a large white tent erected in a grassy field near a beautiful lake reflecting the golden-red rays of the setting sun. Tiki torches are lit to keep away mosquitoes. Tiny twinkling lights, soon to sparkle in the dark, edge the tent and supporting poles.

Marissa suddenly stops in her tracks so abruptly that I almost run into her back. "Brett!" She waves wildly when she spots him until he has no choice but to acknowledge her. I'm so hoping that spending time with someone as cool as Carletta will make him see the light.

I notice Carletta is smiling and looks radiant until she recognizes Marissa. When her smile falters, I catch her eye with a just-let-Marissa-try-something-bitchy reassuring look. Carletta's slight smile in my direction tells me she understands my meaning. In her large designer sunglasses and fancy clothes, Marissa probably will not put two and two together, or even remember her former maid's name.

"Brett!" Marissa gushes. "I was hoping to run into you."

"You don't say . . ." His bored tone has Marissa bristling a bit, but she does the shoulder wiggle and then seems to let it pass. With an arched eyebrow she gives Carletta a once-over and then extends her hand. "I don't believe we've met. Marissa Clayton." She says her name as if she's someone important. I suppose in her own mind she is.

"Carletta Arce. A pleasure, I'm sure." Her lips twitch just slightly, and I have to cough to hide my laugh.

Marissa's golden eyebrows draw together and she gets a don't-I-know-you? look on her face, but when she opens her mouth, Cody, bless his heart, interrupts her. "So, what is this all pertaining to?" he asks smoothly, but with just enough edge to let Marissa know that we have important things to do, such as eating a funnel cake with cherries.

"Let's grab a glass of wine and I'll share," she says. Then off she goes, assuming we will follow like little sheep.

I know Carletta can't see me roll my eyes behind my sunglasses, so I slip off the glasses and carefully store them in the case. Then I give her an eye roll worthy of the situation. "Wouldn't it be funny if we turned around and left?" I whisper to Carletta. She snickers behind her fist, but of course we follow anyway. Still, it would be funny . . .

The tent has long, linen-covered tables laden with fancy food. People in here are dressed up and bejeweled, and I have to wonder if their toes are aching like mine. Plus, it's darned difficult to walk in heels on the soft ground. Pretty soon I'm going to get charley horses in my calves from walking on the balls of my feet. I'm thinking about saying to hell with it and slipping my sandals off, but I spot Mason Worthington looking especially Colonel Sanders-ish in a white suit, so I decide I'd better be good. His wife is wearing a silky, flowing kimono-style dress that billows out at the arms while she talks. If a good gust of wind comes along she might just go airborne. Audrey Rose Mitchell gives us a tinkling two-fingered wave but then goes back to a lively chat with her blue-haired lady friends. I swear I hear the word *penis* mentioned.

Marissa's friend Katie Morgan is weaving slightly, making me wonder if she has had one too many glasses of wine. Her sudden loud laugh confirms my suspicion. I'm trying very hard not to wish that she does something extremely stupid that's caught on camera and ends up on YouTube.

A stiffly walking waiter brings us a tray of flutes holding what turns out to be champagne. The bubbles tickle my nose and I almost sneeze. After we all have a glass in our hands Marissa decides it's time for her big revelation. It's just a gut feeling, but when she presses her lips together and takes a deep breath I'm pretty sure I'm not going to like whatever it is that she has in mind for Cody and Brett. I take a big sip of my champagne and wait.

"Well," she begins, "because I've done such a *tremendous* job chairing the Cottonwood Charity Ball . . . not my words mind you, but straight from Mayor McCord's mouth"—with a hand to her chest, she adds this as a sidebar before continuing—"I've been asked to head up the fund-raising events for the botanical gardens and arboretum. I tried to decline with the charity ball coming up so soon, but Mayor McCord insisted."

I nod, while trying desperately to care. I have to avoid looking at Carletta so I don't laugh.

Marissa takes a delicate sip from her flute and then continues. I wish we had bourbon with some kick instead of lightweight champagne. "Well, our previous chairperson," she begins, and then leans in and whispers so that we all have to lean in too, "whom I won't name but was horribly incompetent, hired for a benefit concert a band that cancelled at the last minute." She makes a face as if she's sucking a lemon. "So I had to step in and do an event that could be pulled together quickly . . . something fun but that will generate considerable money." She pauses dramatically while we wait with bated breath . . . well, not really, but she thinks we do. I'm still dreaming about the funnel cake.

Cody takes off his sunglasses. "Marissa?" he prompts.

She holds her champagne flute to the side and waves her other hand in excitement. "I'm holding a bachelor auction!"

Brett slides his Oakleys to his forehead and both men are shaking their heads. "You mean like when chicks bid on us?"

Smiling brightly, she nods. "Yes!"

"You're kidding, right?" Cody asks, for once forgetting to be polite.

"No, I'm dead serious." She narrows her eyes and answers Cody defensively before reining herself back in. "Listen, I had to come up with something quick. I know it's a little . . ."

"Cheesy?" Brett provides.

"I was going to say *done before*, but in my rather extensive research I found that it's still an excellent way to raise money. With the right men involved, women with money tend to get carried away."

"Are there enough people around Cottonwood to pull off an event like this?" Brett asked.

"I'll have to expand my horizons a little, but the short answer is that yes, I will be able to pull it off *if* I get enough quality men to lend a . . . hand." She presses her lips together and then asks, "So, can I count on you two? I've arranged for a limo service to bring the bachelors to the event. Tuxedos will be provided. And I've arranged for dinner and a limo for you and your date . . . all donated, of course." She adds this tidbit with pride. "That's how it's done. Of course, the publicity for the participants will be worth the time and trouble. I know it's last-minute, but I'll have press releases and posters everywhere. So basically all you have to do"—she shrugs her narrow shoulders—"is agree."

Brett and Cody look to Carletta and me as if we should comment, but before either of us can utter a word or two like *hell no* or *over our dead bodies*, Marissa says, "Oh, surely you ladies won't protest. It's for such a good cause, after all! And of course you can always bid on them if you choose to attend the event." She gives us a sly wink. "Or on someone else for that matter, if Brett and Cody choose not to participate."

"I don't know . . ." Cody frowns, making me wonder if her little challenge bothers him. Oh, there goes my wishful-thinking gene kicking into high gear again.

"I'm convinced I can raise a cool twenty grand at least." She snaps her fingers. "In one easy evening." Marissa turns to Brett. "That kind of money could provide the bird blind and greenhouse your science department at Cottonwood High has requested."

Wow, she's good, I begrudgingly admit to myself.

Brett hesitates but then nods. "Okay. Count me in."

Marissa gives him a wide smile and then arches an eyebrow at Cody. "And you?" Her tone has a hint of a challenge that to me is as good as a dare, but he still hesitates.

"This isn't my sort of thing. I'd rather write a check."

"But that would be the easy way out, wouldn't it?" The words are out of my mouth before I can stop them and suddenly all eyes are on me. It's just that I can remember kids with money in school who could write a doggone check for things when I'd have to scrimp and save. Still, I didn't have to say so out loud.

Cody nods his head and says, "You're right. Marissa, count me in too."

"Why thank you, Cody," she says, and takes the opportunity for a big pushing-her-breasts-against-him hug. She then reluctantly turns to me. "And . . . thank you too, Jolie," she says in a small, rushed voice.

Carletta gives me a tiny nudge with her elbow.

"What, no hug for me?" Brett asks, but all he gets is an air kiss. His indulgent glance at Marissa tells me he isn't quite over his lame attraction to her. Ugh! I want to smack him upside the head.

"Well," Marissa says briskly, "I'll get the details to you ASAP. I'm putting this all together at the speed of light." She takes a deep dramatic breath and then drains her champagne. "I must be off. I have a couple more potential bachelors to approach."

"May I suggest one?" says Carletta, who has been virtually silent up until now.

Marissa seems as if she isn't quite sure how to react. "Mmmm, I have a list," she politely responds, but does her shoulder-shake telltale sign again. I'm guessing she had some control issues. "Well . . . okay. Who?"

"Wyatt Russell."

I turn and blink at Carletta, but she doesn't have the nerve to look at me.

"J-Jolie's father?" Marissa looks at her empty glass as if she's wishing for more.

Carletta nods. "He's probably a little older than the bachelors on your list, but he's handsome, charming, and rich. If you think about it, the demographics of the women who will participate might find him quite desirable and cough up some big bucks."

"Good point," Brett says, and we all stand there while Marissa is put on the spot.

"I . . . um . . . ," she stutters.

Carletta steps in again. "And since not many people will know who he is, Wyatt will be sort of a mystery man, creating some buzz," she says smoothly. Once again I'm impressed.

Marissa suddenly perks up and takes notice. "Are you in public relations somewhere?" She angles her head. "You do look familiar."

"I just snagged her as a personal assistant," I jump in and explain.

"Ahhh," Marissa says, "so you have a vested interest." She taps her temple. "Smart thinking." Although she doesn't look totally convinced she says, "Where is your father, Jolie?"

"He's running a booth with Abigail Marksberry."

"Oh." She seems surprised and I try not to let it bother me. "Well then, I guess I'll head that way and approach him." She glances at Cody as if to see whether he thinks having my father a part of the event would be desirable.

Cody seems a little bit amused by the whole thing, and again I'm seeing a more relaxed side of him than I thought was possible. "I think Wyatt would be a hit, as long as you're okay with it, Jolie?" He turns to me with a more serious expression and I'm touched that he's concerned that I would be upset to see my daddy considered an eligible bachelor.

"I'm fine with it. Daddy needs to have fun."

"Okay then. I'm off!" Marissa finally seems convinced. Almost, anyway. I want to assure her that Daddy won't do anything to embarrass her, but knowing my father, I can't really promise that. If he accepts her request, I'm sure it will make things interesting. He can be a real ham when he wants to. Shaking my head, I can picture him now . . .

"Are you sure you're okay with this, Jolie?" Carletta asks as soon as Marissa is out of earshot. "I should have asked you first. It was just too much fun to see Marissa squirm," she admits, but then glances at Brett to see if she overstepped her bounds. Her eyes widen. "Oh, and do you think your father will mind?"

I roll my eyes. "Daddy really is a big ham. He'll eat this up. It's been fun to see his sense of humor back in full force."

"But . . . ," Carletta begins softly.

I put a reassuring hand on her arm. "I hadn't realized until recently what Daddy must be missing in his life. Mama has been gone for a long time and this sounds trite, but I know she would want him to be happy," I insist firmly, but then I have to swallow hard.

Cody surprises me again when he slips his arm around my waist and lightly kisses the top of my head. His show of concern and public affection feel so wonderful that I smile up at him. "Thank you."

He returns my smile and looks at me with such warmth that I find myself leaning against him. His arm tightens a fraction, drawing me even closer to his side. "Just what are you thanking me for?"

"For understanding." For holding me . . . for making me feel like a desirable woman.

"Hey," Cody says to Brett and Carletta, "would you two mind if Jolie and I scoot out of here? I promised her a cruise with the top down."

"Not at all." Brett gives me a see-he-*is*-into-you look and of course I blush like crazy because for the first time I think Brett might be right.

With questioning eyes, I look over at Carletta to see if she seems comfortable with my leaving. "Go on." She makes a shooing motion with her hands. "Enjoy the evening." She leans in close to give me a hug and whispers, "I'm fine. Have fun but be ready to dish later."

"You too," I whisper back before pulling away.

"See you later," Cody says, and then whisks me from the tent without hesitation even when it's clear that several of the so-called very important people wish for him to stop and chat. Could it be that Cody Dean can't wait to get me alone?

Holy cow. I guess I'm about to find out.

18

Barefoot and Breathless

"Oh my goodness, Cody, this feels amazing!"

"Let me know if I'm going too fast."

"Are you kiddin'? I love it." I stretch my arms up in the air and let the wind slap against my palms. "Whoo-hoo!" Out of the corner of my eye I spare Cody a glance to see if I'm getting a little too wound up, but he's smiling as if he's having fun too. "I always wanted a convertible, but the closest I ever came was driving a tractor down the road. And let me tell ya, it didn't go this fast or hug the curves the way this baby does."

"Well, you can afford one now, you know."

I shrug. "Yeah, I know. Someday I'll get me one." Big talk, but I doubt if that will ever happen. No matter what, I'm still a pickup kind of girl. This is fun, but it just isn't . . . me.

"I could take you out car shopping," he offers while expertly making a sharp turn.

"Okay," I agree.

"Or truck shopping," he says with a quick grin at me before returning his eyes to the winding country road.

Laughter bubbles up in my throat. "Ha! Now you're talkin'." When my hair flies in my face I wind it around my fist. "You're getting to know me pretty darned well, Cody Dean."

"Yeah, I am."

"What . . . that's all you're gonna say?" Maybe it's the champagne in my blood or the wind in my hair, but I suddenly feel a bit bold and carefree.

"Are you fishing for compliments?"

"Well, hell yeah."

"Okay. How about the more I know you, the more I want to know you more?"

"Hmmm . . ." I angle my head as if pondering. "That's a whole lotta *mores* if you ask me, but I'll take it."

"There's more where that came from." When he laughs I turn toward him, thinking I'd love to have my fingers in his windblown hair and my mouth on his neck. When he suddenly slows the car down he catches me staring, but this time I don't blush. Instead, I smile slowly, hoping that his thoughts are going in the same direction. "So just where are you taking me, Cody?"

"To my place."

My heart beats fast. "Oh?"

"Are you okay with that? I guess I should have asked and not simply kidnapped you."

"No, that's fine. I'd love to see your home." I am, in fact, curious.

"Good, because we're almost there."

"I had no idea that you lived this far outside of Cottonwood."

He downshifts and turns up a narrow one-lane road that circles up a steep hill. "I like the privacy and solitude after the stress of work. The big back deck overlooks the woods. Although I usually don't arrive home until fairly late, it's my favorite place to unwind." He smiles at my expression. "Okay . . . what?"

"I don't know. I was expecting something more urban. I guess I'm a little surprised."

"Good. A lot of people, including Brett, think they have me all figured out." While he doesn't say this harshly, I can hear a measure of hurt in his tone. "There's more to me than making money."

"I can relate, Cody. It's not fun, nor is it right to be stereotyped for any reason whatsoever." It's humbling to realize I'm guilty of this as well.

He reaches over and gives my knee a squeeze. "I understand that now more than ever."

"Me too," I admit as he pulls the car to a stop. "Wow," I breathe, and lean closer to the windshield to get a better look out the window. In the waning light I can still make out a rustic but gorgeous wood-framed and fieldstone home perched on the side of a cliff, overlooking tall pines and thick woods.

Cody points at the majestic house. "This is where you'll find . . . ," he begins, but then shrugs and shakes his head as if embarrassed to reveal so much of his emotions.

"The real Cody Dean?"

With a small lift of his shoulders he kills the engine and then reaches over to pick up a wayward lock of my hair. While absently rubbing it between his fingers he says, "Mmmm, yeah, I guess you could say that." He puts his index finger beneath my chin and tilts my head up. "Are you ready to find out?"

My heart thuds hard. On the surface his question seems innocent . . . general. But I think we both know something has been simmering between us all evening. As if reading my mind, he slides his hand beneath my chin and rubs his thumb over my bottom lip. His eyes watch his thumb and then lock with mine. "Yes, I'm ready." Husky, breathless, my voice is laced with anticipation.

With a slow, sexy smile Cody leans over and lightly brushes his warm lips over mine. My eyes flutter shut when he lingers just enough for me to taste his mouth and long for so much more. But in a flash his touch is gone and before my eyes are fully open and focused, he's opening the passenger door and offering his hand.

After helping me up from the low car, he keeps his hand in mine. He guides me in the semidarkness up the brick-paved sidewalk lined with solar lights, but I still have to be careful in my skimpy sandals.

"It's beautiful up here."

"And peaceful," he agrees. A sultry but cooler night breeze ruffles the trees and brings the scent of earth and pine. Above, the inky black sky is sprinkled with stars shining bright like diamonds on velvet. The high-pitched whistle of crickets is the backdrop for other nocturnal animal hoots and howls that break the silence of the summer night.

"Come on in." Cody opens the front door and stands back for me to enter. A lamp is turned on in the corner of the room, illuminating an open floor plan, which in the daytime must feel bright and airy. With a flick of a switch, recessed lighting casts a soft glow while a paddle fan stirs up a welcoming breeze.

"This is really nice, Cody," I tell him.

"Thanks." He seems pleased that I like it and I have to admit it's much more casual than I anticipated. I walk over to a large sectional sofa of deep brown leather that's cool and buttery soft to the touch. Bold red, fringed pillows add a splash of color to an otherwise neutral, masculine setting. A chunky wood and glass coffee table, filled with glossy magazines, matches two end tables with skinny pewter lamps. The focal point, however, is a massive fieldstone fireplace sporting a rustic wooden mantel with a watercolor landscape hung directly above. It's probably an original something or other, but of course I have no clue.

"Gorgeous but with a relaxed feel. The view must be spectacular." I point to the floor-to-ceiling windows on the opposite side of the room.

"It is. You can see Sun Rock Lake below in the daylight. I have a bass boat and small dock at the bottom of my property."

I almost tell him I can't wait to see it, but of course that would mean in the morning . . .

"Sunrises are amazing," he comments as if reading my mind. "The mist rises from the lake and the sun slowly burns it off. It's where I drink my coffee most mornings."

"Sun Rock Lake is pretty. The marina is run-down, but Daddy still fishes over there. I can only imagine." And I do . . . sharing a steaming mug of coffee with his arms wrapped around me from behind. I'd be wearing his pajama top and nothing else. Of course, maybe he doesn't wear pajamas . . . He seems a boxers or naked kind of guy. I swallow a groan.

"Jolie? Are you okay?"

"Sure, why?"

"You're frowning."

"Oh, was I?" I shrug. "I guess it's because these shoes are killin' my feet." It's not really a lie. "My feet feel like they have rubber bands wrapped around them." I know

I'm rambling, but I can't help it. I've got to do something to keep thoughts of Cody naked out of my mind. "I know there's not much to them, but since I'm usually barefoot, I guess my feet just aren't used to tight little leather straps." I glance down and when I look back up, Cody is by my side.

"We can remedy that." He gestures toward the sofa. "Have a seat."

All I can do is nod.

He points a remote at a flat-screen television. Soft, soothing music fills the air with a backdrop of swirling color that's sort of mesmerizing. "I'll be right back."

"Okay," I manage this time. Because my legs are sort of wobbly, I sink down to the soft cushions, glad he didn't see my unladylike flop.

A few moments later Cody returns with two glasses of wine. "Thought this might help you to kick back a little."

"I'm relaxed." Yeah, right . . .

He looks at me over the rim of his glass. "Mmmm, no you're not." He sets his glass down on the coffee table and then kneels down in front of the sofa. "Take a sip of your wine."

I arch one eyebrow. "Are you trying to get me tipsy, Cody Dean?" I'm attempting to joke, but my voice remains breathless, sounding more like an invitation.

His chuckle is low and sexy. "No. I simply want you to sit back and let me rub your feet."

Holy cow. Rub my feet? No one has ever done that before. I swallow hard and then take a big gulp of wine. "Okay." When he slips both sandals off my feet I can't hold back a relieved sigh.

"Better?" With a sympathetic smile he rubs his thumb over the red indentions left by the leather straps.

"Much." I try not to moan but fail. "Mmmm, that feels so good." Then, after gently putting one leg up on the soft leather sofa, he takes my other foot into his warm hand. Starting at the heel, he uses the pads of his thumbs to massage with strong upward strokes. My eyes want to flutter shut, but the scene with his dark head bent over my feet while he works his magic is too erotic not to watch. When I feel as if I'm melting into the soft leather, I take a long pull from my chilled wine. "My feet are happy now. They adore you."

He laughs low, softly, and then exchanges one foot for the other. While he's got my foot close to his face a horrid thought occurs to me. "Oh, they don't smell or anything, do they?"

"No!" His shoulders shake with laughter.

"Good," I say with such relief that he laughs harder. "Wait, you're sure, right?"

"Yes." Cody abruptly stops laughing. "You want me to prove it?"

"I . . . uh . . ."

To prove his point he nibbles on my heel and then licks up my arch before swirling his tongue over the ball of my foot.

My. God.

Then . . . while looking up at me, he sucks my big toe into his hot, so-damned-sexy mouth.

Oh. Dear. Lord.

My breath catches; my heart pounds. And my wineglass almost slips through my fingers.

"Here, let me." As if knowing, he reaches up, takes the glass, and sets it on the coffee table with a soft clink. But if I think he's finished with my feet, I'm dead wrong.

While tenderly kissing each toe, he slides his hand up

over my ankle and starts massaging my calf. He kneads the tense muscle until it's soft and pliant beneath his long fingers and warm palm. Unable not to, I lean back against the leather cushions and try not to slither to the floor. "Surely you have a diploma . . . a master's degree in massage?"

"Yeah, but I bought it online."

I laugh weakly and force my droopy eyes open to look at him. When he puts his index finger to his mouth I say, "Your secret is safe."

"Thank you." He gives me a look of mock relief before taking a sip of his wine. Then he bends his head and turns his attention to my other foot. God, his mouth is cold and wet from the wine but quickly heats up. He licks, nibbles, massages, until I can't help but lean forward and thread my fingers through his hair.

My feet tingle and when he nibbles on the tender inside of my arch, it tickles so much that I try to pull his head up, but he keeps on task until my breath comes in short gasps. I'm warm and yet I shiver. "Cody . . ." When I involuntarily say his name, he looks up. "Kiss me." My request is a mere whisper, but when his eyes meet mine, I see desire reflected in the deep blue depths.

"Gladly." His voice is low, resembling a sexy growl that rumbles over my skin like a hot caress. When he comes up to his knees I tug his head closer and meet his mouth for a long, steamy kiss. He moans into my mouth and slides one hand up my dress to my thigh. His hand feels warm, his fingers firm, calloused and masculine against my soft, tender skin.

I gasp when he circles his thumb higher and higher until he reaches the elastic edge of my lacy thong. He toys, tugs until I'm arching up from the cushions. The

pad of his thumb inches closer and closer to the silk tri-
angle. I'm wet and throbbing, and still he toys and teases.
He kisses me over and over, devouring my mouth, with
fire and passion. Then, when his tongue sinks into my
mouth, he slips his finger inside me.

My hips arch up from the leather, taking his finger
deeper. "God," I gasp when he moves his mouth to my
neck. His finger swirls and caresses while his warm
mouth kisses me just beneath my earlobe.

"Jolie?"

"Mmmm?" I inhale sharply when he slips his finger
from me, but just when I think he is going to join me on
the sofa, he slips his arms beneath me and lifts me up into
his arms. "Wh-what are you doing?"

"Taking you to my bed."

19

While You Were Sleeping

I wrap my arms around his neck and lean my cheek against his shoulder. I'm sure there are reasons galore why I should stop this in its tracks, but right now none of them seem to matter. All I care about is having his bare skin slide against mine.

Cody carries me with ease down the dark hallway and into a huge master bedroom that faces the back of the house and shares the wooded view and the convenience of the deck. What is it about being carried that is the most romantic thing in the entire universe?

"I need to see you," he whispers in my ear, and then pushes a knob with his elbow. Soft, dim lighting illuminates the room and a paddle fan stirs up a gentle breeze. Cathedral ceilings allow for a king-sized platform bed with a tall, sleigh-style headboard in deep mahogany. The furniture is dark, sleek, and masculine without knick-knacks or clutter. Even the walls are bare, leaving the picture-window view to breathe life and warmth into the room. A fireplace is on the opposite wall and I can imagine how romantic and cozy it would feel in the dead of winter.

Cody lets me slide down to his side while he turns down the chocolate brown comforter. "Turn around," he says into my ear. When I do, he unzips my dress and then slowly pushes it from my shoulders. He takes his time, kissing my neck, my shoulders, and trailing downward with the path of the dress. "Turquoise looks amazing on you, Jolie," he says as the dress pools on the hardwood floor, "but your soft skin suits you even better." He slides his hands over my shoulders, down my arms, and then glides back up to cup my breasts.

"Mmmm . . ." Unable not to, I lean back against him, rest my head on his shoulder, and let him explore. My belly quivers beneath his trailing fingers and when he reaches my thong, I inhale sharply and silently thank Carletta for her shopping spree. His fingertip dips beneath the black silk and when he tugs the mere wisp of silk and lace down past my thighs and then all the way to the floor, I have trouble standing. As if sensing this, Cody wraps one arm around my waist for support; then with his other hand he unsnaps my front-clasp bra, and my breasts tumble free.

"God . . ." His breath is warm and moist next to my ear. "You feel amazing." When he slides his hands up to cup my breasts as if they are something precious, I all but melt. While kissing my neck he circles his thumbs over my nipples, sending warm, delicious sensations of desire spreading like wildfire throughout my body. "Ahhh . . . Jolie." With a hot and sexy groan he gently lowers me to cool sheets and then looks down at me. "You are absolutely gorgeous."

Suddenly shy, well, because I'm naked and he isn't, I

catch my bottom lip between my teeth. But when I turn my head and glance away, he leans down and tucks a finger beneath my chin. "I mean it. You are beautiful, Jolie, both inside and out."

"Thank you, Cody." I'm glad this seems something more than physical to him. Making love isn't something I take lightly, and he seems to know it. While I know he has women falling at his feet, I get the strong impression this is something special to him as well.

"My pleasure," he answers with a lingering kiss that has me reaching up to unbutton his shirt.

When my fingers tremble I fumble with the buttons. "Well, hell's bells!"

With a chuckle he takes pity and stands up to finish the job himself. I watch as his chest appears, tanned and defined, making me long to touch his smooth, warm skin. He tosses his shirt to the floor and then makes quick work of his pants, until he's standing before me in nothing but tight, white boxer briefs that leave little to the imagination . . . and I have a very good imagination.

"Your picture should be next to *impressive* in the dictionary," I tell him, and he laughs as if I'm joking.

I'm not.

"Help me," he requests, and then tugs me to my knees on the mattress.

"Okay." But when I reach for his briefs, he leans down and kisses me first before putting my hand on the soft cotton shielding his hard erection. I rub my hand up the rigid length, feeling powerfully feminine that I put him in this condition. Bold now, I cup the weight of him in my palm and then slide my hand back up to where he's straining against the elastic. When I swirl my fingertip there, he leans his head to the side and groans. A muscle jumps in his jaw as if he's fighting for control.

"God . . ." His breath catches when I peel his underwear down, inch by inch, revealing the hot, hard length of his penis. He juts upward, proudly erect, begging for my touch . . . my mouth.

While cupping his firm butt, I shyly lean forward and lick him ever so lightly. Cody groans once more, but although I want to taste and explore more, he sucks in a breath and says, "You're driving me crazy. Right now I want to be buried inside you." Before I can protest, he turns away and sheaths himself in a condom and then gently pushes me back down to the bed. He skims his hands over my bare skin, making me tingle, *shiver*, and when he presses his body to mine, I suck in a deep breath, loving the weight, the pressure against where I want him most . . .

His kiss is hot, hungry, making me wild for him. I run my hands up his back, loving his smooth skin, the ripple of muscle beneath my palms. When he takes a beaded nipple into his mouth and sucks, I arch up from the bed. "Cody!"

"Mmmm." He comes up to his knees, giving me a tantalizing view of glorious male beauty, and then sinks into my heat with one long, breathtaking stroke. He stops while buried deep, as if savoring the moment. Then begins a slow easy rhythm, sending pleasure building, climbing, until I wrap my body around him and love him back with all I've got until our passion explodes. I arch my back, taking him as deeply as my body will allow and kissing him wildly until I come floating back down to earth.

"Ahhh, Jolie." Cody rolls to the side and pulls me

close. With a sigh I kiss his damp chest and then rest my head there. His heartbeat is strong, rapid, while his breathing is still a bit ragged, bringing a satisfied smile to my face. "That was amazing, Jolie." His voice is husky with a sense of wonder, as if loving me was even better than he expected. "You are so sensual, giving . . . and so damned sexy that you just blow me away."

I answer with a long sigh and slip my hand up over his chest and up his neck to hug him.

He kisses the top of my head and pulls me even closer. "Will you stay with me tonight?"

Emotion clogs my throat, but I nod and then manage a husky, "Yes."

"Good. I didn't want to take this kidnapping thing too far." He tilts my head up and kisses me softly, tenderly and then says, "I'll be right back. Don't go anywhere."

"I'll save your spot. Unless, of course someone better comes along."

Cody shakes his head at me and then chuckles after he stands up. Of course, I watch him walk across the room while admiring his naked beauty, namely his butt. When he disappears into the bathroom, I smile and rub my hand over the warm sheet where his body had been. Then I bury my face in the feather pillow, inhaling the musky male scent that mingles with the clean spice of his cologne.

"Ah, good, you're still there." When he returns moments later he turns off the light and slides beneath the sheets.

"Are you kiddin'? You plumb wore me out. I don't think I could move if I wanted to."

"I hope you don't want to." He gathers me close and

spoons his body to mine, and I think to myself that it doesn't get any better than this . . .

"Mmmm, Jolie, you're making me want you all over again," he says into my ear. I can feel the evidence of his statement against my back, but mere moments later I have to smile when I hear his deep, even breathing. I think I'm so sated that I'll fall right asleep too, but I try to stay awake so I can savor the sensation of warm skin against warm skin. His strong arms make me feel safe and secure.

With a sigh I put my hand over his and hug him close. This feels so good, so right, and even though I know we are still in so many ways worlds apart, I also know I'm falling hard and fast for Cody Dean. The thought both excites and frightens me, but with an effort I push away the fear and allow myself to relax in his embrace. I know that losing my mama has left both Daddy and me scared to love without fear of loss, but now that I know what this feels like, I don't want to ever let Cody go.

Take it slow, I warn myself as I start to drift off to sleep. I realize I have a lot more to learn about this high society in which I now live if I truly want to fit in; tonight it's become even more important to me that I do so.

I sigh, then snuggle into the cool cotton pillow and deeper into Cody's arms. I have another one of those surreal I-can't-believe-I'm-here-with-him moments, but then he mumbles something and kisses my shoulder, and I can't help but smile. This is real. I of all people should know that anything is possible. But Cody Dean and me? Who would have thought? Certainly not me . . . and yet here I am.

While my eyelids grow heavy I relive the events of the evening, and then my thoughts start to scatter like dandelion seeds in the wind. I wonder if Daddy is falling for Miss Abigail. They sure looked cozy. My eyes flutter and I wonder if Brett and Carletta will see each other again and if he will give up his stupid infatuation with Marissa Clayton, or the queen of snark as I like to think of her.

I do know one thing for sure: Nobody is going to out-bid me for Cody in the bachelor auction that Marissa has cooked up. I'm dying to know if Daddy accepted Marissa's request that he participate. Something tells me he did, especially if Miss Abigail had anything to say about it. Then, I make a mental note that I have a class with her tomorrow; she does not like tardiness. I found that out the hard way.

Okay, brain, shut off, I tiredly scold myself. But if I drift off to sleep I won't be able to feel the delicious sensation of male heat and warm skin . . . Dang, a girl could get used to this. Mmmm . . . maybe I'll stay awake a few minutes longer . . .

Yawn.

Stretch.

Oh God, he just touched my boob. I hold my breath, hoping he'll do it again.

Finally my eyes slide shut, but then a thought hits me and I open them wide again. Please, God, don't let me snore. I don't do that, do I? Or drool on my pillow. Sigh. I think I do drool on occasion. Groan. Or, you know . . . *toot*! Oh, surely I don't do that, do I? Naw. But then again, how do I know what I do while I'm sleeping? Thinking that I'm likely to do at least one, or heaven help me, *all* of them, I decide I'll just have to stay awake. Yeah, that's the safest plan. I'll just . . . stay . . .

Awake.

Zzzzzzz.

20

About Last Night

"Jolie?" The sound of my name floats like fingers of fog into my brain, interrupting a very steamy dream. With a groan I ignore the intrusion. "Rise and shine . . ." The words drifts in, making me moan louder. I hate cheerful morning people. "Wake up, sleepyhead."

"Mmmm?" I bury my sleepy head deeper into the fluffy feather pillow. "Daddy . . . go 'way," I mumble, and desperately try to go back to my delicious dream.

"Jolie . . ."

"For pity's sake, the chickens can wait for fifteen blessed minutes," I complain, and then fold the pillow over my head. "Gimme a minute." I scoot farther beneath the covers . . . Wait a minute. I don't have to feed the chickens anymore and holy cow . . .

I'm naked.

I know that voice, and it sure isn't my daddy's. I peek out from beneath the covers and encounter the heart-pounding sight of Cody standing there in light blue, low-slung lounging pants and if I'm not mistaken, nothing else. He's cradling a large mug in his very capable hands.

One shoulder is leaning against the door frame and his ankles are casually crossed. Mercy, he looks good enough to eat . . . and I'm hungry.

His damp hair also tells me he's freshly showered . . . oh crap, and I'm more than a little morning-breath funky, I'm sure. I also give new meaning to the term bed head, so I remain in my little cocoon and pretend to fall back asleep. I breathe slow and heavy hoping I'll fool him.

"I know you're awake." Well, crap.

"No, I'm not."

"Right . . ." He has the nerve to chuckle.

"How do you know?"

"Well, the fact that you're talking to me is a pretty darned good clue."

"I talk in my sleep."

"I know."

Wait . . . what? My eyes open wide and I swallow hard. "I do?" I ask weakly. That can't be good.

"Mmmm-hmmm." I see him nod slowly through my little peephole.

"Really? Did I do anything else?" Like drool and snore and oh, dear lord, not that, say it ain't so!

Cody's deep chuckle lets me know I'm being played. Throwing back the covers I sit straight up and sputter, "Why you . . . !" When his eyes widen, I think my hair must really be bed-head crazy, but then the cool breeze from the fan reminds me that, *hello!*

I'm naked!

"Oh!" Yanking the covers back up to my chin, I slide back down and feel heat creep into my cheeks. Silly, since he's seen every nook and cranny of me, but in the light of day it's somehow different, and with the sun streaming thorough the big window it's as bright as can be in here.

"Don't mind me," Cody says in a tone laced with such humor that I have to peek out again. He angles his head to peer back at my eyes.

"Oh . . . just stop." I am sure my hair is sticking up everywhere. I reach up to smooth it down even though I know it's useless because it'll spring right back up until I shower and blow-dry it into submission.

One thing I do know is that I am a restless sleeper, thus the reason for the crazy hair. I have been ever since the passing of my mama, who used to calm me down with her stories. I'm usually up several times during the night and wake at the tiniest of noises . . .

Except for last night when apparently I slept like a baby.

"I take it you're not a morning person?"

I snort. "Oh puh-lease. Cody, I was born and raised on a farm. Early to bed and early to rise and all that."

He arches one dark eyebrow. "You coulda fooled me."

I scoot up far enough for my spiky hair to pop out from beneath the covers. "Wait, what time is it?"

"A little after ten."

"What!" I sit up straight and give him another flash of my breasts. "Are you messin' with me, Cody Dean?"

He takes a sip from his steaming mug that smells really good and then shakes his head. "Nope."

"I missed my etiquette lesson! My ass is gonna be in a sling." I shout before remembering my manners. "Um, I mean, I'm going to . . ."

"Lose your recess?" he supplies with a grin.

"Yes!" I shake my bed head at him and then have to

brush the hair out of my eyes. "Cody, why didn't you wake me?"

He shrugs those impossibly wide shoulders. "Truth be known, I just woke up a little while ago myself."

"Don't you set an alarm?"

He shakes his head. "I don't usually need one. Normally, I'm up with the sun—and cheerful, I might add."

"Oh, you're one of *those*. I bet you whistle or hum."

Laughing, he takes a step closer to the bed. "If it makes you feel any better, I missed a meeting too."

"Sorry."

"It's not your fault," he assures me, but then angles his head as if reconsidering. "No, I suppose it is your fault. You kept me up and wore me out."

I blush so fiercely that I fear my hair might catch on fire. "Sorry."

"Don't be. I haven't slept so soundly in a long time," he says, more to himself than to me, but when our eyes meet he sets the mug on his nightstand and then eases down onto the bed. Reaching over, he tucks a lock of my wayward hair behind my ear and then laughs softly. "I sure shocked a few people by not showing up. I don't think it's ever happened before."

"Really?"

"Yeah, really. How lame is that?"

I frown at him. "It's lame that you're disciplined and responsible? I don't think so."

"No," he answers in his low, husky voice that makes me want to grab and kiss him, but I need to brush my teeth first. "It's lame that I never had a reason to be late until . . . now."

At first I think he's joking, but his eyes seem serious.

"You've shown me that I've been focused on nothing but work for a long time. That needs to change."

"I'm always available to be a bad influence," I joke, but my heart pounds. "Glad to be of service."

Cody's smiles, but then his dark brows draw together. "Jolie, you've made me reevaluate my priorities, reassess my life goals."

"Me?" I try to remember if I've ever been an influence on anyone; nobody comes to mind.

"Yeah," he answers softly. Cody slowly shakes his head and then points to the window. "You know, just about every morning I stand out there on my deck with my cup of coffee thinking about all I have to do for that particular day. It's always pertaining to work. Deals. Money." He inhales a deep breath and then continues. "I look at the view but don't really see the beauty, because all my brain is thinking about is my career." He hesitates and then says, "Today was different."

"How so?"

He cups my chin in his palm and says, "All I could think about was . . . you." While smiling softly he caresses my cheek with the pad of his thumb. "You've made me want to slow down. Laugh." He swings his arm in an arc. "I've got this big house, but I'm rarely home. Another one right on the beach in Florida but I haven't been there since I bought it." He leans back and rubs a hand down his face. "For the first time I understood where Brett was coming from when he turned his back on the corporate world. What good is it all?"

"I've been thinking about that very same thing."

"So give me some answers," he says.

I smile at him and say, "First, get me a big T-shirt and a mug of coffee, lots of cream, light sugar. I'll join you out on that deck of yours and give you my pearls of wisdom if you'll let me."

"You got it." He gets up and walks over to a chest of drawers. After rummaging around he pulls out a big orange shirt and tosses it my way.

"Give me a few minutes and I'll meet you outside," I tell him.

"Okay."

After he leaves I take the shirt. I put my hand to my mouth when I find my underwear and then head to he bathroom. My reflection in the mirror makes me cringe, but I shrug and then have to laugh. "Whatever." After running a brush through my hair and washing up a bit, I locate my cell phone. I decide I'd better face the music and call home. I hate that Daddy must have been worried. Luckily, I get his voice mail, but I know he'll check it soon. I'm sure I'll get a dressing-down when I get home, but I remind myself that I'm an adult. For the first time the thought hits me that I should consider moving out on my own.

"Here you go," Cody says as he hands me a steaming mug of fragrant coffee. He's still in his lounging pants but has put on a T-shirt, much to my sorrow.

"Thanks." I inhale the pungent aroma and then take a bracing sip. "Good and strong, just as I like it."

"I'm not surprised." He smiles over the rim of his mug and then we have a moment of silence while we lean against the wood railing and look out over the woods.

"It is lovely up here," I tell him, breaking the silence that's not exactly uncomfortable, but I think we both have a hard time sharing emotional experiences. I've learned to use humor to mask insecurity or hurt, and I get the impression that Cody holds back his feelings too, but in a quiet, reserved way. After another moment of silence I decide I need to get him to open up, so as Daddy's taught me, I go for the direct approach. "Tell me what's on your mind."

He looks down at his coffee and is about to talk to me, when his phone rings. At first I think he's going to ignore it, but then he reaches into his pocket and pulls out his phone. Glancing down, he shakes his head but then says, "I might as well get this over with." Flicking me an apologetic glance, he says, "Excuse me."

I nod, even though I'm a bit disappointed.

"Hello, Marissa. No, I haven't been screening your calls. Yes, I know the bachelor auction is a week away. Okay." He nods but then rolls his eyes. "Yes, I will. Right. Tonight. Okay. Yes." He flips the phone shut. "Sorry. She gets wound up about these things."

"That's okay," I assure him. "I'm sure there's much more work and planning that goes into these charity events than most people realize." There, that was damned gracious.

Cody nods. "You're right about that. Marissa is good at what she does and probably doesn't get the credit she deserves."

I smile even though jealousy rears its ugly head. "Even though she can be a pain in the ass." My eyes widen and I put a hand to my mouth. "Did I say that out loud? With a lift of one shoulder I say, "Guess I shouldn't have missed that etiquette class."

Cody laughs. While he's tried to make it clear that he doesn't have feelings for Marissa, she's after him in a big way and just so happens to be everything I'm not. I remind myself that although last night was amazing and Cody seems to have growing feelings for me, I still need to be cautious. You can dress me up, but I'm still a little ole redneck farm girl. I should keep that in mind or I'm going to get myself in a heap of hurt. The gap between our worlds seems to be closing, but in so many ways we are still so very far apart.

"Now, back to our discussion," he begins, but his phone rings again. He looks down at the screen and then closes his eyes while shaking his head. I give him credit because he tries to ignore the call, but with an apologetic grimace he gives in and answers the phone. "Dad, what's up?" He rakes his fingers through his hair and says, "I know the meeting was important. Okay. I know that too." He turns from me and he doesn't know it, but this is a telltale sign that makes my heart sink. He paces while he talks, and the relaxed expression he wore this morning while leaning against the door frame has been replaced with a frown. It suddenly hits me like a sucker punch that this is his life . . . and I'm not sure that he *can* change any more than I can alter who I am.

Ohmigod. I swallow hard when a lightbulb goes off in my head.

I don't want to change. The shoes, the purse, the designer clothes that cost the earth . . . are so not me. And never will be. Bringing the mug to my mouth, I take a sip of warm coffee in an effort to dislodge the lump that lodges in my throat. I look over at Cody with a sense of loss and sadness. Although we have something special between us, I still don't see how I could ever be the type of woman he ultimately needs in his life. "Well, damn," I say beneath my breath.

But I suddenly know what I need to do . . . what I want to accomplish but have never had the time or opportunity to do so. While Cody talks to his father and then to someone else, I sip my coffee while a plan forms in my mind. I know what I need to do. Now I have to muster up the courage and take action.

By the time Cody wraps up another business conversation, my mug is empty. "Sorry," he apologizes with a small smile. He seems distracted and a little upset.

"Cody, it's late. I should let you work."

He looks at my face in a searching way. My heart pounds with the hope that he'll protest and tell me he's blown off all of his meetings and whatever else he had to do in order to spend the day with me. "I have some things I need to attend to, Jolie. But I still want to have our talk."

"Okay." I muster up a shaky smile, but the phone calls seemed to have broken the spell we were under. Reality has intruded into our magical night of unbelievable passion.

He takes a step toward me. "There are some business issues I just have to attend to."

I wave a dismissive hand. "I understand."

He looks at me as if he's going to say something more but doesn't.

"Listen, do you have some regular-style boxers that would work as shorts for me? I don't want to come home in the dress I wore last night, ya know?"

"Sure. I'll round something up and a smaller shirt too."

"Thanks." When I hand him my coffee mug, our fingers brush and again I feel the familiar tingle at his mere touch. When he looks at me a bit startled, I have to wonder if he feels it too.

But just a few minutes later I'm in his Audi and he's taking me home. I notice that he's dressed for business, making me feel silly sitting here in his boxers, even though they are soft and comfy. Music fills the slightly awkward silence and although the wind is in my hair, the magic from last night is gone. Cody seems preoccupied, distant, and my heart sinks.

It isn't until we're almost to my house that I realize I've left my dress and shoes behind. Wiggling my toes I look down at my feet and have to laugh.

"What?" Cody asks, and seems relieved to hear my laughter.

I shake my head. "Seems I've left my shoes and dress at your place."

"I'll get them back to you."

"No hurry," I tell him. He gives me a troubled look that I can't quite read.

"I doubt I'll ever wear those shoes again," I admit, even though it was worth it to get the erotic foot massage. I leave that part out. "I won't be needing them any time soon, I'm sure." Like never.

Cinderella, it seems, has turned back into a redneck.

Oh well, it was bound to happen.

It's awkward again when he pulls to a stop in my driveway. He kills the engine and turns off the radio. After a moment of weirdness, I decide that if this isn't going to go beyond last night, I want to have closure . . . and one last kiss.

"Cody, about last night."

He looks at me with question and what seems like anticipation.

I swallow, lick my lips, and then say, "It was amazing."

"Jolie—"

"And I don't regret it." I pause because the next part is hard to say, but when I open my mouth he puts a finger to my lips.

"I want to see you again," he says firmly. "You know that, right?"

I nod. I also know it will never work, but I can't get the words past my lips.

"Good." He seems so relieved that I can't finish what I should say.

I put a hand on his arm. "I know you're in a rush. I can let myself out."

He doesn't seem to like the idea but nods. "Okay. I'll call you," he promises.

I nod again and then, because I might never feel his touch, his kiss, I lean over and press my lips to his . . . just briefly, but I feel it all the way to my bare toes. "Bye, Cody."

21

A Long Time Coming

Without looking back I hurry to the garage and punch in the key code. Thankfully Daddy's truck isn't there and the house is quiet. I'm chock-full of emotion, but I rush up the stairs, hoping to hold off crying until I reach my bedroom. I'm doing fine until I encounter Rufus in my room. When I see his sad face I promptly burst into noisy tears.

"Whoof!" He gives me a where-have-you-been-and-what-the-hell-is-wrong-with-you? look.

"Nothin'," I tell him with a loud sniff. I hardly ever cry because my daddy could never handle my tears, so I learned how to keep them in. I guess it's been building for a long time because it's as if the floodgates are bursting. "I'm f-f-f-f-fine!"

"Woof! Woof!" He isn't buying it.

I flop down onto the bed with my arms flung to my sides and stare up at the ceiling fan until it makes me feel kind of dizzy. I sniff and swallow, trying to get myself under control. "This is stupid," I grumble. After a shaky intake of breath I think I have the tears at bay. In fact, I'm not even exactly sure why I'm crying . . .

Oh yeah, I'm crying because even though I've been learning manners and fashion and all that good stuff, I know I'll never be happy wearing outlandishly expensive clothing and designer shoes that pinch my feet. I miss fishing, four-wheeling, poker, and pig roasts. Summer means softball and corn hole, not stuffy lawn parties in fancy-ass dresses.

"Well . . . hell!" Hot tears slip from beneath my eyelids and slide down my temples into my ears. Rufus barks. "I'm okay!" I gurgle since tears are welling up and pooling in my throat. I know I should sit up, get control of myself, and calm my dog.

But I don't.

I lie there and cry.

Rufus finally breaks the rules and tries to jump up onto the bed, but his short legs won't cooperate. He whines and is able to put his front paws on the edge of the mattress and gaze pleadingly at me. "Oh . . . okay." I lean over and with a grunt I heft him up onto the bed with me. "Don't get used to it. You know I don't like dog hair in my bed and slobber on my pillow."

Rufus flops down next to me and gives me a wheezing sigh. I absently pet him while thinking about everything. Finally, after my tear ducts are bone-dry, I clear my throat and sit up. You know where we need to go," I tell him. "To the shed."

"Woof!" His ears perk up since he knows what it means, and he scrambles to the edge of the bed but looks down with fear in his droopy eyes.

"It must suck to have such short legs," I tell him with a gurgled laugh. "Here you go." I help him to the floor. I should change from Cody's boxers and T-shirt, but I suddenly don't have the energy. A masochistic side of me seems to want the torture of wearing his aftershave-scented. clothes. I know. I'm a glutton for punishment.

"Come on, Rufus." I head down the stairs and pause in the kitchen to snag a bottle of water for him and an Ale-8-One from the fridge. The only soft drink bottled and brewed in Kentucky, it was my mama's favorite. She wouldn't drink anything else, and I have to admit that the sweet fizzy drink with a hint of citrus and ginger is still a favorite of mine too. The unique recipe is supposed to be a closely guarded secret. Like Mama, I prefer my Ale-8-One in the bottle. Grabbing one, I pause to take a sweet, cold swig. The familiar taste is soothing and as always, reminds me of my mother.

"Come on, Rufus. You know where we're goin'."

"Whoof!" He trots after me past the pool and into the back part of the property toward the tool shed, one of the only remaining reminders of our old farm. Tears again well up. I swallow hard to control them, take another cooling swig of my soft drink, and open the door. I pull the string for the overhead lights and leave the door open for more light and fresh air. The old windows crank open and there's an oscillating fan that stirs up the musty air. After pouring water into a bowl I keep out here for that purpose, beneath an old coffee can I locate the key that opens an old cedar chest. I look at the small key connected to a blue ribbon that was mine as a child and stare at it for an emotional moment.

"It's been too long since I've been back here," I whisper to Rufus, but I'm really talking to my mother, and myself too. While Rufus laps up his water I slide the key in the lock and listen to the scratchy creak as it unlocks.

When I open the lid, as always, my heart lodges in my throat. This is where I keep the dozens of sketches for my mother's nighttime stories that I've drawn over the years. Then, with shaking fingers I pick up the letter from the publisher who wants to buy them.

I sent off several of the books when finances got so tough that we needed extra income just to make ends meet. After several rejections, the letter of acceptance came just before we sold the farm. Because we then no longer needed the money, I wasn't sure whether I wanted to sell Mama's stories or just keep them close to my own heart. But now I wonder if the offer still stands. If so, I now know what I hope to do.

I want to have the stories published in my mama's honor, but the difference is that now I want all of the proceeds from my end to go to charities benefiting needy kids . . . oh, how my mother would love that!

With trembling fingers, I sit down and open a book. My hand immediately goes to my mouth when I look down at the pages. We didn't have air-conditioning in the farmhouse, so on hot summer nights my bedroom windows would remain open. The nocturnal sounds of various animals used to scare the pants off me, so my mama would lie down beside me and give the hoot owls and the raccoons and coyotes cute names and personalities. Suddenly Harley the Hoot Owl, Robbie the Raccoon, and Casey the Coyote weren't frightening at all. Mama had to have been exhausted after a long day of farm work, yet she never complained, never scolded.

She simply loved.

"Tell me again, Mama!" Even now, as I open a book of sketches and read the story I can hear her soft, soothing voice. I remember slipping my small hand into her hardworking, calloused grasp and a sense of peace settling over me. At first, I didn't want to share her with the world, but these stories need to be read, shared . . . treasured.

As I turn the pages I realize that my sketches aren't sleek and professional, but the editor said they had an honest quality that was charming and beautiful. He wanted to keep the sketches raw and untouched. The writing, he said, was simple and easy for a child to understand and relate to, but with subtle humor that would entertain the parents reading the stories to their children.

"Ah, Rufus, I hope I haven't waited too doggone long." I know my time frame. I hope to have a substantial check for the Cottonwood Charity Ball to give in my mother's honor. I want to make my father proud and to show the upper-crust Copper Creek neighbors that there is more to us than meets the eye. "In other words, Rufus, I'd better get on the stick."

After carefully returning the book to the stack, I keep the letter so I can muster up the nerve to call the editor. When the key is back beneath the coffee can, I sit down to finish my soft drink.

I also know that after the Cottonwood ball I need to move out on my own. I've been thinking about it lately and I know it's time.

"Okay, Rufus, let's go. We've got us some work to do."

22

Deal . . . or No Deal?

I'm so busy that the next week passes in a blur. Simplicity Publishing is thrilled and so enthusiastic when I contact them that I know my decision to sell Mama's stories is the right one. They adore the idea that I will be giving my end to charity and promise to get the books published as fast as possible and to get behind the project with a big Christmas push!

I haven't told anyone except for Carletta, but the news is bubbling up inside me so much that I have a difficult time sitting still.

"Jolie!" Miss Abigail warns while we practice dinner table etiquette. "Please stop fidgeting with your silverware."

Pressing my lips together so the news doesn't spill out, I nod sheepishly. "Sorry."

"You're supposed to be engaging in polite conversation, but your mind seems to be elsewhere." She rolls her hand up in the air as if my thoughts are somewhere up there.

"Everything okay with you, baby doll?" Daddy asks, and they both look at me with a measure of concern.

God, I so want to tell them!

"I'm fine."

Miss Abigail and my daddy exchange a look. "Wyatt?" She gives him a pleading tell-her expression and they suddenly have my full attention.

Daddy's cheeks flush, but he nods and then says, "Baby doll, I have something to announce."

I put my hand to my chest. Are they going to move in together? Get married? Holy cow, is Miss Abigail pregnant? My heart thuds.

"Wyatt, do you want me to tell Jolie?" Miss Abigail asks gently.

"No . . . no." He shakes his head.

"Daddy?"

He clears his throat and then announces, "Abby and I are . . . dating."

"Oh." After my wayward thoughts this is a little disappointing.

"Does that upset you?" Daddy asks, obviously mistaking my dull response for uneasiness.

"Oh, good heavens, no!" I assure him, totally ignoring the polite-conversation rules of using my indoor voice. "This is wonderful news. And to be honest, I saw it coming a while ago." To prove my point I jump up and give Miss Abigail a big hug. She, in turn, totally disregards her prim and proper rules and we hug while hopping in a circle as if we're on a grade school playground.

Daddy shakes his head. "You two look plain silly," he says gruffly, but when I glance his way there are tears swimming in his eyes.

"Oh, hush up and get over here," I tell him, and suddenly we're all three hugging like . . . a family. And it feels good.

"I'm so relieved," Miss Abigail says with a sniff.

"Told you it would be okay," Daddy tells her.

"I know!" she admits, "but I wanted to be sure."

I like her even more because my feelings matter so much to her, and I give her another reassuring squeeze. "Oh my goodness! Miss Abigail!"

"What?"

I look down and then back up at her. "You're barefoot!"

She looks down at her perfectly manicured toes and then grins at me. "Shoes, I've come to discover, are overrated."

"I hear ya!" I hold up my hand for a high five.

Daddy grins at her. "Do ya know that Abby can cast a line like a pro?"

When I raise my eyebrows at her she shrugs but blushes at his compliment. "After countless hours of your patient instruction," she says to him.

Daddy holds his index finger and thumb a couple of inches apart. "I'm this close to gettin' her to bait the hook."

She wrinkles her nose. "We'll see about that one." But then she turns her attention to me. "Thanks for being so sweet. It means the world to me."

Daddy looks at her with adoring eyes.

"You know," she says with a shake of her head, "I've been trying so hard to find a way back into this society that I was booted out of, and now I realize so many of them are"— she leans forward—"ass-hats."

Ass-hat is one of my daddy's favorite expressions, but coming from Miss Abigail it has me laughing so hard that I just might pee my pants. "Oh, dear lord." When I get my laughter under control I say, "You got that right." I inhale a deep breath. "But I've found there are some good people too . . . You just have to sift through the ass-hats."

Miss Abigail does her tinkling laugh that has Daddy smiling. "True. I just had to get rid of the chip on my shoulder to find that out. I have your father to thank for that."

"Oh, Abby . . ." He leans in and suddenly we're hugging again.

"Hey! How come I wasn't asked to join in on this hug fest?" Carletta asks as she enters the kitchen. She had been working hard on a press release for me. She stands there for a second with her hands on her hips while tapping her toe.

"Get over here, princess," Daddy says, and urges her with an outstretched arm.

"That's more like it," Carletta says with a grin. "I would ask what's going on, but of course I've been listening."

When she joins our circle I give her an elbow while laughing at her honesty. "So, what took you so long?"

"Are you kidding? I wanted to give you your privacy, for goodness' sake."

We all laugh and hug, and I think to myself that this is one of the happiest moments I've experienced in a long time.

"What do you say we blow off this lesson and hang out by the pool?" Daddy asks Miss Abigail.

"Excellent suggestion, Wyatt." She turns to us. "Girls?"

Carletta gives me a questioning rise of her eyebrows.

"Are you finished with everything for the day?" I ask her.

"Pretty much," she says with a nod.

"Then let's head for the pool." When she looks uncomfortable with my suggestion I say, "You can make up for lost time later if you need to."

After glancing at his watch Daddy says, "I have a bachelor auction rehearsal at six o'clock."

"Oh, Wyatt!" Carletta puts her hand to her mouth. "I'm sorry if I got you roped into that."

Daddy waves a dismissive hand her way. "Naw, it'll be fun to have women fighting over me."

Miss Abigail clears her throat.

"Um, I mean it will be fun when Abby wins the bid." He jams his hands in his pockets and rocks back on his feet. "Course you might have to dig deep in your pockets," he teases.

"I'll break open my piggy bank," she responds dryly.

"You better have more than one," he shoots back, and they banter back and forth as they leave the kitchen, completely forgetting about Carletta and me.

"They are too cute. They just crack me up," I tell Carletta. "Hey, speaking of the bachelor auction, we will *not* let Marissa win the bid for Brett or Cody. Deal?"

Carletta frowns. "I'm not comfortable spending your money, Jolie."

"Oh no you don't. Think of it as working for me, if you have to. Sky's the limit, okay? Do *not* back down."

"If you win the date with Cody you have to go, Jolie." I groan.

Carletta shakes her head. "I don't get it. Why are you blowing him off? He's obviously into you." She puts her hands on my shoulders. "And I can tell by the look on your face that you're in love with him. Don't even try to deny it."

I lean against the high back of the oak chair for support. "Okay, I fully admit I love him. But Carletta, I'm not what he wants or needs in a . . . wife. He needs someone to host dinners and cocktail parties. To parade around in designer clothing. I tried all of that and it's fun, but it isn't me." I shake my head sadly. "We just don't have a future and it's too painful to date him knowing that."

"You don't know jack."

I look down at the floor. "Oh, but I'm afraid I do. Now that Daddy has found happiness and I've sold Mama's stories, I have a sense of purpose . . . a reason for all of this money that I couldn't get comfortable with." Closing my eyes, I swallow hard. "It's time that I move out from under Daddy's roof and live my own life."

"Jolie . . ."

I put up a hand. "I'll win Cody at the auction. And I'll go out to dinner with him as closure."

"What about the charity ball?"

"I want you to go with Brett."

"Jolie!" She draws my name out and puts her hands on her hips.

"Yes, Carletta. I plan on showing up late by myself and giving Marissa the check in Mama's honor."

"And then you're leaving?"

I nod. "Keep this under your hat, but Daddy's got a little fishing camp up by Sun Rock Lake. I'm going to spend some time up there while I figure things out. I think I might build a log cabin or something like that. I've been eyeing some property near there overlooking the water." I shrug. "The marina is getting pretty run-down. If Daddy's on board I'm even thinking about making an offer to buy the place. We could turn it around. I could see Daddy running it and maybe giving fishin' lessons."

Carletta taps her index finger to her cheek. "Hmmm, I

think you might have a connection with a developer." She arches one eyebrow, but I shake my head.

"I'm thinking about log cabins. More like a fishing camp or retreat. Dean Development wouldn't be interested in anything like that. But like me, Daddy needs a purpose . . . He can't remain idle. It simply isn't him. I think he would love this idea. I've just got to spend a few days up there and walk the lake . . . do some sketches."

"When have you been doing all of this thinking?" Carletta asks.

"At night when I try to sleep." I shake my head. "I've been having insomnia lately." In fact, the last time I peacefully slept through the night was with Cody, but I'm not about to give Carletta that information.

"You're crazy, you know. Cody loves you."

"I entertain him and we have chemistry, that's for sure." I shrug. "He's never said that he loves me though, Carletta."

"I can see it in his eyes when he looks at you, Jolie," she insists. "He adores you."

"But it doesn't matter if I'm not right for him." When it looks like she's going to argue, I shake my head while gripping the chair harder. "Don't you see? There's no reason to move forward with something that's never going to work in the end. It would be too painful."

"Ah, now I know what's going on here. You're afraid."

"I'm not afraid," I insist even though she's nailed me. "Just realistic. My stint as redneck Cinderella is nearly over."

"Um, Jolie, you're forgetting something here."

"What?"

"Cinderella lived happily ever after."

I swallow the doggone lump that keeps lodging in my

throat. "Except this time the shoe doesn't fit. I'm Justin Boots, not Kate Spade high heels."

Carletta fists her hands on her hips again, but this time leans forward too. "Jolie Russell, you're as stubborn as an old mule. But I've said my piece. The rest is up to you."

"Let's forget about all this and go for a swim. Oh, and by the way, you'll still be my personal assistant. I need someone now more than ever with the books being published."

"Oh, I'll work my tail off as your publicist and anything else you need. We'll learn as we go and I'll work hard in school, but I'm a quick study . . . and of course I'll have you looking great at book signings!" Carletta hesitates as if she wants to say more about Cody but then nods. "Okay. I'll shut up about Cody Dean. For now."

"Thank goodness! There are swimsuits out in the pool house. Let's go round some up."

"Okay," Carletta says a bit glumly as we head out the door. "It's just that—"

"Carletta! Give it up. Please. Let's talk about your love life instead. Things seem to be heating up with you and Brett."

She rolls her eyes. "I don't know. I think he still has this thing for Marissa."

"Then that boy's just plain stupid."

Carletta laughs and we pause to high-five, but then she frowns.

"What?"

"He doesn't know that up until now I was just a maid."

"And you think that matters to Brett?"

Carletta shrugs.

"So you don't practice what you preach?"

"Apparently not, but I'll make a deal with you."

"Why don't I like the sound of this?" I ask as we enter the pool house.

"It's not that bad," Carletta says as she goes through my bathing suit drawer. "Don't you own anything but tiny bikinis?"

"Put one on!"

"Right! I don't have your skinny-ass body."

"I'm not a skinny-ass and you'd look amazing in one of these."

"I'm going to hit you."

"You don't give your curves enough credit." I toss her a more modest red two-piece.

While holding it up she wrinkles her nose. "Okay, back to my deal. I'll make sure I win the bid for Brett if you bid on Cody. But we have to go through with the date. Okay?"

"I already said I would."

"But give him a chance, okay? None of this closure crap."

"Carletta . . ."

She raises her eyebrows. "Deal or no deal?"

I groan. "Okay . . . *okay!* Deal."

23

"Holding Out for a Hero"

I look around the pre–bachelor auction cocktail party with a sense of wonder. "Okay, so Marissa is a genius," I begrudgingly comment to Carletta and Miss Abigail, who now wants me to call her Abby. Even though she's dressed in a classy black sleeveless dress with pearls at her throat, there is a softness that makes *Abby* now suit her . . . even though I keep forgetting.

Carletta nods in agreement. "She sure pulled this all together in no time and I have to admit the movie hero theme rocks." The country club ballroom has been tastefully decorated in black and gold. A raised platform with a catwalk is at the end of the room and rows of chairs have been set up in place of tables. We each have a heart-shaped paddle to raise as we bid.

"Do you know who Daddy is dressed up like?" I ask Miss Abigail, I mean Abby.

"He wouldn't tell me." She rolls her eyes but then grins. "But I found a whip and a hat."

"Indiana Jones?" Carletta guesses, and Abby nods.

"I believe so."

"I have no idea who Cody is going to be," I admit.

"You would if you hadn't avoided his calls," Carletta accuses with a wag of her finger.

I take a cheese puff offered by a passing waiter and then pop it in Carletta's mouth. She wrinkles her nose at me but has to shut up and chew. "I've been busy," I remind her, which is true, and she of all people knows it. The publication of Mama's books is going full speed ahead but I had no idea how much work it would entail. I love it, though, and I can't wait to see the finished product on the bookshelf.

I snag a stuffed mushroom stabbed with a fancy toothpick and carefully take a bite so that I don't get anything on my little black dress that Carletta insisted I purchase during another shopping excursion that made my head spin. Delicate gold hoop earrings match my thin gold bracelets that tinkle together on my wrist. I'm wearing my mama's heart-shaped pendant necklace that has a way of calming me down whenever I reach up and touch it. Simple and yet chic is how Carletta described my outfit. In keeping with simplicity she clipped my hair into a sleek ponytail at the nape of my neck but then flipped it over one shoulder. I have to admit that I like it even though I whined about how long it took her to flatiron my hair into submission.

"You two look amazing," Abby comments.

"And so do you," responds Carletta, whose hair is bigger and her dress a little lower cut than mine. "You have such a classic sense of style, but you make it seem effortless." She shakes her head in adoring wonder.

Abby puts her index finger to her lips. "Shh, it's certainly not without a tremendous amount of effort," she admits. We all three laugh but then turn our attention to the stage when the lights dim and Marissa makes a dramatic entrance. She's wearing a deep red evening gown that matches her deep red smile.

"Good evening, ladies! Welcome to the Cottonwood Country Club's first annual bachelor auction! Would you all please take your seats." She waits while we sit down in our chairs and then continues. "As you know, all, and I do mean *all* of the proceeds from the auction will benefit the Cottonwood Botanical Gardens and provide additional funding for the extensive project that will include a greenhouse and bird blind for our area schools!"

After another round of applause, Carletta whispers in my ear, "That girl can work it."

"Don't I know it," I whisper back.

"Now, y'all have a paddle like this one." She holds hers up. "And yes, ladies, when the auctioneer takes over, I too will be bidding on these most eligible men. You didn't think I would get left out of the fun, did you?" she coos, and is it my imagination or is she looking right at me? "So dig deep into those purses, okay ladies?"

Carletta and I glance at each other and nod.

"Our bachelors have arrived via limo from Caston's Costume Shop, where they have been outfitted as our most exciting action movie heroes!" The song "Holding Out for A Hero" plays ever so softly in the background. "Then, after you have a chance to read their profiles in the brochures that you will find on your seats, which by the way, were generously donated by Dean Development, the second round will begin! Our handsome bachelors, dressed to kill in tuxedos, will come back out on stage, and ladies . . . you'll get to know them just a little bit better! Then dig deep and bring out the plastic, because shortly after that the bidding will begin!" After some whoops and catcalls from a few overly excited women who have been drinking, she continues. "The winners will be whisked away via limo to various area fine-dining spots highlighted in your brochures. Each of you will bet on a certificate to dine at one of them. Again, all of the restaurants have donated the dinners, but please tip your servers accordingly. That's all they've requested in return for the generous gift!" After more applause Marissa holds a silencing palm up in the air. "Did you hear that?"

The buzzing of conversation and laughter stops.

"Oh no!" Marissa pauses and cups her hand to her ear. "Did you hear . . . *thunder?*" When her eyes widen, a hush falls over the crowd . . . Marissa's ability to control a room full of women who have imbibed a few cocktails is impressive. "What's going on?" she asks when a sudden breeze kicks up, fluttering the curtain and blowing out over the rapt audience. "Everybody stay calm!"

I look at Carletta, who widens her eyes and shrugs her shoulders. Even Miss Abigail, I mean *Abby*, seems enthralled. Thunder rumbles in the distance followed by lightning crackling on the midnight blue curtain directly behind Marissa. The thunder rumbles louder and then louder still. The lights suddenly go out completely and lightning flashes like strobe lights in the background.

"Ladies!" Marissa shouts into the microphone. "I do believe a storm is brewing . . . and oh my goodness!"

"It's raining men!"

The pitter-patter of rain begins and then slides into the Weather Girls' old-school disco song. The lights come up and the curtain parts, revealing a stage full of bachelors in movie hero costumes.

"Everybody up!" Marissa shouts, and soon all the

ladies are on their feet dancing and singing the lyrics, "It's raining men! Hallelujah!"

Abby surprises me by doing the bump with Carletta; I have to admit I thought this would be stuffy and boring, but boy was I wrong. While the song blasts, the bachelors strut their stuff one by one down the catwalk. Daddy is dressed as Indiana Jones. When he gets right in front of us he cracks his whip, making us laugh.

We see the likes of Zorro, Batman, and Neo from *The Matrix*. I elbow Carletta when Brett saunters down the catwalk as Captain Jack Sparrow. He gives her a Johnny Depp wink as he pivots and flips his braids and dreadlocks. Someone got roped into Robin Hood in tights. Will Turner musters up a big cheer . . . and then, ohmigod, it's Cody looking suave in a dark suit. At first I don't know who he is until I spot the martini glass in his hand. "Bond," Carletta says in my ear, "James Bond, and damned sexy!"

My heart beats faster when he looks down from the catwalk and makes eye contact with me. Suddenly, I need to be a Bond girl. Of course, it's readily apparent that I'm not the only one in the audience with the same desire nor am I the only one with money . . .

"You are not going to lose the bid for him," Carletta says in such a determined tone that I have to laugh.

"Not on your life." I lean over to Abby. "We have to win Daddy too!"

She grins and pulls a gold credit card out of her purse. "Your father gave me strict instructions."

"Then do whatever it takes!" When she gives me an expression of indecision I remind her, "This is for a good cause." Then I add for good measure, as if I know all about such things, "And a tax write-off. So keep that in mind."

"I will," Abby promises. She looks so serious about the situation I have to smile. When I think of the unusual circumstances through which she came into our lives, it's truly amazing. I should thank Brett for suggesting that she polish up Daddy and me. But when I look at her radiant face beaming with happiness, I have to wonder who taught whom the most.

"Okay, ladies, here's one last look at our dashing soon-to-be dates," Marissa announces while "It's Raining Men" fades into "Holding Out for a Hero." "Take some notes while our bachelors take one more quick walk before changing into their evening date attire."

When Cody walks back down the catwalk and does a snazzy little turn, saluting his martini glass in the air, I'm miffed at the *ohhs* and *aaahs* from the crowd and have this sudden urge to stand up and shout, *He's mine, so back off.* But then I remind my jealous self he's not mine and that if I win the bid, this will have to be our last date. Bummer. There'd just be no use dragging anything out between us.

Panic wells up in my throat at the thought of losing him forever and for a glorious moment I tell myself I'm crazy for not giving it a shot. I smile, relieved, but then I look around at the designer dresses. Expensive perfume lingers in the air and I know with absolute certainty that this lifestyle is not me and never will be.

This is Cody Dean's world. Not mine. When I try to picture him in worn Wranglers and slinging mud on a four-wheeler I just can't . . .

So, I'll give myself tonight and then move my life in a direction that's no longer pointless but that makes me proud. With that in mind I glance at the glowing faces of

Carletta and Abby and decide to make this a night to remember.

"Ladies!" Marissa says loudly so as to be heard over the laughter and chatter. "May I introduce Randy Wade, our auctioneer?"

Randy steps forward and tips his black Stetson.

"Sorry, ladies, he's not up for bid this evening." A good-natured moan ripples through the audience even though Randy's belly laps over his big silver belt buckle. Marissa holds up her palm in an effort to quiet the crowd. "But Randy has graciously donated his professional services, so let's give him an appreciative round of applause!" When the clapping fades Marissa announces, "Okay, let the bidding begin!"

"Macho Man" is piped through the speakers while colorful spotlights swirl and flash. Then one by one the bachelors enter the stage, this time decked out in black tie. My daddy looks so dashing that I just have to put my fingers to my mouth and give a whistle so that he knows it's his crazy daughter. When Abby looks at me I think she is going to give me a stern don't-do-that frown, but instead she laughs and slaps me a high five before giving Daddy a shrill whistle of her own.

Carletta laughs but then puts her hand to her chest when Brett walks our way. "Damn, he's looking fine," she says in my ear.

"You got that right." My whistle, it seems, broke the ice and the crowd of uppity ladies gets a little rowdy. But when Brett gets some catcalls and whistles, Carletta's eyes narrow. Since I know how she feels I give her knee a sympathetic pat. "I got your back," I whisper in her ear, and she laughs.

Daddy and I have been to several auctions, so I think I'm prepared for the action . . .

I couldn't have been more wrong.

Paddles are hefted in the air as soon as the previous Zorro, whose real name is James Proctor, is introduced. When he arches one eyebrow and unbuttons his tux, the ladies go wild. After he struts the catwalk he stops to pivot, and you would have thought he were Jon Bon Jovi the way the women are reacting. Paddles are hefted into the air and Randy Wade is having a difficult time keeping up with the bids. My eyes widen at Carletta. Bidding on farm equipment did not prepare me for this. I get so caught up in the moment that I raise my paddle to up the bid to five hundred dollars!

"Are you crazy?" Carletta elbows me and hisses in my ear, "What are you doing?"

I shake my head and look at my paddle as if it has a mind of its own. "Danged if I know."

"You don't want to have dinner with Zorro, do you?"

I shake my head. "No."

"Then put your paddle down!"

Yikes! Luckily I'm outbid. While the next two bachelors are auctioned off, I hold my paddle in my lap and watch the pandemonium. Then I get so excited when Daddy walks out on stage that I raise my paddle. Carletta prods me again and Abby laughs. I shrug my shoulders and have to feel proud when the ladies go crazy for my daddy, who is looking dashing in his black tux. The white collar of his starched shirt shows off his tan, and when he pauses at the end of the catwalk and winks, the ladies cheer! Bidding goes crazy, but Abby hangs in there. Her eyes narrow at a big-haired blonde directly across from

us who seems determined to win my daddy. Judging by
the diamonds dripping at her throat, she can afford it.

"Don't let up," I tell Abby when the bidding reaches
one thousand dollars. When she balks I lift her hand in
the air for her. Daddy, I notice, is eating this up with a
spoon and preening like a proud peacock.

"I'm going to kick his butt," Abby grumbles. That
sounds so funny coming from her that I toss my head
back and laugh. Daddy, ever the ham, lifts his hand and
runs his fingers through his hair, raising the bid another
hundred. When Abby catches his eye she lowers her paddle as if she's done bidding, and he immediately sobers.
Then, walking over to our side of the stage, he blows her
a kiss.

She rolls her eyes and raises her paddle high. She
closes the bidding when she ups the bid by five hundred
dollars and wins my daddy for a date when she's already
won his heart. But instead of getting angry, Daddy laughs
and blows her another kiss. This time she blows him a
kiss back, drawing a big cheer from the crowd.

"Your father is a hoot," Carletta comments with a giggle. "Not to mention charismatic and cute in a John
Schneider kind of way, and John Schneider, by the way,
looks even better than when he was Bo Duke. No wonder
the women are going nuts." She taps her chest. "I knew I
was right." With a laugh she leans her shoulder against
mine and gives me a little shove.

I have to admit that Carletta's right. It's fun to see
Daddy up there in the limelight enjoying his fifteen minutes of fame. With a sigh, I reach up and touch Mama's
locket and feel a bittersweet pang of joy.

Abby smiles when she wins the bid at two thousand
and then turns to me and swipes fake sweat from her

brow. "Whew! Glad that's over. Of course, I don't know if your daddy's swelled head will even fit into the limo," she grumbles, but I can tell she's secretly pleased that all the ladies wanted him too. "Marissa will be eating crow on that one," Abby adds with a sly smile. "Ha!"

I groan inwardly at the mention of Marissa's name. Up until now I had forgotten all about her, but I just know she's going to bid on Cody and maybe Brett too. I look around and spot her checking off things on a notepad, but when Brett's name is called, her blond head snaps up and the stage has her full attention. "Get ready to rumble," I tell Carletta, who is poised with her paddle.

Brett looks bodacious in a black, three-button, single-breasted notch with a satin lapel. His vest is a very light pastel green that adds a splash of color. Although his hair is slicked back, he has a dark five o'clock shadow, giving him a dangerous bad-boy edge that has several women using their heart-shaped paddles as fans. Carletta blinks up at him, forgetting for a moment to bid until I nudge her with my elbow.

The bidding is fast and aggressive, making Randy Wade's voice announce at lightning speed. By the time Brett flashes a big grin at the end of the catwalk, the bidding is way over one thousand dollars. When Carletta looks nervous I give her elbow an upward lift.

"Ohmigod, Jolie! This is crazy."

"Go another hundred."

"No!" When she refuses, I raise my own paddle, but then Marissa raises the bid another fifty. I shoot a challenging glare her way and poke Carletta with my elbow.

Carletta responds and the bidding war is now between her and Marissa. A hush of anticipation falls over the previously noisy crowd. Whoever is doing the lighting kicks up the drama with a swirling spotlight sweeping the stage in large arcs.

"Fifteen hundred?" Randy rattles off, and Marissa raises her paddle. "Sixteen hundred? Sixteen fifty?" The crowd watches as if it's a tennis match. "Seventeen hundred? Seventeen fifty."

"Two thousand!" Marissa shouts, and all eyes then turn to Carletta who gives Randy a nod to twenty-one hundred. Marissa looks nervous and starts to raise her paddle, but with a negative shake of her head backs down. This means one thing to me: She's going after Cody.

Carletta turns to me. "This is insane."

"Yeah but that was fun!" When she shakes her head but appears relieved, I remind her, "It's a good cause."

"I know, but still!"

I angle my head toward the stage. "Look at him. He's worth every penny!"

"I hope so," she says, but then puts a hand to her mouth.

"You go, girl," I tell her, but then my attention is turned to the stage when Cody Dean, the final bachelor, is announced.

"This is going to be an all-out war," Abby warns me. "Not only is he the prince of Cottonwood but the last guy up for grabs, and I have a feeling Marissa planned it that way." She wags a finger at me. "Do not let her win."

"Don't worry," I answer, but my heart pounds hard. Marissa is a pro at this sort of thing and has a determined expression on her face when the bidding begins.

The competition for Cody is like a feeding frenzy with the paddles flapping in the air so aggressively that there is a cool breeze stirring up the room. Audrey Rose Mitchell and her friends are part of the fray, but when the bidding approaches three thousand, they start to drop like flies. Marissa, however, is tenacious, hanging in there like a bulldog.

I'm starting to feel kind of silly that I won't throw in the towel. Tossing around this kind of money is still hard for me, but I remind myself it's for a good cause and that I'm giving back . . . but still!

"Thirty-three hundred dollars going once, going twice!"

"Jolie!" Carletta and Abby both poke me at the same time. My palms sweat, but I raise my heart-shaped paddle.

"Thirty-five hundred!" My voice rings out, strong and determined.

Marissa glares.

I raise my chin a notch.

Her paddle inches up and then with a sigh she shakes her head at me as if I'm crazy.

"Woo-hoo!" Carletta cheers.

I shake my head and put the paddle in front of my face.

Abby laughs and pulls the paddle down. "Dress, three hundred dollars. Shoes? Ninety-five dollars. Cody Dean, thirty-five *hundred* dollars. The look on Marissa Clayton's face?"

"Priceless!" Carletta and Abby shout together.

Marissa, looking a little bit peeved, puts a smile on her face and heads up on stage. "Thank you, Randy, for a job well done. Ladies, let's give our auctioneer a big round of applause!" She stands back and waves her hand in a dramatic arc toward Randy Wade and then claps her hands.

"My pleasure," Randy booms into the microphone, and then tips his cowboy hat. "I think y'all need to give

Marissa here a show of appreciation too. She worked her little tail off."

Knowing that Randy is right, we all give her a loud round of applause.

Marissa waves a dismissive hand at Randy but beams with pride. "And now, one last look at our brave bachelors," she says with a deep red smile. "Guys, come on back out and take a bow!"

The colorful lights dip and swirl while "Holding Out for a Hero" plays softly in the background. The women applaud wildly while the bachelors line up and collectively bow as if they're at the end of a Broadway play. Daddy winks at Abby, who in turn blows him a kiss. I have to wonder if she's ever done such a thing in public before.

"Let's go collect our men!" Carletta says when the lights go bright.

"Yeah, baby!" I give Abby and then Carletta a high five and a big smile, but now that it's time for the actual date I'm a little nervous. Cody is in a tuxedo and we're going to an intimate, upscale restaurant that's bound to be romantic. I tell myself to be strong and not to give into an attraction that will only lead to heartbreak. Cody needs to know I no longer have the desire to fit in but rather to stand up, stand out, and be counted. My life has changed, but with the publication of Mama's stories I now have a sense of purpose and the confidence that goes with an accomplishment that will allow her memory to live on while raising money for underprivileged children.

The man I choose to spend the rest of my life with will have to accept me as I am . . . a fun-loving, hardworking little ole redneck and damned proud of it.

With that in mind I march up to Marissa and write her a big fat check before going on to claim my date.

24

A Rose by Any Other Name . . .

"I feel like I'm at the prom," Cody comments when we're required to stop for a photo.

"I never went," I admit, and then wish I hadn't.

He looks at me in surprise. "Why? I can't believe no one asked you."

I smile for the camera and after we walk away I tell him. "It's true. I was a total tomboy and didn't have a clue, and Daddy sure didn't either, bless his heart. Besides, we didn't have the money for a fancy dress anyway." I shrug as if it didn't mean anything to me even though I cried the night of my junior prom.

He leans next to my ear and says, "Well then, this can be your prom night." Oh, why does his voice have to be so deep and sexy and why does his warm breath have to make me tingle? Why? And why did he have to go and say something so danged sweet that I just want to kiss him? Why, why *why*?

"The ticket price was a little steep for a prom," I tell him with a roll of my eyes. "You woulda thought you were George Clooney or somethin'." Yeah, right, George has nothing on him. There, if only my sense of humor kicks into gear I'll be okay.

"I thought for a minute you were going to drop out of the bidding," he admits, and I try not to feel so good that he wanted me to win so badly.

I give him a nudge with my elbow. "Yeah right, you were hoping for Audrey Rose Mitchell. Admit it." I don't mention Marissa and he's smart enough not to either. Instead, he laughs as we head out the front of the mansion to the circular driveway, where the limos are waiting in an impressive line. I smile when I see Carletta getting into a white stretch limo with Brett.

When Daddy and Abby wave to us, Cody turns to me. "Are those two dating?"

"Yep, can you believe it?"

Cody's dark brows draw together. "What do you mean?"

"They come from very different backgrounds, Cody."

"That shouldn't matter," he says firmly. I nod as if in agreement but avoid his eyes. I'm saved from commenting further when the limo driver comes around and opens the door for us.

The interior is dark and cool. I slide onto the leather seat across the back and look around in wonder since I've never been in a limo before. Small lights lining the sides of the interior give off just enough illumination to make it seem cozy and intimate even though we can see the driver up front.

"What restaurant are we going to?" I ask as we pull away from the curb. "I forgot to look at the certificate."

Cody clears his throat. "Actually, I hope you don't mind, but I'm having dinner catered to us at my gazebo. Call me selfish, but I want to have you all to myself."

I angle my head in question. "But Cody, the gazebo is in the center of town."

"I have one in the side yard at my house."

My heart thumps hard. "Oh." He isn't going to make this easy on me.

Disappointment flickers in his blue eyes when he mistakes my dilemma. "If you'd rather not"—he looks down at the certificate—"we could go to Peppi's Italian Bistro."

"No, it's not that."

When Cody covers my hand with his, I try to keep my body and heart from reacting. "Then what is it, Jolie?"

I swallow hard and give him a small lift of my shoulders. How can I tell him I'm falling in love with him but know I'm never going to be the kind of woman he wants? I've known this for a while; yet I bid on a date with him and here I sit in a limo! Oh right, because I wanted closure. I'm an idiot. "Wait, so you were sure that I'd win the bid? Or were you going to do this romantic dinner for anyone?" I'm half teasing but curious too.

While scratching his chin he says, "Well, now that you mention it, I *was* hoping for Audrey Rose . . ."

"Sorry about your luck."

Cody laughs. "Well, keep this under your hat, but I have a confession to make."

I angle toward him on the leather seat. "What?"

His grin turns a little sheepish. "Yeah, I was sure."

"Oh, really now?"

"I told Marissa it was the only way I'd do the auction."

"Wait." My brows draw together. "You've lost me."

Cody nibbles on the inside of his cheek for a second as if he doesn't want to totally confess. "Marissa wasn't exactly bidding on me."

"Huh?"

"She was in a manner of speaking bidding *for* me. I told her to outbid anyone except for you . . . with my money of course. But that I would go to dinner with you and you only."

"Wait, but she bid against me."

He grins. "Yeah . . . she had a vested interest in doing that, didn't she?"

"Oh . . ." A lightbulb just went off in my head. "So she bumped up the bid a bit for the cause, but you two had a deal that I was going to have dinner with you even if she won. I get it now. I would tell you that you were wrong for doing such a thing, but it's for a good cause."

He arches an eyebrow. "And?"

I purse my lips but then confess. "Daddy had the same kind of deal going on with Abby, and I made sure that Carletta ended up with Brett. Are we all gonna burn in hell for our underhanded deeds?"

"For donating thousands of dollars to charity?"

"Okay, I feel better now."

Cody leans his head against the leather seat and laughs. "There isn't a person on this earth who I enjoy spending time with more than you, Jolie Russell. I hope you know that."

I smile, but a bittersweet feeling washes over me and sinks like a rock to my stomach.

"Ah . . . Jolie." When he reaches over and caresses my cheek with his fingertip, my heart turns over in my chest. "There's something going on in your head I need to know about. I can feel it. But would you do me a favor and just enjoy tonight?"

"Well, it *is* my prom."

Cody slides a fingertip beneath my chin in a gesture

I'm beginning to expect and love. "So, will you come to my gazebo and have a romantic dinner with me?"

"Why do I feel as if I'm in an episode of *The Bachelor*? Are you going to offer me a rose in the end?" I know I'm using humor as a shield, but it's my only defense. I want to give in to the moment and melt into his arms, but I'll regret it later for reasons I can't even begin to understand or explain.

Cody shakes his head. "I've caught bits and pieces of that show, so I know the premise." But then he gently tilts my head up. "Believe me, there's no other competition." His blue eyes aren't teasing but serious, and for a heart-stopping moment I think he might tell me he loves me. I hold my breath, knowing that if he says it, I'm a gonner. I'll wear Kate Spade shoes, diamond tennis bracelets, and host dinner parties.

And I'd be miserable.

"Cody, you're right. Let's just enjoy dinner, okay?"

He hesitates as if knowing something is wrong but then nods his head. "All right," he agrees. "So you're accepting my rose?"

"For tonight," I tell him softly.

For a moment he appears troubled by my response but then smiles as if he suddenly has a plan. "I'll take that as a yes."

"Cody . . ."

Ignoring my plea he says, "We're here."

"Oh!" I hadn't noticed how far we'd come. "So we are." The driver, who looks like Alfred from *Batman*, comes around and opens the door to assist us out. "Thank you."

"My pleasure, ma'am. Enjoy your evening. Sir." He turns to Cody and bows.

"Thank you." After Cody gives him what I'm sure is a hefty tip, he puts his hand to the small of my back and leads me to his side yard. There is indeed a white gazebo surrounded by thick, lush hostas and day lilies and deep pink azaleas laden with blossoms. To the left is a gurgling fountain, which feeds into a decorative pond full of colorful koi.

"This is lovely, Cody."

He smiles. "Yes, another part of my home that I never take the time to appreciate and enjoy." He grasps my hand and draws me closer to the pond. "That is, until now."

The thought sneaks into my brain that maybe Cody can change, much in the way Abby has with Daddy. But then I remember our night together and how his cell phone kept him occupied. When he missed the meeting with his father it was a major big deal. As much as Cody wants to stop and smell the roses, I don't know that he will . . . or even if he can, and I don't want to fall into false hope again.

As if reading my mind he wraps his arms around me from behind and hugs me close. At first I resist but then give in and lean against him. He kisses my head and then with a soft sigh he moves his mouth to my neck and lingers there until my eyes flutter shut and my head rests back on his shoulder.

"You smell good . . . taste delicious." His arm tightens around me and he continues to nuzzle my neck. "God, I've missed you."

"Me too," I whisper, but I feel as if a vise grip is squeezing my chest. My heart starts a major war with my brain:

This could work. Give it a shot, my heart tells me.

This is Cody Dean. He runs a major company and needs a corporate wife, my brain fires back.

He could kick back . . . learn to delegate.

Yeah, right . . . Cody? Not even . . .

It could happen! my heart insists.

But what if I give him my love and then lose him? my brain asks.

He won't die like your mama! my heart says.

You don't know that, answers my brain.

Don't live in fear, finishes my heart.

"Talk to me," Cody murmurs in my ear.

I swallow the moisture clogging my throat and squeeze my eyes shut. Then, after getting my emotions under control I say, "Let's have dinner, Cody. Enjoying the evening sounds like a good plan and I don't know about you, but I'm starving."

Cody goes very still but then says, "You're right." He kisses me briefly, "Let's eat."

I nod, hoping the food won't stick in my throat, but instead of leading me to the gazebo, Cody turns me around, lowers his head, and kisses me . . . softly, gently, sweetly, until I wrap my arms around his neck and sink into the kiss. He cups the back of my head and deepens the kiss until my ability to resist evaporates like raindrops on a hot summer sidewalk. With a sigh, I thread my fingers through his hair and give in . . .

A moment later he lifts me up into his arms and carries me across the lawn and to his front door. He fumbles with the lock and then suddenly we're inside his house. His long legs gobble up the distance to his bedroom, where he gently eases me to the bed. He stands there looking down at me in the hushed light of the room.

No words are spoken.

I watch while he removes his tuxedo jacket and carelessly lets it slide to the floor. He makes quick work of his vest, his tie, and then unbuttons his starched shirt. When his tanned chest appears against the white shirt, I think there couldn't be a sexier sight in the world. Unable to stop myself I come up to my knees and slide my hands up his bare skin and then press my mouth to the base of his throat. Pushing the stiff cotton aside I kiss his chest, letting his dark, silky hair tickle and tease my tongue.

With a quick intake of breath Cody slides the clasp from my ponytail and then, with a deep sigh, slides his fingers through my loose hair. When I lift my gaze to face him, he lowers his head and kisses me with such passion that I have to hold on to his shoulders for support. Then, after pulling his mouth from mine, he sends his shirt to join his vest and jacket, quickly followed by his pants. When he's standing before me in beautiful masculine splendor, I slide my hands everywhere . . . over his glutes, up his back to his wide shoulders. While watching his expression, I trail the tips of my fingers over his chest, down his torso, and over abs that tighten and ripple beneath my exploration. When the back of my hand barely grazes his erection, he inhales sharply. His eyes close when I close my hand around him . . . and oh, he feels so hot, silky smooth, and powerful.

His hand reaches behind me and unzips my dress. Gently, he pushes the fabric over my shoulders until my black bra is exposed. He swallows hard and then cups my breasts, letting his thumbs caress the soft swell spilling out over the lacy cups. My nipples tighten, and with trembling fingers I reach up and unsnap the front clasp.

"You are beautiful." His voice is barely audible, sounding like the rustle of sheets over bare skin. I swing my legs to the floor, holding on to him while he pushes my dress to join his tuxedo. I shimmy out of my panties and then press my skin to his.

God.

When my nipples graze his chest I'm filled with deep desire that slides like slippery hot fudge down my body. Cody scoops me up onto the bed, turns away briefly, and then, sheathed in a condom, joins me. When he glides his body over mine I reach up and wrap my arms around his neck. With a moan he dips his head and devours my mouth with a passionate kiss that has me arching up to press closer. Then, with one slick, powerful stroke he's buried deep, stealing my breath and capturing my heart.

Cody makes love to me thoroughly, tenderly, taking his time. Knowing this might never happen again, I savor his kiss, his caress, and each and every stroke. The passion builds slowly, making my release achingly, hauntingly bittersweet.

We doze wrapped in each other's arms and then finally have our dinner by the light of the moon. I'm wearing his boxers and T-shirt once again and he's in gym shorts and shirtless. Our fancy dinner is instead casual and easy, and I wish the night would never end . . .

Much later, when I'm sleeping in his arms, my heart whispers, *This doesn't have to end, you know*.

"I know," I mumble back.

"I love you." Wait. I know that deep, sexy voice.

My heart thumps hard and my eyes open wide. Did he just say what I think he said? "Cody?"

"Mmmm?" His arm tightens around my waist and he nuzzles my neck. I wait, but all I hear is even breathing.

I start to ask him again if he's awake, but it's obvious that he isn't. So . . . do I wake him? Then what? Ask if he just said that he *loves* me? I open my mouth but then clamp it shut. No way. I mean, what if he didn't say it? I could have been having a wishful-thinking dream. Or maybe Cody was dreaming? Or talking in his sleep?

Well . . . now what?

I decide that I'll have to just stay awake and find out if he actually talks in his sleep.

I listen to him breathing. I scratch my nose. Then my foot itches, but I don't want to scratch it and wake him, so I grit my teeth, hoping it will go away. But it gets worse, so I end up ever so lightly scraping my toenail over the itching spot on the instep of my foot. Ahhh . . . better.

My eyelids start to droop but then open wide when his hand brushes over my breast. A warm, tingly shot of desire makes me sigh and snuggle my butt closer. Maybe he'll wake up and make love to me.

Oh, stop, Jolie, I sternly tell myself. You wanted closure, remember? When a frustrated groan escapes me, Cody stirs but doesn't say anything, even though I hold my breath, listening really hard.

When he remains silently sleeping I start to relax again. God, it feels so good in his arms . . . and then a hot tear slides down my cheek. My brain reminds me that ending our relationship now is for the best. But my heart?

My heart is breaking . . .

25

Pillow Talk

"Could you be any grumpier?" Carletta complains as she zips up my strapless teal evening dress.

"I'm not grumpy."

She gives me a deadpan stare and then looks to Rufus for support.

"Woof!"

"See!" Carletta says.

"Oh, so now you can understand doggy talk too?"

"Apparently."

"Traitor," I accuse Rufus, but he's been none too happy about my recent move to this cabin overlooking Sun Rock Lake. I try not to think about the fact that Cody's big house is perched atop the ridge almost directly across the water, only miles away as the crow flies. "I know you're moonin' over Misty, but that little hussy has been cheating on you, Rufus!" I turn my attention back to Carletta. "Okay, so I'm a little on edge. We did copy edits all week and may I remind you I just talked my daddy into sinking more than a million dollars into this here run-down lake and marina."

"It's an awesome idea. I've never seen your daddy so excited."

"But what if it flops?"

She puts reassuring hands on my bare shoulders. "It won't. Especially if you get Dean Development involved."

I give her a look.

"I'm just sayin'."

I nod, but panic wells up in my chest and squeezes so hard that I find it hard to breathe . . . oh wait, it's the damned strapless bra that's cutting off my wind. "This danged bra is killin' me. Maybe we should have gotten the next size up?"

Carletta sighs. "Yeah, if you wanted to have a wardrobe malfunction."

I have to grin when I remember my other malfunctions with Cody. "It's not like it hasn't happened before. Well, I won't be at the ball long enough to show my breasts to anyone, thank goodness."

Her face falls. "Oh, Jolie, can't I talk you out of this? Brett says Cody is beside himself since you haven't been returning his calls and has been mean as an old bear. Don't you get it? You two belong together!"

"We do not!"

"Well, you're sure as hell miserable without him!"

"I'm not! I'm just . . . stressed."

"Well, you shouldn't be living in this itty-bitty cabin." She swings her hand in an arc. "Mercy!"

"It's not itty-bitty and I like it. Besides, I plan on building something closer to the marina after the development begins. This is temporary. But it's the perfect place for writing and sketching." I tug at the beaded bodice and wonder if I can get away without wearing a bra. Probably not. "So . . . um, did Brett say if Cody is going to the charity ball with anyone?" I try to ask casually, but my voice sounds unnatural even to my own ears. "Not that it matters, of course," I quickly add. "I'm just, you know, curious."

"Right, just curious," Carletta repeats dryly, and then inhales a deep breath. "Brett says Cody might not even go."

"What?" My jaw drops and I forget to use Miss Abigail's, I mean Abby's, indoor voice. "He has to go! It's Dean Development's big yearly gig. They are the main sponsors."

Carletta stops fiddling with my hair and raises her palms in the air. "Don't shoot the messenger. I'm just telling you what Brett said."

"By the way, how are things with you and Brett going?"

Carletta looks at me in the mirror of the bathroom, which is spacious compared to the bathroom in my old farmhouse but small compared to the one in Copper Creek. "Progressing nicely, Jolie, even though he is Brett Dean and I'm little ole Carletta Arce. Once upon a time I was intimidated by that, but someone," she says absently, and then taps her cheek, "oh yeah, it was *you*, told me it didn't matter that I was a mere maid and he was from millions." She continues to tap her cheek. "Oh, and your daddy and upper-crust Abigail Marksberry are doing just fine too, despite their different backgrounds. They are all living proof you can change. Switch things up. You've even gotten me"—she jams her thumb toward her ample chest—"at nearly thirty years of age, going back to school. Now there's a reality show waiting to happen."

"You'll do fine. I bet you make the dean's list!"

"It seems as if you are the only one hung up on meaningless nonsense, Jolie! Have you ever heard of practicing what you preach?"

Okay, so she has a point, but of course I decide to argue anyway. "Carletta, may I gently remind you that Brett turned his back on his millions and is happily teaching school? And have you noticed that Miss Abigail, I mean Abby, has slowly but surely morphed into a refined but barefoot and jeans-wearin' redneck?" Redneck might be stretching it but still . . .

"My point exactly!"

Wait, it was supposed to be *my* point. "What do you mean?"

"Jolie, you've already seen firsthand that people can change, adapt, adjust their lifestyle if it means that much to them. You never gave Cody a fighting chance. He's hurting, Jolie. Brett says so."

"Oh God, please don't play that card." My eyes well up with unshed tears.

"It's true. I've seen him. He looks like hell."

"Stop! I'll never fit into his world and you know it!"

"What? And then he'll dump you? Leave you?" She gently puts her hands on my shoulders and meets my gaze in the mirror. "Or get sick and . . ."

"Oh, stop!" I put my hands over my face. "Please . . . just stop."

Carletta comes around and pries my hands away from my eyes. "Sweetie, I can't imagine what it must have been like to lose your mama at such a tender age. Even though your daddy is a wonderful man, he was busy running a farm and you must have felt lost."

I nod and confess. "All I had were her stories to keep me company and ease the pain. God, I was so afraid that

Daddy would die too . . . and I would be alone. Like the Boxcar Children. Isn't that silly?"

Carletta's gentle brown eyes mist over with moisture. "Not at all. But don't let your past interfere with your future, even though it's easier said than done."

"I know . . ." I swallow hard but then say, "I no longer care so much about fittin' in, that's for sure. I've found purpose. Meaning."

"You've found love too. If you'll let it happen. Have you ever thought that Cody could change too? Slow down and live his life differently?"

Yes, but I won't admit it to her. "Right, can you see him in a John Deere hat and Wranglers?" I snort.

"Okay." She raises her palms in the air again. "I've said my piece and now I have to go home and get ready for the ball too." But then she sighs. "Jolie . . ."

"Carletta!"

"Okay!" She looks down at Rufus. "Maybe you can talk some sense into her."

Rufus rolls over and hopes for a belly rub.

"Ew! You know I don't do belly rubs."

Rufus gives her an I-thought-it-was-worth-a-try sad expression.

"Okay, chickie, I'm outta here. I'll see you tonight, I hope, if only briefly."

I nod. "I'll get there in time to give Mama's check to Marissa."

"Okay."

As soon as she leaves, my smile fades. I look down at Rufus and he whines. "No, we are not going to mope around here. I'm sick of moping. Misty is wrong for you and Cody is wrong for me. Got that?"

Rufus looks up at me with droopy, who-are-we-kidding eyes.

I slip out of my evening dress and decide to take a nap until it's about time to leave. I hate the fact that Cody might not be attending the Cottonwood ball, but I firmly tell myself it's not my fault. After carefully hanging up the dress, I lie down in bed and hope for blessed slumber. The soothing pitter-patter of rain on the roof, coupled with my exhaustion, makes falling asleep easy.

When I wake up it's dark outside. I'm confused for a moment as I try to clear my thoughts. Then it dawns on me. "Oh crap!" Rufus, whom I've allowed to sleep in my bed since we're both scared up here at night, raises his head. "Rufus, how did this happen?" Panic washes over me and I turn to look at the alarm clock on my nightstand. "It's almost eleven o'clock!" I scramble from the bed, flip on the light, and start running around in circles, accomplishing nothing until I stop and take a deep breath. "Okay, the ball is from eight until midnight. If I hurry I can get there in time to present the check. Just calm down, Jolie."

I stay calm for about ten seconds and then start running around again like a crazy person. But less than fifteen minutes later I am in my evening gown with the check in my little clutch purse and headed out the door.

"What?" I stop in my tracks on my front porch. The rain has turned my gravel driveway to rocks swimming in mud. With a groan I look down at my delicate sandals and shake my head. "Now what? I can't have mud ooze onto my toes." I inhale a deep breath, trying to calm my panicking self, and spot my cowboy boots perched next to the porch swing. I had taken them off after a hike a few days ago. I hurry over to the swing, sit down, slip off my sandals, and shove my feet into the boots. No socks kind of sucks, but I'm in a hurry and I'll change as soon as I get to the country club anyway.

Hiking up the hem of my gown, I hurry to my pickup truck. Tossing my purse and sandals onto the seat, I shift the truck into drive and roar down the windy road.

The parking lot, of course, is packed, and no attendant is in sight. "Well, hell's bells." Since I plan on being there only for a few minutes anyway, I park the old truck in front of the mansion, grab my purse and shoes, and all but run up the sidewalk. I go as far as to open the front door when I remember my muddy boots. "Damn!" But at least I have the sandals dangling from my fingers, so I hurry over to a big wicker chair next to the door and tug my boots off. I notice with a cringe that the hem of my dress is muddy, but there's no fixing that. After slipping on the sandals, I take a deep breath and head inside.

I hear dance music filtering down from the ballroom upstairs. I pause to calm my thumping heart and wonder if Cody came or not. Then, holding up the soiled hem of my dress, I ascend the staircase and hope to enter the ballroom unnoticed. All I want to do is present the check and letter to Marissa and then leave.

At first I think I've accomplished slipping in unnoticed since most of the people are dancing, but someone grabs my arm.

"Wanna dance?" A stranger, who has clearly had one too many, sways toward me.

"No, thank you."

"C'mon." His grip tightens.

"No, thanks," I tell him tightly while trying to decide whether to stomp on his foot or give him an elbow in the gut. I'm thinking both, when a deep, all-too-familiar voice interrupts my decision-making process.

"Excuse me, but she is with me," Cody says firmly, and gives the dude a look that makes him slink away.

"I had it under control," I tell him.

Cody grins, making my heart turn over in my chest. "That's what I was afraid of." He gently but firmly grasps my elbow and leads me toward the dance floor.

"What do you think you're doin'?" I ask him.

"Having the last dance with you."

"You know I'm not much of a dancer," I argue feebly.

"I don't care," he answers in my ear. "The only thing that got me here tonight was the hope of having you in my arms." He draws me into his embrace and onto the dance floor. "I've been watching, waiting . . . hoping you'd arrive."

"Cody . . ."

"Shh." He puts a finger to my lips. "Give me this, okay?"

I nod and then slide my hand into his, but I immediately know it's a mistake. Having him hold me feels too good. When a smooth-voiced singer croons "Can't Help Falling in Love," I melt into Cody's arms. The lyrics make a huge lump form in my throat and when he kisses the top of my head, a tear slides down my cheek. This is too painful. I should never have come here tonight, and it takes everything in me not to bolt from the dance floor; but as if reading my thoughts, Cody tightens his hand on mine and draws me in even closer. Inhaling a shaky breath, I close my eyes and rest my head on his shoulder. Lost in the lyrics, I sway to the music and allow myself this memory.

The familiar citrus-and-spice aroma of his aftershave

teases my senses and creates a longing that has me sliding my fingers over the nape of his neck. When he sighs into my ear, I thread my fingertips into his hair and I know without a doubt that I love this man.

"Jolie, I've missed you so much," Cody says when the song ends. "You look beautiful, by the way."

When I gaze up at him, my heart lurches when I notice faint but visible dark circles under his eyes. It breaks my heart but I say, "Cody, this world . . . isn't me."

"Jolie . . ." He takes my hand. "Do me a favor and come with me." I nod, not wanting to be spotted by Daddy or Carletta, and let him take the lead. He draws me outside of the ballroom, away from the crowd and the noise, and then says, "I understand where you are coming from, but listen, we have to talk."

I nod. "Okay, but will you do something for me first?" It's almost midnight and I want Marissa to have the check before the ball ends.

He nods. "Sure."

I open my purse and give him the envelope with the check. "Give this to Marissa, okay? There is a letter of explanation in there."

"All right."

Standing in the shadows, I watch Cody walk away. At first I fully intend to wait for him to return, but as I watch women glittering with diamonds and pearls walk past me, panic bubbles up in my throat. "I can't pretend to be something I'm not," I whisper. With my hand to my mouth, I hurry down the staircase and then rush out the door. Thankfully, my truck is waiting, so I heft up my dress and hop inside.

Of course, my brain and my heart argue all the way home. I intermittently sob and cuss while I let them duke it out. But by the time I'm standing on my front porch, one thing is for sure.

My heart won.

If Cody loves me, he won't want me to be anything other than who I am. And truthfully, I can hold my own at a dinner party or four-wheeling in the woods. Carletta had me nailed. Fear has been holding me back. "Well, enough of that horse pucky."

When I hear Rufus scratching at the door I open it up. After he lumbers sadly out the door I flop down into a rocking chair and say, "Okay, I have a confession to make."

He looks up at me.

"Misty hasn't really been cheating on you."

"Woof!"

"I just thought, you know, that it wouldn't work out." I sigh. "Tomorrow we'll have to go and tell Mason Worthington that the puppies Misty's carryin' are most likely yours."

He wags his tail.

"There's gonna be hell to pay, you know. But it'll be worth it to be with the one you love, right?" I think of the Elvis song I just danced to and say, "I guess as crazy as it seems, some things are just meant to be." I reach down and scratch him behind the ears. "Okay, I guess we should get inside while I figure out what my next move should be. I sure hope I haven't screwed things up royally." But when I put my hand on the screen door handle I hear the deep rumble of a car engine. My heart pounds as I turn around. Sure enough, Cody's little Audi is rumbling up my muddy driveway.

Unable to move, I stand there and watch him unfold his long legs from the small car. Instead of wearing his tuxedo, he's in jeans and a T-shirt. He reaches inside the car and puts a ball cap on his head. Then I notice with a grin that he's carrying my muddy boots. When he gets closer I see that the green baseball hat sports the John Deere logo, and I know he's been talking to Carletta.

"You left something behind at the ball, Cinderella."

"Thank you," I say rather shyly, and take the boots from him.

"Would you do me a favor and put them on?"

I look down in question at the muddy boots but then toe off my fancy sandals and shove my feet into the cowboy boots. "There," I tell him. "Okay, are you going to explain?"

"You don't have to give up who you are to be with me, Jolie." He puts his warm hands on my bare shoulders. "You've proven you can hold your own on a ballroom dance floor. I understand you're raising money for needy children in honor of your mother and keeping her stories alive."

"Marissa read the letter out loud?"

He nods. "She actually got choked up."

"Wow."

"Yeah, you've been an influence on more people than you realize." He hesitates and then says, "Your father cried."

I put a hand to my mouth.

"I also understand from talking to your daddy that you're going to develop this lake into a fishing camp."

I nod again.

"I know a pretty good developer if you're interested in talking."

"Oh . . . so *that's* the reason for your visit?" I tease.

He grins. "Hardly."

"What, then?" My voice is breathless.

"I love you, Jolie Russell. But then I already told you that."

I suck in a breath. "Wait . . . you weren't talkin' in your sleep?"

He shakes his head. "I don't talk in my sleep. I was planting that seed inside your brain, hoping it would grow." He hesitates and then says, "Did it work?"

I narrow my eyes at him. "That was kinda underhanded."

"I was desperate."

"Hmmm, planting a seed in the head of a farm girl. Clever idea."

"Listen, I know you're a farm girl at heart. I understand that. Neither of us has to give up who we are. But Jolie, we can blend our lives, our personalities. You've made me want to slow down, enjoy life."

I put a hand on his arm. "And I understand I don't have to feel guilty having money. I just need to do good things with it." I look down at my muddy boots peeking out from beneath the fancy teal hem, and everything suddenly makes perfect sense . . . well, in my head, anyway. "Oh . . . I get it," I tell him gruffly.

"I knew you would. Do me a favor—don't ever change. Having you in my life has made me a better person." He reaches around my waist, picks me up, and twirls me around until I'm laughing and dizzy with happiness.

When he stops my world from spinning, I wrap my arms around his neck and say, "I've been so afraid. Fighting it. But I love you, Cody."

"I know." He grins. "You *do* talk in your sleep."

"I do not!"

"Do too." He scoops me up in his arms.

"Just where do you think you're takin' me?" I ask.

He removes his baseball cap and puts it on my head. "To bed."

"Good, then I'll prove to you I do not talk in my sleep!"

"Oh no, you won't."

"How's that?" I arch an eyebrow, knowing where this is going.

"We won't be doing any sleeping . . ."

I toss my head back and laugh, causing the John Deere hat to fall off my head. We both look down and see that it's fallen right beside the fancy silver sandals.

"You are my little redneck Cinderella," he says, and then dips his princely head to kiss me.

Once upon a time, a beauty queen met a brooding former rodeo champion. . . .

Read on for a sneak peek of LuAnn McLane's next Southern fairy tale,

He's No Prince Charming

Available October 2009 at penguin.com and wherever books are sold.

"Eeeeeee! Dropping her purse with a thud, Dakota screamed and then shouted, "Get off, get off, *get off*!" While dancing in a circle she slapped at the spiderweb she had walked into upon entering the musty cabin. "Eeee!" With another squeal she tugged at the cobwebs sticking to her hair and then frantically brushed at her arms. "Oh . . . oh!" Feeling itchy, she wiggled and squiggled, imagining there were baby spiders crawling all over her body.

"Okay, okay, settle down," Dakota scolded herself while taking shallow breaths. "Oh-kaaaay . . ." After a moment her rapid heartbeat calmed a bit, but then she felt a tickling sensation, as if something were crawling between her shoulder blades. "Oh God!" Wincing, she reached behind her back and slid her hand up her shirt, but the tiny tickling persisted just out of her reach. "Grrr . . ." She arched her spine and tilted back her shoulders in a move that would have made Cirque du Soleil proud, but then in desperation tugged her T-shirt over her head. She slapped at her back with the sleeve and sure enough flung a big black spider into the air. "I knew it! Okay, now where did you go?" With a shudder, she squinted down at the hardwood floor.

With the curtains drawn, the room was in semidarkness, with the only real light slicing in through the open front door. "Aha, there you are!" Nervously twisting the T-shirt in her fists, Dakota crept forward with the intention of smashing the spider beneath her flip-flop. She even went as far as to raise her foot but then stood there balanced on one leg, looking as if she were doing a karate pose. Closing her eyes, she swallowed hard and glared at the spider—but then she imagined the imminent pop and squish, and her foot remained poised in midair. "You can do this," she whispered fiercely, but could not bring herself to perform the deed.

Dakota concentrated hard and dug deep for her killer instinct. "Okay, here goes nothing," she murmured, gritted her teeth, and was about to end the life of the spider—

"Are you okay?" A deep voice from out of nowhere questioned.

Jarred from her focus on her task, Dakota's head whipped up and she let out a startled, "Eeeee!" She dropped her shirt, lost her balance, and smashed the spider with an audible *splat*. Her eyes widened at the tall figure standing in the open doorway, blocking most of the waning sunlight. "Oh, God. Ew!" She kicked off her flip-flop, which was soiled with spider guts, and blinked up at the giant man standing in the shadows. Well he wasn't a *giant* . . . maybe six-two or -three, but to Dakota's five foot four—and that's on a big hair day—he seemed huge and sort of . . . looming. His dark hair reached nearly to his shoulders and equally dark stubble shaded his square, unyielding jaw. A black T-shirt stretched across a well-defined chest and seemed to test the limit of the short sleeves, which revealed bulging biceps. Faded jeans, ripped at the knees, hugged muscled thighs.

"What made you scream?"

"Um . . ." Dakota inhaled a calming breath and was beginning to think she was in her overreacting, fight-or-flight mode when she noticed—*Oh dear lord!*—he had an ax by his side! "I uh . . ." With a gasp, she started backing away, thinking it had been a while since she had come home to Pine Hollow Lake and perhaps things had . . . changed.

"Hey, I'm not going to hurt you," he promised in a deep voice that sounded a little bit insulted.

I just bet that's what all the ax murderers say, Dakota thought while wondering if she could scurry past him and run for the hills. She suddenly felt as if she had stumbled into a B horror flick and was Sarah Michelle Gellar. "I know karate," she bluffed, hoping he had mistaken her pose and screams for some martial-arts moves. Fat chance, but it was worth a try. "So just back off!" Dakota quickly removed her other flip-flop and held it up over her head as if it were a samurai sword.

Yeah, right—even though it did kill the spider rather handily, the flimsy rubber wouldn't do much damage to the dude in the doorway. Still, knowing it was all in the attitude, Dakota wielded her weapon with all the fearlessness she could muster—which unfortunately wasn't much, so she narrowed her eyes and added in a low and lethal tone, "I'm serious."

"Are you, now?"

"Yes," she said in a whisper of warning, and waved the flip-flop so hard that the fake daisy adornment fluttered to the floor and landed near the man's feet as if she had just thrown down the gauntlet. Not good. "So just back off," she decided to add.

After a brief moment of silence the dude in the doorway laughed, making Dakota feel as silly as she must have looked. Well, at least his laughter didn't sound sinister—more like a rusty rumble, as if he hadn't laughed in a long while and needed to be oiled like the Tin Man. His laughter somehow eased Dakota's fear but then she became a little miffed at his amusement. She was trying to come up with something haughty to say when she suddenly remembered that she was standing there in her skimpy lace demibra with the little lock and key charm dangling between the pink cups. With her low-rise jeans hugging her hips, she realized she was giving him quite an eyeful. With as much dignity as she could muster, which was none at all, she scrambled over to her T-shirt and hastily tugged it over her head.

"Okay," Dakota said with her hands on her hips, "just who do you think you are, busting into this cabin without so much as a knock?" She asked this in a snooty tone, since now that she had come to her senses she was pretty much convinced that he wasn't a crazy backwoods killer. She noticed her shirt felt funny, and she realized she had tugged it on backward and hoped he didn't notice.

He scratched the side of his chin. "Well, the fact that you screamed several times had something to do with it. Pardon me for asking, but just why *did* you scream? And why were you only half dressed?"

Dakota lifted her chin a notch. "If you must know, I was attacked by a spider."

"Attacked?" he asked drily.

She once again narrowed her eyes at the amused inflection in his voice. "Yes," she answered primly, and then explained, "I walked straight into a huge cobweb and the spider"—she paused to demonstrate the hugeness by forming her arms into a circle—"crawled beneath my shirt."

"So that's why you were half naked?" He leaned one shoulder against the door frame and crossed his arms over his wide chest.

"I wasn't half naaaa-ked!" she sputtered, and felt heat creep into her cheeks. After nine years in L.A., her Southern drawl suddenly returned with a vengeance. "And I have, I'll have you know"—she widened her eyes and put a hand to her chest—"aracnaphelia."

"You mean arachnophobia?"

"Whichever one means that spiders scare the ever living daylights out of you." She waved a hand in the air, wishing he would come out of the shadows so she could get a better look at his face. Maybe it was because she was so used to metrosexual men, but for some reason his rough-around-the-edges appearance was making her female hormones kick into high gear. Feeling a little self-conscious at her wayward thoughts, she averted her gaze and looked around. "This place needs a good scrubbing."

"Well, this isn't a Holiday Inn. Look, I'm not sure where you were heading, but you must have made a wrong turn. You're at Willow Creek Marina and Fishing Camp. This particular cabin belongs to Charley Dunn, the owner's father. The owner lives in L.A. and hasn't been here in years," he explained, but then suddenly stood up straight. "Wait, who are you?" he asked bluntly, even though Dakota could tell he had just put two and two together.

"Dakota Dunn, Charley and Rita Mae Dunn's daughter." While angling her head to the side she peered at him more closely, wishing the lighting in the room were brighter. "Are *you* Trace Coleman?" She had seen pictures of the ex-bull-riding star, and the man standing before her did not look like a former hotshot PBR champion, but then she remembered her father telling her Trace had been forced from the dangerous sport due to serious injuries.

"Yes," he answered tightly.

Embarrassed at her incredulous tone, Dakota forced a smile. "Well, it's nice to meet you. My father tells me you do a bang-up job running the marina." She moved a couple of steps closer to him and was about to offer her hand, but to her amazement he didn't make any move to enter the room or to welcome her there.

"So, are you just checking up on things? Passing through?" Any hint of amusement or friendliness was suddenly gone, replaced with a distinct you-don't-belong-here attitude.

"No, I'm moving in." Dakota answered a bit stiffly. "I need some peace and quiet for a change," she added, leaving out the fact that this marina was the only thing left in the world that she owned and she had nowhere else to go unless she headed to Florida and lived with her parents. *No, thank you.*

"Oh." He seemed annoyed. "But it *is* temporary, though—right?"

Dakota shrugged since she didn't really know the answer to his question. She certainly hoped so since living in a fishing camp cabin was a far cry from her house in L.A. It wasn't necessary, though, to explain to Trace Coleman that her bubblegum pop days were long gone or that her record label had released her several years ago.